Ghosts & LIGHTNING

Ghosts & LIGHTNING

Trevor BYRNE

CANONGATE

Edinburgh · London · New York · Melbourne

Published by Canongate Books in 2009

1

Copyright © Trevor Byrne, 2009

The moral right of the author has been asserted

First published in Great Britain in 2009 by Canongate Books
Ltd, 14 High Street, Edinburgh EH1 1TE

www.meetatthegate.com

British Library Cataloguing-in-Publication Data
A catalogue record for this book is available on
request from the British Library

ISBN 978 1 84767 329 9

Typeset in Bembo by
Sharon McTeir, Creative Publishing Services

Printed and bound in Great Britain by
CPI Mackays, Chatham ME5 8TD

Mixed Sources
Product group from well-managed
forests and other controlled sources
www.fsc.org Cert no. TT-COC-002341
© 1996 Forest Stewardship Council
FSC

For Louise and Brian
(for love and life and everything else)

CITY OF YOUR BIRTH

—Ma's gone. Jesus Denny, yeh have to come home.

Your sister's words from the night before like some spiralling mantra, her voice slurred by drink and small-sounding, a lifetime away. You hadn't heard the accent for months.

Dublin.

Home.

You ended the call and still the words were there, dancing, odd and sad and haunted.

—Ma's gone.

The nighttime ferry was packed, the mostly Irish passengers drunk and raucous, the eastern European crew hovering on the edges of things, tired and wary. You sat with your bag between your knees and watched.

And so you're here.

You pass through Dublin ferryport's unmanned ID checkpoints, your sports bag awkward and heavy as you shift it from one shoulder to the next, a tinny female voice on the loudspeaker announcing something with a Polish accent, something about luggage, the need to take care and a lack of liability, before being cut off as the automatic door sucks shut. Cold, salty air and a slight breeze. Behind you the ferry looms huge against the night sky, the Irish

Sea beyond an immense glittering darkness. A bus is waiting, humming in the dark, a small huddle of people with bags and suitcases crowding the doors. You wait your turn and struggle onboard, drop coins into the machine, a copy of the *Evening Herald* open on the driver's lap. You haven't thought about that paper for a long time. He nods without looking up. You sit by the window and a young man sits beside you, although there are other empty seats. Excitable, jumpy, his hands wringing about themselves in a bony flux. He's wearing faded jeans and a tight and battered leather jacket, his blond hair cropped and his beard patchy. The smell of sweat lurks behind his cheap deodorant. His pupils are black holes.

—Grand to be home, wha?

You nod, the bus shunting forward.

—Can't beat it, says the young man. —Over the water were yeh? Obviously, yeah. Fuckin ferry port, isn't it? Swansea I was in. Deadly little city. Small like but cool, yeh know? Great fuckin craic. And this mad bird I met, oof. Should o seen her, Welsh lass. Fuck sake. Off her trolley she was, pure mental.

The crumbling docklands pass by. Strange that so dilapidated a place can exist in this city, these odd dark shapes and leaning gates, these silent, haunted buildings. What was before, what's left behind.

—Took her back to her place, few vodkas and that. She was pissed up like. Place was a bit of a kip yeh know? But fuckin hell yid wanna see this bird, absolutely fuckin stunnin. Mad like but gorgeous, deadly fuckin bird altogether, tellin yeh.

Past the Point Depot and onto the quays. The lights of the city, the gothic and angular Ulster Bank headquarters

2

across the Liffey like some huge and squatting medieval folly, throbbing, malevolent. The young man licks his dry, cracked lips and grins.

—Up for everythin she was, oof. Came fuckin buckets. Bet the arse off her. She'd a kid in the other room though, which was a bit annoyin like, yeh know? Cryin and that.

Through side streets, the walls grey and close. Dimly lit apartment windows. Flashing neon signs, people hurrying along and others idle, loitering. A man on a street corner, his face briefly lit by the flickering flame of his lighter. Black, dark-eyed, his hair braided. Then nothing, a shadow reclaimed.

—She starts goin on about the kid, then. Had to give yer woman a smack in the end. Fuck that. Not interested. Yeh have to let them know who's who, course yeh do. Some fuckin ride though, I'm tellin yeh, oof.

The bus stops. You stand and the twitching man beside you does likewise.

—Last stop this, is it?

You nod and pull the bag from the stairwell, step off the bus. A crowd of drunk teenagers stumble past, laughing and whooping, mock fighting. You walk on, the curious statue of Joyce to your right and then, towering above it, above everything in the city, the Spire, an immense silver needle pricking at the belly of the night sky. Cars and buses glide past on either side, O'Connell Street bustling with drunks and revellers and dotted amongst these the tall broad forms of gardaí, streetlight flashing from their jackets.

—Fuckin dyin for a drink are you? Wanna grab a scoop like? Auld Dub or somethin, yeah? Although it's a bit touristy now, mind. Could do the Foggy Dew instead if yeh want, always jammers in there.

He is standing to your left, his eyes on a passing woman in a short red skirt, her arms crossed beneath her breasts.

—Yeah?

You shake your head and step forward, crossing the road first to the Spire and then the GPO. The young man follows, unperturbed, shucking and winking at passersby, nightmare shadowside of a life you have long lost any love for. A longhaired man in a Chelsea jersey pisses against one of the GPO's Ionic columns, still pocked with British bulletholes, and a shout goes up from a garda in a deep Donegal accent. The man breaks and runs with his penis flopping, his mates laughing on the corner of Middle Abbey Street some yards behind you.

—C'mere t'me yew, ya dirty fucker! C'mere!

The garda's shoulder catches you as he bustles past, spinning you. Your bag hits the ground.

—See that? See yer man there pissin? Fuckin madman. Fuckin mad town this, isn't it? Fuckin deadly.

You haul up the bag and walk on, your shoulder straining and your bicep aching dully. Past McDonald's, past Burger King and across Bachelor's Walk, over O'Connell Bridge and past Fitzgerald's on the corner, the mingled raucous sound of bodhran and fiddle and tin whistle spilling out, then into the new Super Valu where you buy a bottle of Sprite from a young sad looking Chinese woman with pink hair, not to drink but to break into the last fiver you've got in your pocket for bus fare.

—Yer not goin home are yeh? Grab a few scoops and a few youngwans, no? Tellin yeh man, fella like you, betcha the birds are all over yeh. And anyway I've a plan B if the natural charms don't work, yeh know? Lookit.

The young man slips his hand into his jeans pocket and surreptitiously pulls out a small bag of pills. He winks and grins his toothfucked grin.

—Know wha I mean? Stick a few o these in their drink and yer fuckin Casanova. Any bird yeh want, any way yeh want. Oof.

The 78a pulls in and you step onboard, the young man still on the path behind you, arms out, a puzzled look on his face.

—No? Yer missin out, man. Tellin yeh. Yer fuckin missin –

The doors collapse inwards and you head upstairs, taking the front seat, watching the streetlamps shimmer on the Liffey below. The Ha'penny Bridge is thronged with people crossing the river. A woman crouches and drops something into a Styrofoam cup at the feet of a sleeping man and passes into the crush. The upstairs deck of the bus is empty. You pin the bag between your legs and lean your head against the buzzing window.

City of your birth; Dubh Linn, the Black Pool. The bus kicks into life. You're almost home.

THE FACTS WILL DESTROY YOU

Wha d'yeh do when yer ma's gone, like? I can feel the sadness comin back, an echo o that horrible raw hurt from the day I got back from Wales. I pulled aside these pale blue plastic curtains and there's me ma, lyin in the bed. Her face was different somehow. Have yeh ever seen someone yeh know after they've died? This weird thought jumped into me head – the crap-lookin waxworks in that museum in town, the one near Parnell Square. I remember goin there years ago, with me ma, I was about nine or ten and yeh only really knew who each waxwork was supposed to be from the context. Yeh knew George Best cos o the hairdo and the old-fashioned United jersey, and the Pope cos o the robes and the little hat, that kind o thing. That's what I thought of in the hospital – that me ma didn't look like herself, not really, but I knew it was her cos me sister Paula was standin beside her shakin and sobbin, her face streaked with mascara. And the ring on me ma's finger, a ring me nanny gave her. Smooth. White gold.

I took her hand. It was cold. Freezin. The woman who washed us and loved us and dragged us all up. Hands that weren't her hands.

Jesus, me ma's gone.

That simple and that fuckin complex.

★

I'm after forgettin me key so I have to ring the bell. No answer. I ring again and then I remember we need a new battery. I knock instead. And again. About eight years later Paula answers.

—I'd the radio on, sorry, she says. —Eamon Dunphy. He's bleedin wired to the moon that fella.

She's still in her dressin gown, the pink one with frilly bits, and she's wearin a battered pair o Homer Simpson slippers that used to belong to me. Fuckin image o me ma, Paula is. It's freaky how similar they are. Me ma was beautiful and I suppose Paula is, too. They look exactly like a woman from this book I've had since I was a kid, a book me uncle Victor brung down from the North . . . she might o been Cúchulainn's wife, actually; long, thick blonde hair, high cheekbones and a lovely nose that'd probably look a bit too big on a face less impressive and regal . . . a trinity of warrior women, me ma and Paula and the woman in the book. Well, if the ancient women of Ulster dressed in Top Shop, like. And, in Paula's case, if they had dipso tendencies and swore like fuckin sailors.

She looks at me bag and smiles.

—Ah, get chips, did yeh?

—Yeah.

—Yer a life saver. There's fuck all in that press.

We go inside. Paula gets a couple o plates out and rummages in the sink for forks. She pulls out two and runs them under the tap, dries them with a tea towel. The sink's piled up with dirty plates and cups and glasses and all sorts. The kitchen in general – the whole fuckin house, actually – looks stale and sad. Me brother Shane was around last week, checkin up on us, like – he called the

7

place a disgraceful fuckin kip and, even though he does me head in, he's right. It's fuckin awful lookin. Without ma the place is fallin apart. I think that kind o prompted him to arrange the meetin with the solicitor. Well, that and the smell o money.

Paula sways a bit as she walks over to the table with the plates.

—You fuckin locked? I say.

—No.

—Yeh are, I can tell, Paula. Jesus.

—I'm not locked.

—How many yeh had? What're yeh drinkin?

—I had a bit o that vodka. A little bit.

—Fuckin hell, Paula.

She smiles. Her eyes have that floaty look. She sits herself down carefully at the table. Probably no one else'd even notice that she's drunk, but I'm well used to her. She reaches across the table and takes up the bundle o chips and opens it up on her plate, the paper a big greasy rose unfolded in front of her.

—Ah, a spice burger, deadly. Thanks. Haven't seen these in ages.

—Yid wanna sort yerself out, Paula. The state o yeh.

She waves a chip at me. —Jesus, lighten up Denny. I'm grand. Fuckin hell. Hair o the dog is all. She pops the chip into her mouth. —What's the story, so? she says, mid chew.

I scratch me chin. I want to have a go at her about the drink, make me feel a bit better about meself, but fuck it, I'll leave it. —We're lodgers, I say.

—Lodgers?

—Yeah. From next week. Me, you and Teresa. Or tenants or wharrever.

—Is there a difference?

—Dunno. We've to pay rent anyway.

Paula tilts her head and makes her unimpressed face, absentmindedly shakin a load o salt over her chips. —Supposed to leave it by the fuckin graveside, are we?

I'm not in the humour of arguing with Paula so I let that slide. Stress is the last thing I need after that horrible fuckin meetin with Shane and the solicitor.

—The rent goes to Shane, I say. —He owns the house like, that's wha the solicitor said. Sure we knew that anyway. The solicitor said we'd be able to get rent allowance off the dole.

—What's he gonna do with it?

—Give it to charity. Wha d'yeh think?

—That's a fuckin . . . are yeh serious?

—That's wha the solicitor said, Paula.

—And wha did you say?

—Wha could I say? Shane paid the mortgage off so it's his, it's all kosher. It was all sorted with ma, like. Before . . . yeh know.

—So he's keepin the money?

—Yeah. Obviously.

—He's actually keepin the rent money?

—Yeah, Paula. Yeh listenin? It's his. It's his house.

Paula thinks for a few seconds. She cuts the spice burger with her fork. —He could let us have it just as easy, she says, eyes on her burger. —The rent money, like. I mean, he's got his own fuckin house, he could give that rent money back to us. Or split it, even. Sure it's no skin off his nose if the mortgage is paid off. That's all profit.

—Say it to him.

She looks up at me. —I will. He can hand that rent straight fuckin back. Greedy fuckin bastard's rollin in it. I'm not payin rent to live in a ghost house.

—Don't say that to him.

—Wha?

—Don't say fuckin 'ghost house' to him. Jesus. Cop on, will yeh? Yeh know wha he's like. He's already on the warpath cos o the state o the place.

—Denny, it is. It's a fuckin ghost house. I'm tellin yeh.

—Okay. Wharrever. It's a ghost house.

—Exactly. And here, another thing, if we're payin rent then he's the fuckin landlord and that means he has responsibilities. He can get a new hoover and sort the oven. And he can fix that fuckin toilet, the fuckin smell'd drive a funeral up an alleyway.

—He was lecturin me today about havin people over and that, though. He's not gonna do anythin when he knows we've got loads o people dossin here and all the rest.

—The fuck does he care?

—That's wha he said. I'm just tellin yeh.

—Fuckin miserable bastard.

I pour the curry sauce in a zigzag over me smoked cod. This is startin to do me head in now. Between Shane and Paula, like. No fuckin peace. No fuckin life this, I'm tellin yeh. Back from Wales to this. Jesus.

—I'm just tellin yeh wha he said, Paula, I say. —Yeh could o come and had all this out with them there and then but yeh were happy enough here knockin back vodka so just fuckin . . . stressed out to death in that solicitor's office, I was. Yeh know I hate places like that.

Paula tucks her hair behind her ear. Somethin's happenin, I can tell – she's thinkin . . . the cogs and gears in motion, makin some sort o mad, we're-all-gonna-end-up-homeless decision. She's smilin again. Bad news, man. Bad fuckin –

—Know wha we need? she says.

—G'wan. Can't wait to hear it.

—A séance. We're gonna have a séance. Talk to the ghost. Get Pajo to do it. Serious.

I shake me head. —Mad. That's all I can say, Paula. Fuckin . . . madness. Yer mental.

Paula laughs.

★

A couple hours later I see Pajo through the window, strugglin at the front gate, a big green satchel on his back. He eventually manages to get the gate shifted (it's gone a bit wonky and scrapes along the concrete) and walks up the garden to the door, disappearin from view. I'm watchin The Simpsons in the front room, one o the older, good episodes, so I wait for a knock before I get up, but after a couple o minutes there's still nothin. He must be tryin to ring the bell. It occurs to me to just let him keep ringin and, hopefully, he'll give up and fuck off. I keep tryin to square that with meself, morally. I mean, wha if I hadn't o noticed him at the gate? He would've been ringin the broken bell for ages and I'd never have noticed – nothin Machiavellian, just bad luck. Or good luck, really. I feel dead bad, though. After another few seconds I get up and step over the basket o Paula's washin by the coffee

11

table and head for the hall. I can see Pajo's skinny shape in blurry silhouette behind the glass. I open the door.

—I was ringin for ages, says Pajo.

—The battery's gone, I say. —Yer lucky I clocked yeh.

Pajo's an old mate o mine. I've known him and his brother Maggit since we were kids. He got into heroin when he was sixteen or so but he's been on methadone for a few years now, left the needles behind. Although that's just swappin one ball and chain for another if yeh ask me. It was mad; for a few years no one really seen much of him – he was off with junkies and all sorts, shootin up in parks and squats in town. He doesn't really talk about it. We knew he was on gear but there was nothin yeh could say to him; the few times I tried he just looked dead sad, dead ashamed. He's a real soft soul, Pajo.

He's standin in the doorway and even though it's cold he's sweatin slightly and he looks delicate, like he'd break if he fell, a thin gothic doll with his lank green hair tucked behind his ear, so many chemicals in and on him he smells like a breach o the Kyoto Agreement.

—Is Paula in? he says.

—Will I not do?

—Well, it was . . . she was sayin about a séance. Like, organisin somethin.

—Yeah, I know. She's up in the shower. Come in.

Pajo steps in behind me.

—D'yeh want tea or somethin?

—D'yeh have any cappuccino?

★

Paula's hair is still damp and she's wearin the Reebok tracksuit she bought off our mate Ned's stall yesterday. She's sittin on the armchair with the basket o washin on her lap, pickin through her and Teresa's knickers and all sorts, no shame at all. Me and Pajo are on the sofa. Pajo's lap is burdened as well, but with a pile o dog-eared books on spiritualism and ghost sightings and Buddhism, and, on top o that, an A4 pad, into which he's scribblin notes in his big, dopey-lookin handwritin. When Pajo writes he only ever uses capitals, like he's tryin to convince himself that whatever he's writin is solid and worthwhile.

—Right so, says Pajo. —We need to, like, establish some stuff before we can . . . em . . .

He makes a vague gesture with his hands. —Before we decide what's the best way to deal with . . . this . . . situation.

Paula nods, carefully drapin a red bra over the arm o the chair.

—There's loads o ways, like, of approachin paranormal situations like this, says Pajo. —Like, a séance, a Ouija board, a –

—Psychologist, I say.

—Shurrup Denny, says Paula.

Pajo looks at me, then at Paula, and then carefully writes somethin on his pad.

—Wha yeh writin? I say.

—Notes. Just for like . . . reference.

He taps his head knowingly and I shake mine.

—Don't mind him Pajo, says Paula. —He has no sense o wonder at all.

—Wha? I say. I don't know why I'm even risin to this; I know Paula's just tryin to annoy me. —I do have a sense o

13

wonder, I say. —I just don't believe in fuckin ghosts, that's all. It doesn't make any —

—What's the big deal, then? says Paula. —Why are yeh so freaked? Yer more freaked than me and you haven't even heard anythin.

—Yeah, it's not because, like . . . I'm not afraid, though. It's psychological, isn't it? It's in yer head.

—Yer sayin more about yer own psychology than mine, Denny, says Paula, and she makes that annoyin 'crazy' gesture, pointing her index finger at her temple and makin little circles. Paula's referrin to the fact I was foolish enough to tell her that me worst fear is goin mad. Not that I expect to go mental or anythin, it's just . . . it's freaky, the way yer head works. I mean, if yer mad, ghosts and monsters, they exist; they're real, or they might as well be. I have an auntie, Denise, me ma's youngest sister, and she's schizophrenic. She sees demons in mirrors and all sorts. Me cousin Martin, her eldest, told one time that Denise attacked him with the bread knife cos she said he was hidin horns under his Nike cap. I mean, fair enough, he *is* always wearin baseball caps, but as far as I know it's to hide his recedin hairline, not fuckin horns. And then Denise saw that film Child's Play on Sky Movies and convinced herself that dolls had evil spirits inside them and burned all o her daughter Susan's Barbies in a bonfire out the back garden. They say madness runs in some families so sometimes I worry that Paula might be losin it. And then I start to convince meself that *I* might be the one goin mad cos I'm thinkin about it all too much, obsessin on it.

Which reminds me – *stop fuckin thinkin about it, Denny.*

Pajo flips onto a new page in his pad. —So go on, Paula, he says. —What is it, exactly?

He's bein kind o hesitant, which isn't unusual for Pajo, but I can tell he's enjoyin this. He's mad into this kind o thing; life after death, ghosts, yetis, any and all religions. Basically, anythin there's fuck all proof for, Pajo'll believe it. Almost like he's definin himself against the world in some way.

Paula looks up at the ceilin, to where her and Teresa's bedroom is, and then back to Pajo.

—It's . . . well, as far as I'm concerned, there's a presence in the house. She looks at me. —A definite presence. Definitely.

—D'yeh know she was drinkin vodka when I came back at half two today, Pajo? I say.

—Ignore him, she says to Pajo. —There's definitely somethin. A hundred per cent.

—Have yeh seen anythin? says Pajo.

—No. I . . . no, I haven't *seen* anythin. Just, like, felt somethin. And heard it as well. That's the worst. It's under the beds.

—Did it say somethin? asks Pajo. —Or was it just noises?

—Said somethin.

—Is it a fella or a girl?

—Now this is the freakiest bit. This is fuckin . . . it's a fella. It's male, like, but it's *pretendin* to be a girl. It's puttin on a girl's voice. How fuckin mad is that?

Too fuckin mad if yeh ask me. The ghost of a man pretendin to be a girl, hidin under Paula's bed. For fuck sake.

And this goes on for an hour or so. Madder and madder. Wild speculation and wilder interpretations. Pajo says he'll have to look some stuff up, consult charts and websites and all kinds o shite, but they've agreed on it – they're gonna do it, they're gonna have a séance. And they want me and some of our mates to be there. It'll help attract the spirit's attention, accordin to Pajo; a bigger group, more energy to feed off.

Pajo packs up his books and pad and heads off. Me and Paula sit there for a while. I need to be distracted. Paula heads upstairs. I turn on the telly and watch Takeshi's Castle.

★

Next mornin there's a scream from upstairs and I drop me spoon into the bowl o Cheerios I've only just started and hop over the bollixed vacuum cleaner and skid into the hall and grab me brother Gino's hurley, then it's up the stairs three at a time and I bash open Paula's door and there she is, standin in her Snoopy nightdress with her back to the window in the middle of a pile o clothes and shoes with her hand to her mouth, shakin.

—Wha the fuck's goin on?

Paula looks at me and then looks at the wardrobe and I get a horrible tingle shootin up me spine.

—Wha, Paula? Stop fuckin around will yeh.

—Oh Jaysis Denny. Look behind the wardrobe.

I step into the room, the bed unmade with a pair o jeans laid across it and the telly in the corner babblin low down, Jeremy Kyle pronouncin judgement on a scaldy lookin fella in a denim shirt. There's a vodka bottle on the window ledge, the sun behind it, and a few crumpled Bulmers cans. Dolls everywhere. Them weird porcelain ones with real-lookin eyes and hair.

Paula inches along the wall towards me.

—Fuck sake Paula, I say, me heart hammerin. I glance at the wardrobe. I can feel sweat on me back.

—Get it Denny. Oh Jesus. Get it out. The bleedin size o the thing.

I edge cautiously forward. I don't want to but I do. There's some grinnin horror waitin for me and I'm edgin me way closer to it. Like in a fuckin film or somethin. A wizened, crouched old man with a little girl's voice. Jesus. I grip the hurley two-handed.

—Wha is it, Paula? Fuckin hell.

—Just get it!

I turn and look back at her.

—I swear to fuckin god, Paula, if it's –

—I was pickin up me jeans. Icky ick. A bird or somethin. Jesus. A bat.

I stop and look at her. —A fuckin bat? Wha the fuck are yeh on about?

—A bat. Some mad flyin thing.

—I thought yeh were bein fuckin murdered by the . . . yeh tryin to give me a bleedin heart attack?

—Shurrup. Get it.

Paula scurries behind me on tiptoe and out the door. She pulls it almost shut, half her face visible.

I stop about six feet from the wardrobe. Me heart's goin ninety now. The doors are open and there's knickers and socks and all sorts spillin out. A pile o cardboard boxes are stacked haphazardly at the back and there's a china doll in a blue dress with a massive skull fracture sittin on top, smilin. I avoid eye-contact with it.

Paula sticks her arm into the room and points, her eye wide open. —Behind it, she says. —It's hidin. Grab that torch there. Shine it at it.

I set the battered old hurley down against Paula's bed. The torch is a chunky yellow Bob the Builder toy.

—Where'd yeh get this?

—Ant'ny left it here.

Anthony's me mate Maggit's son. I pick the torch up and crane me neck forward, tryin to see round the back o the wardrobe. There's somethin black stickin out, about half an inch. The tips o somethin's wings, I think. I've never seen a bat before. Well. I saw a few in the zoo. They were mad-lookin, stalkin upside-down across the ceilin.

—That's it, says Paula. —Shine the torch.

—For wha? Why?

Paula doesn't answer. I don't know why the fuck I'm doin it – the bedroom light's already on – but I lift the torch and point it at the little wing-tips and click the ON button, and immediately the wharrever-it-is scuttles back behind the wardrobe.

I turn and look at Paula. —Did yeh see that?

—Sicko!

I turn back to the wardrobe and I'm just about to take another step towards it when the wings poke into view again.

—Fuck, I say. —Lookit that.

—I am lookin. Shine it again. It doesn't like the light.

—It's not a fuckin mogwai, Paula, I say. But I point the torch at it anyway, feelin a strange combination of freaked-out-ness and curiosity, and click the button.

It scuttles out o view again.

—That's mad, I say.

—Kill it!

—I think it's a moth.

—The size o the thing, Denny! It must be a bat or somethin. Don't they suck yer blood?

—Shh.

Paula points in again, her hand waggin up and down. —It's too brainy to be a moth. Moths wouldn't hide, would they? They're stupid.

I step over a shoebox and press me face against the wall and peer along the gap at the back o the wardrobe. It's dark and greasy, clogged with hairballs and wadded up socks and all sorts and I can see the fat black shape o the bat or moth or wharrever the fuck it is, scuttlin about in the gloom.

—How many legs do moths have? I say. —This thing has loads.

—Dunno. The bastard's fuckin trespassin anyway. Killim. It's his own fault.

—I think it's a moth. Fuckin huge though.

—He was in me jeans the dirty fuckin bastard. Icky icky. He's fuckin dead Denny I'm tellin yeh. He's gettin it sooner or later.

I toss the torch onto the bed. —I can't get him when he's behind there and me Cheerios are goin soggy. I'll get him after.

I back out o the room and start down the stairs. Paula softly shuts the bedroom door and grabs her housecoat from the banisters and hurries down after me.

★

—What's with the fuckin giant insects everywhere? says Paula.

I rinse me bowl under the warm tap and set it down on the drainin board, a token effort at cleanin up. The sun's spillin into the kitchen, watery and lemon-coloured. Looks like it's gonna be a pretty nice day. Cold like, but dry and clear.

—Wha giant insects?

—That moth upstairs. And that big spider yeh showed us over the back door. Probably more.

I shrug. —Dunno. Spiders are arachnids, anyway. Dunno wha moths are.

—Dirty fuckin tresspassin pervos, that's wha. I'm gettin a spray. This place is a bug hutch.

—Spider provider, I say, smilin.

—Alien ant farm, says Paula.

She clinks her spoon against the steamin teacup and lifts it to her mouth. Takes a little sip. —I got a fuckin fright, she says. —Serious, he flew right up at me. Yeh can smile all yeh want but I'm tellin yeh it's not nice, flyin into yer face. What's the point o moths?

—Dunno.

—They've no point. They're pointless. Kill the lot o them.

—I thought someone was murderin yeh yeh mad fuck. Or yer fuckin ghost was after yeh.

Paula shakes her head. —No, she says, like she needs to confirm it. —Just that moth. Bastard.

—I'll sort it out after.

—Never openin them windows again. He must o flew in.

—Yill get over it.

Paula sets down her tea and digs out a lump o butter and tries to spread it on her toast but all she does is bludgeon the bread into raggedy bits.

—This butter's solid.

—I know. We should get Low-Low next time. It's softer.

—Yeah. We should.

Paula squashes the butter back into the tub and takes a bite o the dry toast. It's half nine in the mornin. Nothin's changed. She sits there, starin through the patio doors at the back garden. Nothin's gonna change, either. Her legs are crossed and one hand's restin on her stomach. She looks tired and sad. Her hair's hangin limp around her shoulders. If it wasn't for the moth she probably wouldn't be up till after twelve.

—We have the place the way it is, Paula, I say. —We're gonna have to do somethin.

Paula says nothin.

—I honestly do think yer drinkin too much, I say.

Again, nothin. I hate when she does that. Ignores me. Makes yeh feel like a kid. Yid swear we were still in our teens, like, and I was askin her to turn off Sweet Valley High for Zig and Zag and she'd be sittin there brushin her hair, pretendin she can't hear me. Always been that way. Sometimes things are cool, or they seem like they are, and then . . . ah sure who the fuck am I kiddin? She's me sister. I'm her brother. It's just the way things are, isn't it? In an age when to be deeply philosophical is José Mourinho sayin sometimes yeh get three points and sometimes yeh get none, but then again sometimes yeh get one, maybe I'm overanalysin things.

—What's the story with that ... like, this under the bed stuff? I say. —Is it for real or what?

—Yeh just want me to humour yeh, Denny. I'm not gonna. Yeh know I'm not.

—Yer mad.

—Wouldn't have it any other way.

★

I was seventeen and Paula was eighteen when she told me she was gay. She didn't make a big deal of it or anythin, just came straight out with it.

—I'm gay, Denny.

Just straight up, like. I was eatin a battered sausage and I nearly choked. It took me a few seconds to get it down, then I skilfully re-routed the conversation:

—Eh, did yeh get these in J.J.'s or out o the van?

—Denny?

—Wha?

—I'm a lesbian.

Paula never bothered with skirtin round issues. It still sounded weird hearin her say 'lesbian' though. Gay was bad enough, but lesbian was a hundred times worse. It sounded like a medical condition.

—Since when? I said.

—Since always, Denny.

She took a deep drag on her cigarette and blew the smoke out through her nose. She was wearin a denim jacket and jeans, her hair newly dyed a bright, shiny purple.

—Have yeh got a smoke? I said.

—You don't smoke.

—I do.

Me own confession was a bit less drastic than Paula's but that was all I had. She rummaged through her handbag.

—I've only two left, she said, but she tossed me one anyway. I put it to me lips and lit up, inhaled shallowly. Me ma was out at me mad aunty Denise's. She wasn't that mad at that time, though. Me ma would've killed me if she saw me smokin.

—Are yeh sure? I said.

Obviously that was a stupid thing to say. It was like somethin a character on The Wonder Years would blurt out. But that was the only reference point I had, the telly. Me ma and da never talked about lesbians. Not to me, anyway.

—Am I sure? Yeh fuckin serious?

Paula shook her head and turned her attention to Richard Whiteley. There was hurt in the look, though, mixed with the nonchalance, the defiance.

—I don't mean it like that, Paula. I just mean, like –

— Just leave it Denny.

She was still staring at Countdown. Paula hated Countdown, she said it was a show for nerds. Carol Vorderman was doin a sum. I fancied Carol Vorderman, a bit. She looks nicer the older she gets. I wanted to retrieve the situation, though. I didn't want to fuck things up.

—Have yeh got a girlfriend?

Paula stubbed out her cigarette. The way she did the stubbin, it was a statement: she bludgeoned the cigarette butt, a tiny act of violence.

She lit another cigarette and pursed her lips.

—I'm not messin, I said. —Just wonderin, yeh know? Seriously.

Fuck. It was dead embarrassin. Me sister was a . . . wha had Maggit called them? Dykes? I took a drag on me cigarette to calm down. Smoke curled in front o me eyes.

—Have yeh?

—I do as a matter o fact.

Paula's eyes were still on the screen. Maybe she was someone I knew, this girl? That would've been a bit weird. I didn't know any lesbians (except Paula, of course, and it seemed like I didn't know her at all), but maybe there was another surprise comin. Maybe it was someone I went to school with. Maybe someone off the road?

—Who?

—Yeh wouldn't know her.

—Well go on so.

—Her name's Teresa.

—Where's she from?

—Town.

—What's she like?

Paula rolled her eyes, then looked at her cigarette.

—She's nice, she said. —I like her.

I nodded. Wha the fuck else was I supposed to do? Congratulate her? And then somethin occurred to me.

—Wha about Harry?

—Wha about him?

—Does he know?

—About Teresa or me bein a lesbian?

—I don't know. Either.

—No, I don't think so.

I broke off a bit o me sausage. I could feel the grease coolin on me fingers.

—Maybe he has an idea, she said. —I don't know. I don't fuckin care either. He's a fuckin prick anyway.

—Took yeh long enough to say it.

I hated Harry Cummins. He was a leery bigheaded gimp and he'd taken a lend o Wrestlemania XII off me and never brought it back up. Bret Hart versus Shawn Michaels was on that one, the Iron Man match. I fuckin love that match. People'll tell yeh it's crap, that it goes on for over an hour and nothin happens in it, but that's why I love it – the slow build, all the holds and jockeyin. I was fuckin ragin Shawn Michaels won though. He fuckin loves himself.

—Well it's said now, said Paula. —I'm finished with him as of tonight. I told him. He can go fuck himself for all I care.

—Yer well shot of him.

—Yeah.

—The bleedin head on him. Fuckin knock a wall down with that head. He should hire his head out to builders, demolish a few walls.

Paula laughed.

—His head's somethin else, isn't it? I said. —Fuckin mallethead. It was deadly gettin to slag Harry off. Even before that night I knew Paula wasn't really mad into him, but she'd still never let yeh say boo about him. Even down to the videos I lent him: I'd say it to Paula and she'd look at me like I had two noses; for some reason Harry Cummins wasn't to be discommoded. Even if he robbed brand new wrestlin videos on yeh. Well, second-hand from Chapters, but they were new to me.

Paula turned to me. —Giz a bit o that sausage.

—Yeh can have it. I'm not hungry.

—Wonders never cease.

—How'll I get me videos back?

—I think he lent them out.

—To who?

Paula shrugged. Then she laughed. I looked at her for a few seconds, then I laughed as well. The videos were gone. But fuck it, so were a lot of things. I was glad.

★

The moth – and it is without doubt a moth, even if it is a freaky fat fuck nearly three inches long – is squattin still and upside-down on the ceilin o Paula's bedroom. Like them bats at the zoo. Paula's resumed her vantage point behind the door. I edge closer to the centre o the room, eyes glued to me prey. I'm slidin a kitchen chair along with me hip and I have a rolled up Vogue magazine in me right hand, although I'm not gonna whack it, like . . . I'm just gonna give it a nudge and see wha it does. I have the windows wide open, so hopefully it'll just fly the fuck off and that'll be the end of it.

I manoeuvre so that I'm nearly directly below the moth and stand carefully up on the chair. The moth's big and fat and dark brown and its legs are thick and hairy. Two weird-shaped antennae movin slightly. The wings are downy and –

—Watch it doesn't fly into yer face.

—Shush.

—They do. They don't know wha they're doin.

—Just shush, will yeh?

I slowly reach up towards the moth, tiltin me wrist back for leverage so I can kind o flick the thing away from me.

—Close yer mouth, says Paula. —It might go in yer mouth. It doesn't care if it dies. It knows no better.

—Shurrup, I say, although fuck it, I might as well close me mouth. Imagine that thing in yer gob? Fuckin sick.

Right. Here goes. Just a little tap. I plant me feet square on the padded seat o the chair and reach slowly towards the moth. The Vogue magazine is about five inches from the thing, Angelina Jolie warped and stretched on the rolled-up cover, and the moth still hasn't budged. Well, it's turnin slightly, in little jerky circles, like an anti-aircraft gun gettin its bearins.

—Get it!

I look at Paula. —I am gettin it, I say and turn back to the moth and out o nowhere it hurtles at me all flappin whirrin wings gigantic in me vision and I can feel it brush me face, soft and hairy and meaty and me legs jellify and I let out a stupid yelp and fall backwards off the chair onto the ground with a huge crash and the moth bashes against the window random and bat-like and Paula bolts and legs it down the stairs half screamin and half laughin.

—I told yeh I told yeh I told yeh Denny, they always go for the face ick ick ick ick!

GHOSTS AND LIGHTNING
CAST NO SHADOW

Fuckin hell, I've never seen rain like this before. Hurryin along a twistin Wicklow mountain road, eight miles from Enniskerry, three soaked and stoned intruders from the city. Teemin rain and roilin grey skies and a dull flat buzzin noise like static, like the sound yeh get off the telly when it's not properly tuned in. All around us a sodden earthy smell and behind it the faint tang o rusted iron. There's sheep huddlin in the fields beyond, black-eyed and watchin placidly, unmoved. I take a gulp from the bottle o wine I bought at the cornershop in the village and spill as much as I get in me mouth. The bottle's so wet the label's peelin off and I have to press it to me chest to make sure I don't drop it.

—I swear, yer fuckin gettin it buddy! FUCKIN BIGSTYLE!

Maggit spits the threat at the rumblin sky. His face is upturned as he runs and his eyes are half closed against the downpour; the fucker'd fight the rain if he could. Such mad fuckin rage inside Maggit, his shaven head and angry mouth, the lips pale and stretched, a lopin, cursin, tracksuited shape in the wild evenin, the tent packed high on his back. Ahead o me, Pajo is quiet and wide-eyed, turnin in circles as he jogs, amazed and awed by the sky's raw and sudden fury, the dozens o badges pinned to his denim jacket clackin like maracas.

Shane's been ringin me all day, the missed calls stackin up. Fuckim. A few hours ago we were in Dublin, in Eamonn Doran's for wha we assumed was the night, downin pints and fightin off the creepin dark and now we're here, in the arse end o nowhere, soaked and runnin. I couldn't face the thought o goin back to the house, the staleness and fuckin sadness of it all. Me ma's absence weighs on yeh like a sack o sand back there. We bought a cheap tent from an army surplus shop on Capel Street and hopped on the 44 outside Trinity College, spur o the moment job. Shots o vodka from the cap at the back o the bus, rain on the windows. Unusually for Pajo he had no pills on him so he bought a handful o herbal ecstasy from the hemp store, which has BZP or somethin in it, and I'm startin to come up on the two I popped, me teeth, legs and arms all warm and tingly. Feels nice, like there's a spell on me, protectin me from the cold; an invisible cloak wrapped tight around me.

—Didn't I fuckin tell yeh about the rain? says Maggit. —Didn't I fuckin say? Yeh can't be fuckin told, d'yeh know that?

Maggit's referrin to the fact that I said not to bother pickin up rain gear, but balls to that. Who needs to keep dry when yiv this mad stuff in yer bloodstream? Fuckin class this is.

—Fuck it man! I shout.—C'mon and dance!

I catch Maggit by the sleeve of his tracksuit top and twirl him, brief thin fans o red water springin up and fallin round our soppin feet.

—Dance yeh cunt! Yeow!

Pajo claps and laughs, the three of us beneath the swayin branches of a huge and ancient oak, raindrops fallin fat and sparse about us and ragin beyond. Red mud on the narrow road and the mountaintops wrapped in rags o mist. Maggit pulls away from me and shrugs the tarpaulin bag o tent poles from his shoulder, droppin them at Pajo's feet.

—Right, your fuckin turn. Yiz mad fucks.

Pajo grabs the bag two-handed and swings it up and over his shoulder, tiltin backwards with the awkward sudden weight before I grab him. I givvim a wink and he winks back.

—Sure we'll just pitch here then, I say. —Yeah?

—Me bollix, says Maggit. —Lookit them fuckin sheep Denny, yid wake up and one'd be in the fuckin tent eyeballin yeh.

—Don't be a clown.

—Balls, they'd give yeh the evil fuckin eye Denny, fuck that. Not sleepin in a field with sheep, no fuckin chance.

—Right so, I say, and I bound ahead, another surge o the pills washin through me. Where the fuck I'm goin I don't know but I start howlin as I run, like a madman from ancient times, a drugged up ancient clansman howlin at the wind, at sheep and bowin trees, at the whipped and tossin clumps o nettles, me hands above me head, clappin and spinnin and howlin still, howlin at the sheer fierce fuckin beauty and madness of it all, o the trees and rain, o the silent grey mountains and me gobshite friends, the oddness o things, the wonder of it, the sheer and mad and funny beauty.

★

Still buzzin I follow a narrow gravel path that leads off the main track and come to a garden, huge with a whitewashed bungalow at the bottom almost hid by high bent grass and overgrown bushes. I vault the gate and the others follow. There's an amber glow from the kitchen window and a shape movin, potterin back and forth. I look back over me shoulder.

—This do yeh?

—A bleedin garden?

—A garden or sheep, up to you. We'll be quiet, yeah? Just get the tent up and skedaddle first thing.

We're crouchin in the rain behind a blackberry bush. Maggit scratches his ear. Pajo's still smilin aimlessly, grindin his teeth at the same time in a weird, rictus, shiftin grin. I stick me head slowly above the cover o the bush. The shufflin shape is an old woman, forty yards away and oblivious, her hair long and white in a single braid hanging over her left shoulder. She reminds me o me nanny Cullen, me ma's ma. I touch the ring she gave me ma, the smooth white gold. It's her hair, mainly, that reminds me of her; me nanny Cullen never went for that blue rinse, short hair bollix. I run a hand through me own soppin hair. It's gettin long now, like; needs a cut. I duck back down.

—Just keep it down and we'll be grand, yeah? We'll be found dead out here if we keep this up, fuckin pneumonia like. Leave the place as we find it though, yeah?

—Right, says Maggit. —Fuck it. Fair enough.

Pajo shrugs. —Cool.

I take the bag from Pajo and slide out the first o the tent poles, then point it at Maggit, a blunt and wonky sabre.

—Grab that.

31

He does, and far off I hear the huge and darkly swellin grumble o distant thunder. The sound comes from a great depth, or it seems like it does anyway, to me, underwater, long and low and deeply sonorous. Somethin stirrin. Some immense and ancient form o life.

★

—Giz the flask over, Maggit, I say.

Maggit's lying on his side, readin *The Adventures of Huckleberry Finn*. I brung it up with me and I'm surprised to see him readin it. Books aren't his thing, yeh know? His upper body's pokin out of his sleepin bag, his long, wiry arms almost covered in dark blue tattoos. He has the Liverpool crest on his right shoulder and Che Guevara on his left. He's wearin his glasses and they make him look older than he is, his lips silently shapin the words. He shifts and grabs me Adidas bag, then throws it over.

—Hardly any left, he says.

Pajo's rollin up a joint and his fingers make me think of a documentary I saw a few days ago, with this close-up of a spider's legs as it rolled up a fly. Pajo's wired to the moon, but in a completely different way to Maggit; there isn't a hint o violence in Pajo. He's as serene as they come. And a bit frazzled, as well, to be honest; a bit addled, like. Black and white, these two. They don't even really look that similar, cept for the eyes.

—There y'are, Denny, says Pajo, passin the joint to me. Pajo's collarbone is pushin against his skin like it's tryin to force its way through.

I take a long, deep drag. Nice. I take another and then hand it to Maggit. Maggit closes over the book and takes the joint, regardin it for a few seconds between thumb and forefinger, then takes a quick puff. He nods his head and passes it back to Pajo, who taps the ash into an empty Monster Munch packet.

Pajo skootches over and sits beside me. His hair's brushed back over his head and his slightly yellow, misaligned teeth are bared in a big grin. He takes a heroic drag on the joint and offers the smoulderin remains to me. I wave it away.

—Yeh sure?

—Positive man, I'd be snoozin in no time.

Pajo nods. —Cool. Sound. Very wise.

I stretch and crack the bones in me neck.

—Preposterous, isn't it? says Pajo.

—Preposterous? Wha is?

—The weather.

Preposterous. Yid never catch anyone cept Pajo sayin that. It's not even really that preposterous at all, this weather in November, in the mountains. But yeh have to laugh. Madman, our Pajo.

Pajo's inspectin the inside o one of his soaked Doc Marten boots. Behind me I can hear Maggit readin, whisperin to himself. We're all knackered. Fuckin cold, as well. The BZP's wearin off, like. This was probably a dopey idea, comin up here.

—There's a few things we'll need for the séance, says Pajo

—Wha?

—A few things, like. Emm . . . trappins and that. I'll have to get a few things together.

—Like wha?

—Just . . . emm . . . there's a special candle. And yiv to have a strong-smellin spirit. Whiskey or wharrever.

33

—Right.

—Yeh have to do it proper, like. Yeh can't just mess around with the paranormal.

—Paula said it might be a revenant, I say. —Wharrever difference that makes. None.

—Well. There's different types.

I shake me head. —Yer a sky pilot.

—There is, though. There's, like, poltergeists, spectres, wraiths. And there's this Swedish one, a gjenganger. I don't think it's one o them, though. They'd probably have an accent.

—I suppose they would, yeah. Like ABBA.

Pajo nods. —Don't be, like, afraid or anythin Denny.

—I'm not afraid.

—Well . . . OK. Good. There's nothin to be afraid of.

—There's nothin there at all for fuck sake.

Pajo shrugs. I do feel a bit edgy, though. I mean, out in the middle o nowhere like this, fuck all protection. I saw a sheep's skull in one o the fields, big empty eye sockets and all its teeth still in place. Fuck that. I turn away from Pajo and look at Maggit.

He's still readin.

It's mad that. Maggit readin. Not that he's stupid or anythin. He's a canny bastard but he's not what yid call a scholar. Still, it's cool all the same, seein him gettin into a book. Lookin forward to askin him about it, actually. Havin a chat like, yeh know? I've known Maggit forever but we're dead dissimilar in loads o ways, and I think we're driftin. I wonder, sometimes, if we'd still be in touch if I hadn't o had to come back from Wales. If me ma hadn't of . . . like . . . and if I'd o stuck it out and got a decent job, or a qualification or wharrever. He never rang me while I was over there. Although I was only gone a few months so I suppose yeh can't make too much of it.

Me big plans. Off to Wales. Get a job. Get some money and go to university. Meet someone. Someone nice. Didn't happen. Dunno why I thought it might.

There yeh are, anyway. Must o stepped on a snake somewhere. Slid back to Dublin. Square one. Or Wicklow at this exact moment, which might be square two, or even minus one. Ah sure, details. I'm fucked either way.

Outside there's a small white bird dartin through the air from tree to tree. I think it's a lark but I wouldn't stick money on it. Shane or Gino would know. Gino especially, he's mad into birds.

Anyway. Busy oul thing, this lark or wharrever it is. Keeps dartin from the trees on one side o the garden to the other, dodgin raindrops. Then onto the roof o the bungalow and a low dip over the grass, dead close to the tent then back to the first tree. I can hear the whirr of its wings. It just keeps doin that, over and over, like it's castin a spell or somethin. The old woman could be a witch and the lark, or wharrever, her familiar anyway, is layin some strange curse on us, some witch's hex.

—Lookit that, I say.

Pajo puts down his boot and looks up.

—Wha?

—The bird there, lookit.

—The white one?

—Yeah, lookit the way it's flyin. Watch.

We sit there for a few minutes, our eyes dartin after the bird.

—Mad, isn't it?

—Yeah.

—Maggit.

—Wha?

—Lookit this out here. Wha kind o bird is that?

Maggit closes the book and shifts slightly, the evenin's dyin light catchin in his glasses. His head and jaw are stubbled. The glasses make him look strange, kind o . . . I dunno, vulnerable or somethin. Not that I'd say that to him.

He takes off his specs and peers past me and Pajo.

—Where?

—There, look. That white one on the bungalow, on the roof there. See it?

—The roof?

—There, look. Put yer glasses on.

—They're not fuckin binoculars Denny. Where?

—Look, there. Yid wanna get yer eyes tested again.

I meant that as an observation, the thing about the eye test. As advice or wharrever. But as soon as it comes out of me mouth I know it sounds like I was slaggin him. Maggit looks at me for a second, scopin me out, annoyed, then scratches his ear and sinks back down into his sleepin bag.

—Just sayin man, I say. —I don't mean like –

—I can't see the fuckin bird Denny, right? he says, without lookin up. —Poxy fuckin trip.

—Ah c'mon, says Pajo. —Don't start gettin cranky and, like . . . yeh know? Relax the cacks, lads. Deep breaths.

I nibble on one o me biscuits and shrug.

—Don't be so sensitive man, I say, and I wanna say more but fuck it, there's no point. For a harchaw Maggit's feelins are very easily bruised. Sometimes, anyway. Other times he'd laugh it off, slag yeh back. Fuckin impossible to know which road he'll take. Ah, sure. Rough and smooth, yeh know? Way o the fuckin world, isn't it? Too right, man. Too fuckin right.

★

It's freezin and we're swayin in the semi-dark o the tent, cross-legged and face-to-face like peace pipe smokers, three pale and bony totems grinnin at each other over Pajo's Euro-Stretcher lamp. I'm absolutely, completely and utterly spaced. I drum me fingers on the now empty biscuit tin. I'd love another Jammie Dodger. Ah well. Our shadows are lurkin behind us, full o mischief and intent, flickerin, shiftin as we shift, dark and stretched second-selves on the tent wall. Goin on about wrestlin for ages, the topic dredged up out o the past – The Undertaker and Bret Hart and Shawn Michaels. The mad spectacle, the pomp and lunacy. Undertaker was my favourite, Bret was Pajo's and Maggit's was Shawn. I've always loved wrestlin – the heroes and the villains and the stories they told with their bodies. The sound o the rain's heavy now and so's the hash's thick sweet smell and outside and above us, all around us, the deep sad sound o the night wind. Maggit and Pajo's faces are alive with smoke and shadow. *Huckleberry Finn*'s on me lap. It's an old copy, used to be me mad uncle Victor's.

Pajo shifts his weight and farts. It's dead loud and ripe and fruity. I don't mind cos Pajo's farts are basically odourless. Maggit's are toxic. We launch into a fit o deep and gulpin laughter. Seems like the funniest thing in the world, which is another sign o how far gone we are.

—Fuckin noise o that, says Maggit.

Pajo grins. —It's about yer posture, like. If yeh tilt a bit yeh can get great ones.

—Is that wha they teach yeah at yer Buddhist classes?

—Nah. Just, like, found out.

I brush a few crumbs off o the book's cover.

—Wha d'yeh think o the book? I say.

Maggit chews on a mouthful of Garibaldi. He washes it down with a swing from a bottle o wine. He's still on his detox. He reckons he's gettin a bit of a belly, which he is, so he's off the beer. I tried to tell him that detoxin on wine's not that likely to make a difference when yeh drink it by the bottle but the cunt knows it all, apparently.

—It's good, he says, noddin at the book.

—Yeah?

—Yeah, yeh know yerself, I'm not really mad on bukes. It's good.

Pajo reaches over and I hand him the book. He flips it in his hands, his fingers long and pale, and they get me thinkin about somethin else I saw on telly recently; they're like the vampire's fingers in Nosferatu, Pajo's are, that old black and white film. Not as long, obviously. I think they overdid it with Count Orlock's fingers actually, made him look a bit comical.

Maggit's chewin on another Garibaldi. He swallows loudly and says:

—Did I ever tell yiz about the time I caught a goblin?

—Wha?

—Did I ever tell yiz about the time I caught a goblin?

—Caught a goblin? Wha yeh on about?

Maggit sits forward and tilts his head, poppin the bones in his neck.

— Yeah, he says. —At this bird's gaff, like. I was on a bender with Tommy Power and Rochey, few days on the booze and all sorts. We ended up back at this bird's gaff in Tallaght.

—A goblin. Is this a joke? When was this?

—You were in Wales. Wait and I'll tell yeh. The three of us were wrecked like, in ruins. Then this bird, this hippy kinda bird like, breaks out the mushroom tea. She picked them herself, Dublin mountains job. Worst thing I ever did, drinkin that tea. Yiz know me and hallucinogenics. Specially cos I was drunk already and full o Red Bull. I lost the head like, ran out the door. This was broad daylight now as well, it was early in the mornin. We'd been up all night. I thought I could hear people talkin about me, slaggin me off, these whispery voices. It was weird, horrible like. Rochey was callin after me from the garden but I was fuckin gone, scarpered. So I ended up in this park I think, out near the mountains yer woman's house was, fuckin sweatin, freakin out, seein faces in the bushes, these mad demonic faces, eyes and all this, voices in me head, callin me a waster, a loser. Never doin mushrooms again, tellin yeh. So anyway, there I am goin mad and, out o nowhere I see this little fuckin goblin wearin a pair o dungarees standin in front o me, lookin up at me. Swear to fuckin God, now. This little goblin standin beside a bench lookin up at me.

—Like, a hallucination or wharrever?

—No. Listen. For real, like. This little goblin in dungarees. And soon as I saw it the voices stopped. Just stopped dead, silence. So I walked over and grabbed it. Caught it, like, cos I was thinkin to meself, it's the goblin that's after stoppin the voices. I grabbed it up and ran through the park and back to yer woman's house. It was cryin on the way, wah wah, all this, a mad little thing with round eyes, tears streamin out, but like I said, it was after gettin rid o the voices so happy days. The front door was still open so I put the goblin in the front room and called into the kitchen. Look wha I'm after findin, I says to them, so in comes the hippy bird and Tommy and Rochey. A fuckin goblin, I say. For real. So they follow me out and Rochey opens the door to the front room, pops his head in and then looks back at me. You for fuckin real, he says. And he looks fuckin horrified, yeh know? Yeah, I says. That's a fuckin Down syndrome kid yeh fuckin head-the-ball, says Rochey, yid wanna get her back where yeh found her before yer done for fuckin kidnappin. But I was too out of it, I crashed out in the kitchen, talkin to the spoons, off me mallet and wrecked tired as well. The hippy bird and Tommy took the kid back to the park and found its ma. They told her she'd wandered off so she was glad to have her back, no hassle, sorted. She was takin her to school. Like, a special school or wharrever, I suppose.

Maggit starts on a new Garibaldi. —Mad, wha?

—Yer a fuckin waffler.

—Swear to fuckin god, Denny. On Ant'ny's life. I fuckin swear to yeh, it happened. Cross me fuckin heart. Fuckin goblin I thought it was. Thought I was gettin a pot o gold.

—That's leprechauns, says Pajo.

—Yeah, wharrever. Don't they look a bit like goblins, though, them little Down syndrome kids?

—Yer off yer fuckin trolley, Maggit, I say. And I feel a bit fuckin, I dunno, a bit fuckin disgusted or somethin. Maggit's grinnin. Poor fuckin kid, like. Well, assumin that story was actually true. Given a) Maggit's legendary propensity for lyin, even about the most mundane stuff and b) Maggit's propensity to get wrecked and do mental fuckin things, it's a hard one to call.

I lean back, supportin meself with me flattened palms, me fingers spread wide. I saw a thing on telly about kids with Down syndrome years ago. I remember Paula laughin durin it, out o nervousness really, and me ma sayin that yer gift if yiv got Down syndrome is yeh automatically go to heaven. Makes up for the botch of a life (my words, not hers) that yer stuck with, I suppose. Years ago, that was . . . fuck. Time passin, wha? Tick tock, gettin older, yer bones –

—FUCK!

The tent flap rips open and a freezin swirlin wind and rain rushes into the tent. I scramble to me feet, me knee smearin the remains of a Snickers into the floor, then tumble out into the night with Pajo and Maggit behind me. It's fuckin freezin, thunder boomin overhead. The light from the old woman's kitchen clicks on and I stand there in the dark, grass knee-high, me hair flyin all over the shop. Pajo crouches in the grass, pattin the squelchy earth for the lost tent pegs. Maggit's down beside him, scramblin like a madman, and then he turns back to me, glasses agleam with lightnin and his voice high on the wind, a banshee wail through the mountains o Wicklow –

—Ghosts and lightnin cast no shadow, man! he half roars, half laughs. He holds up one o the uprooted pegs, his arm straight above his head, the peg pointed at the heavin sky. I shake me head.

—The fuck yeh up to?

41

There's another deep rollin boom above us and a huge forked flash miles beyond the bungalow. For a split second we're in daylight, but the light's sick and caustic, too white, too severe. I can see the raindrops as they fall, millions o them; it's like lookin up at a streetlight durin a storm, all these drops o rain fallin, minute but separate, individual. Then fuckin deep-sea blackness dives down on top of us and I can hardly see a thing, just shapes and shades o darkness.

—Tellin yeh Denny! Lookit man! In the buke like, d'yeh remember? Ghosts and lightnin cast no fuckin shadow! Member that? Too fuckin right! Fuckin mad or wha!

★

—AHHHHHHH! ME FUCKIN BACK!

Me eyes flick open and I scramble onto me elbows. What the fuck's goin on?

—Out ye come now, boys.

—ME BLEEDIN VERTEBRAE!

—Pajo? Wha the fuck?

—I'M CRIPPLED!

Maggit scrambles hands-and-knees over me and out o the tent. I can't see anythin, just a red and blue gloom. Me head's killin me. Jesus. I always imagine hangover headaches as jellyfish, pulsin away in the pink waters o me brain.

—GERRA WHEELCHAIR!

—A wheelchair he says! Will another rock do ye?

Who the fuck is that? It's a country accent, anyway, pure bogger. Bollix to this. Pajo wails somewhere at the end o the tent. I follow Maggit, pullin the collapsed tent over me head as I go, then flop out into the mornin. The sudden sunlight sears me eyes. There's a pair o mud-spattered but otherwise shiny boots inches from me nose. Two pairs, actually. I look up.

Fuck.

There's two coppers standin over me and Maggit's slightly to the side, in his Liverpool boxers, which looks kind o bad. I told him last night to leave his tracksuit bottoms on. The four of us are in the middle of a small field o wet grass, the sky pale blue above us.

—Calm fuckin down, says Maggit to one o the guards. —We're doin fuck all.

I can see the old woman standin in her porch, her hand to her mouth and a baldy fella standin beside her. The sun's burnin a hole in me fuckin head. One o the guards is holdin a big lump o shale in his hands.

—Did youse drop that on us?

Bit of a stupid question, I know. But for fuck sake, that's a bit much, isn't it? Droppin bleedin rocks on people? The piggy fucks.

—Ah no, says the garda with the rock. —Just dropped out of the sky. Pure fuckin miracle.

The two o them laugh. One o them, the older one, has a turn in his eye. He's rosy-cheeked and double-chinned and his hat's tucked under his arm. His thinnin brown hair is swayin slightly in the wind. Makes me think o seaweed, the way it's wavin. The other fella's much younger and besides the massive, donkey-ish teeth, he's probably wha yid call a good-lookin fella.

I stand up, suddenly conscious o me bare upper body. I hold me left bicep with me right hand, tryin to casually cover meself up. Maggit has no such worries, still arguin away in his boxers. The older copper gives me a dirty look, then Pajo crawls out o the tent behind us. His eyes are sunken and red-rimmed and he's got one hand pressed into the small of his back.

—That's assault, says Pajo as he claps eyes on the gardaí.
—That's battery.

—I'll batter ye now if ye want, says the younger garda. He's smilin, his donkey teeth bared, but you can see the smile for the smokescreen it is; he's twitchin, barely fuckin contained, pure dyin for a scrap. I cup me other hand over me groin.

—Ever hear of private property, boys? says the older garda.

—We were just campin, I say.

—In someone's back garden? This the new thing in the city then?

The younger one's sneerin now. —Fuckin Dublin junkies, he says. —No fuckin class.

—Better than bein a state-owned bogman cunt, says Maggit.

Fuckin hell, no point in goadin the pricks. Fuck that. We've –

There's an explosion in me jaw and I feel me teeth rattle in me head. I hit the grass like a sack o sloppy shite and the oul garda's face appears above me, all the culchie quaintness gone and replaced by a slaverin fat-faced lunatic. I try to curl up and he lays into me ribs with the toe of his boot and fuckin hell, an arcin flash o pain shoots through me. I can see Maggit through me guard tusslin with the younger fella and another boot catches me in the stomach, the breath flyin out o me in a hot, sweet belch.

—That's an abuse o human rights yiz nazis! Pajo squeaks, dancin madly on the spot, skinny and white-skinned, and then I see the bird again, the lark or wharrever, dartin through the mornin sky and flyin towards me, dead on, locked in, ready to catch me final earthly breath.

★

Our money's gone. We'd fifteen euro, roughly, most of it in change, and it's fuckin gone. That was to do us for bus fare once we got back to Enniskerry. Pajo says the coppers must o took it. Now is that fuckin petty or wha? Fifteen poxy euro, the robbin bastards.

We're trampin back along the road we took yesterday. Me clothes are still damp but at least the sun's out, so it's not too bad. Cept the pain in me ribs, like, and the ache in me jaw. The fields on either side a slick and shiny deep green. Loads more sheep. I'm tempted to say this is all the sheeps' fault but to be fair it's not, it's ours. Or more specifically Maggit's, he's the one with the wacko phobias and the big fuckin gob. Wha did he have to say that to the gardaí for?

Pajo's complainin about his foot. He says it's killin him and that one of the gardaí must o stamped on it. He's gettin a bit twitchy as well, cos he needs to get back to Dublin to get his new methadone script.

—Don't know how yer foot's fucked, Paj, I say. —Yeh left us to get fuckin battered.

—Well, I was in the melee, like, he says. —Collateral damage. Yeh know I'm a pacifist. And I was the one got a boulder in the back.

—There's a time and a place for Martin Luther King quotes though, Pajo. Fuck sake. Wha were yeh thinkin?

—I can't, like, get involved, Denny. It says so in the Koran.

—Yeh do know the Koran's not a Buddhist book, don't yeh?

—Ah leavim, says Maggit. —He's no use in a scrap anyway.

I look up at Maggit. He's swishin a thin, leafless branch in front of him, the tent packed high up on his shoulders. There's a small yellow bruise under his left eye.

—We're not talkin about conscientious fuckin objection here, Maggit. This is me, on the ground, gettin the bollix kicked out o me cos o you, while –

—Yeh can't fuck with beliefs, Denny, he says.

He delivers the line with a generous dollop o weight and finality, like he's King fuckin Solomon or somethin.

I slow up a bit and let Pajo and Maggit pull ahead. It's mad, but in a way I'm glad we're in this position. It's to do with the house, really. I'm happy enough out here, even though it's cold and me smokes and socks are damp and me head's bangin. I don't wanna get back just yet. And that stupid fuckin séance thing as well. I'll be fuckin honest here – I'm dreadin it. Totally fuckin dreadin it. Dunno why. It's all just yer mind, isn't it? It's just human psychology. We trick ourselves. We have to, to get by.

That's all it is.

I think so, anyway.

I've had this feelin before, this dread. I was only a kid, maybe seven or eight, and one o me uncle Victor's stories was playin on me mind. I'd been to visit him with me ma and Paula, at his caravan, and he'd told me about the banshee. He was always on about ghosts and fairies and all sorts o mad stuff, and usually I loved it but the banshee was too much – he'd scared the shite out o me. The banshee, accordin to Victor, was an ancient hag with long, dirty hair, and if yeh were unfortunate enough to see her, as he once had in Balbriggan, she'd be pullin a comb through her greasy tangles. But it was those that heard her that had to watch out – to hear a banshee wail was a sign that someone you knew was about to die.

So later on I was sittin in the front room with me ma. It was gettin late but I didn't want to go to bed. I shared a room with Shane and Gino but they were older so they didn't have to go up yet. They were sittin in the kitchen, talkin. Plannin somethin, probably. Paula was up in her room.

—I'm not even tired, I said to me ma. Really I was knackered but I'd worked meself into a terror about the banshee, imaginin hearin her keenin outside me window. Or, worse, lookin in at me, her withered old face smeared up against the glass. Me ma looked up at me. She was sittin at the end o the sofa, the light from the telly on her face. Her hair was tied back. I was sittin at the opposite end o the sofa, me legs curled up under me. Me da was workin a nightshift, I think. Or out drinkin, or chasin women or worse.

—Yiv school in the mornin, me ma said, tryin the obvious first.

—I'm not tired.

—Yer eyes were droppin a minute ago. I was watchin yeh.

—I'm not tired now though.

47

But she wasn't havin it. Often me ma would let us stay home from school if we made some half-arsed gesture, like washin the dishes or lightin the fire. She was dead soft in that way. But if me da was in, and he would be the next mornin, either wrecked from work or hung over, there was no chance – he'd whip us into school. He wouldn't so much as give yeh a hug but he'd never let us miss a day o school.

A few minutes later I was standin at the top o the stairs. I was there for a minute or two when me ma opened the door in the hall below. She walked up the stairs and sat a few steps down from me.

—Is there such a thing as banshees, ma? I said.

—Banshees?

—Yeah.

—Who told yeh about banshees?

I told her I didn't know who told me, I just knew about them. It was like aliens or yetis, everyone knew about them. I didn't want to get Victor into trouble.

—Is there such a thing as them? I asked her.

—They're not real, Denny. They're only stories.

I wasn't convinced.

—They're stories is all, Denny, she said again.

—Victor said a banshee chased him across a field, I said, already forgettin about protectin Victor's identity. I felt bad for a second, then glad it was out. I was startin to hate him for scarin me.

—Don't mind him, me ma said.

—He said though. He told me.

—Victor's a great fella for stories, Denny. He's a space cadet. Wait and I get a fuckin hold of him. Tellin tales to children.

—He said a banshee flew after him. It was white.

—It was probably just a bag or somethin.

—A bag?

That was stupid.

—A plastic bag, she said. —Blowin.

No way. I'd seen plastic bags caught in the wind and they didn't look like banshees. Especially in one important detail.

—Bags have no hair, though, I said. —Banshees have dirty long hair that they comb.

Me ma thought for a second. She knew she had a fight on her hands convincin me. She took me hand, then she smiled and nodded.

—OK, she said. —I'll be honest with yeh. Yeah? Cross me heart.

I nodded.

—It wasn't a bag, she said. —There's no foolin yeh. D'yeh wanna know what it really was?

I nodded again. I felt like I was bein let in on a secret. Like I was a grownup.

—Yeh sure? she said.

—Yeah.

—It was a monkey.

I wasn't prepared for that.

—A monkey?

—A monkey.

—A monkey in a field?

—He was escaped from the zoo.

—A white monkey?

—Yeah, a white monkey. He was Japanese, I think. It was in the news at the time and everythin. Everyone was tryin to catch it.

—Really?

—Cross me heart. There was this monkey over from Japan on a tour. He was owned by the emperor.

—Do monkeys have long hair?

—This type does. They're called longhaired Japanese imperial monkeys or somethin like that. They're rare.

—And it chased Victor?

—Yeah. It was hidin in the fields in Balbriggan. It was wild out there then. Wilder than now, and it was—

—Was there bananas out there?

—No. Loads of apples, though. That's what he was livin off. Victor was comin home from the pub and he did his wee against a tree. Dirty oul fecker. But wasn't the monkey livin in this tree? That was his hideout. He wasn't very happy when he saw wha Victor was up to, so he jumped down and chased him.

—Really?

—Swear to God.

—And where's the monkey now?

—Ah he's back home in Japan. They caught him and sent him back.

—He must be old.

—He is. He has a handy life over there though, belongin to the emperor. He just takes it easy, sits around and that. The only thing was, when he got back to Japan, he wouldn't eat bananas anymore; all he'd eat was oul crab apples from Ireland. Yer uncle Victor sends him one over every Christmas for a present, to say sorry for weein against his tree.

That made me laugh. A crab apple from Ireland for Christmas. I wasn't really sure about wha me ma told me but it didn't matter, I wasn't afraid anymore. That Christmas me and me ma sent a huge crab apple to Japan for the monkey as a present. Well, we wrapped it up and put a little tag and that on it, and addressed it to the emperor's palace in Japan, and me ma took it with her to Ballyfermot when she was shoppin and said she'd posted it.

So that's wha I'll keep tellin meself; that there's fuck all under anyone's bed at home, and that Paula's ghost is nothin, fuck all, an escaped white-haired Japanese monkey.

★

There's a tractor bumblin along in the field to our left, thick black smoke billowin from the exhaust. I've counted three dead rabbits on the road so far, squashed to bits, and four hedgehogs. Meself and Maggit have a game goin; he's countin dead rabbits and I'm countin the hedgehogs. The winner's owed a pint if we ever get back to civilisation. I've never seen a live hedgehog before, only dead ones, so I'm fairly sure the pint's mine. Bit macabre, I know, but fuck it.

—There's another one, five.

It's in the bag. Yid think they'd learn, hedgehogs, acquire over time some race memory that tells them roads are bad, they're populated by gleamin giants that screech and squash, AVOID.

At a turn in the road there's a furry, meat-streaked lump, smeared with dark, blackish blood.

—Rabbit, says Maggit. —Four.

—Bit big for a rabbit, I say. —The thing's three foot long.

—A hare then, says Maggit. —Four.

—A hare's not a rabbit though. I don't get points for rats or wharrever. Yer still on three.

—I think it's a badger, says Pajo. He hunkers down beside it, then looks back over his shoulder at us. —Yeah, he says. —A badger. Pity, isn't it?

He straightens up and the three of us stand round the squashed badger. I feel sad or somethin. It's weird, but a badger seems more relevant, somehow, than a rabbit or a hedgehog. More of a loss. Badgers, like, they're noble, yeh know? Battlers. I saw a thing on telly where these pricks were makin them fight pit bulls, but the badgers were after havin their teeth and claws pulled out. Fuckin sick, like. They still gave nearly as good as they got, the poor fuckers, until these pricks stepped in with cruel-lookin, barbed shillelaghs and whacked them till they let go o the dogs.

—That's a point each then, says Maggit.

—Wha?

—One each for a badger.

—What's the point o that? It's the same difference.

Maggit shrugs. —Dunno. Bonus points.

—Fuck it man, I say. —Leave it. I'll get yeh the pint, yeah?

★

I mash up some holly berries and smear DUBLIN onto a bit o cardboard that Maggit found in a bush, but no one stops to pick us up. By eleven o' clock we've been goin for nearly three hours and Pajo's had enough.

—I can't go on, me foot's gone queer.

—Sit down then. Sit fuckin down and I'll have a look at it, says Maggit.

Pajo shuffles off the road and eases himself over a bit o mangled fence and onto a tree stump. Pure theatrical, like. He's a bit of a hypochondriac. A while ago I called round to him and he was sittin in his gaff, wrapped up in a blanket and sippin a mug o green tea, watchin some David Attenborough thing on telly. He looked wretched. I asked him wha was up.

—I have salmonella, he said.

Salmo-fuckin-ella. He couldn't even just say it was flu. Course, it turned out he had a bog standard cold, but there was no tellin him. He even debated it with Dr McSorley, quotin stuff from ER and Dr Hilary out o the Sunday magazines.

Pajo's mumblin somethin under his breath. It's some sort o prayer by the sounds of it, made up as he goes. I'm not sure wha this whole religion thing is with him. I mean, wha comfort does pretendin to be a Buddhist or wharrever give him? What's wrong with pretendin to be a Catholic like the rest of us?

—Here, I'll take it off, says Maggit.

—Careful, says Pajo.

And, surprisinly, he is careful, teasin out the clump o soggy knots. It's a strange scene, Maggit a bowed and shaven-headed supplicant at the feet of a shiverin, green-haired waif on a country road.

—Yeh OK? I shout over.

Pajo nods.

I stand in off the road and light meself a cigarette with a box o matches from Maggit's rucksack. I have to shield the tiny flame from the wind with me jacket. A car rumbles towards us, muddy red water sprayin from the wheels. There's a middle-aged woman drivin it, pudgy with black curly hair, and she looks worried when she sees us, alarmed nearly; three ravaged pilgrims in off the hills and bent on murder. I give her a big smile as she passes.

—Yiz know wha? I say. —Bollix to this. I'm gettin a fuckin car. Bit o bleedin freedom, like. Independence.

They're not even listenin to me.

—Will yeh stop movin for fuck sake? says Maggit.

Pajo nods and then grimaces as Maggit teases the boot off his foot. There must really be somethin wrong with him, the poor sap. There's a big hole in the heel end of his threadbare green sock.

—That feels miles better, says Pajo.

Maggit stands up, holdin the boot. I step over the fence and take a gander, tryin to assess the extent o Pajo's war wounds. He's rubbin his foot with both hands. A raindrop hits me cheek.

—Yeh alright to go on?

—Ah yeah, just, like, give us a minute.

Maggit turns the boot in his hand and somethin falls out. Sunlight catches it, wharrever it is. Then somethin else. We look down and in the muddy grass there's a small pile o coins.

Our money.

—The fuckin money's in yer shoe, I say.

Pajo looks up at me, genuinely amazed to see the coins spillin from his boot. I swear to god, I have never met a more addled, oblivious fucker in me life.

—The money's in yer shoe yeh clown.

Pajo bites his lip.

—Yeh stupid bleedin cunt, says Maggit, and the boot clonks off Pajo's head.

PLAYSTATIONS ARE STUPID

I'm trampin along Moore Street, shoulders hunched up against the rain, neon and fairylights flashin in the puddles and dodgy-lookin dancin snowmen in every shop window when I hear someone callin me.

—Denny, yeh bleedin deaf or wha?

I turn and it's Ned, half-hid behind a bockedy oul dealer's stall. This used to be the nearest yid get to old Dublin – old Dublin women with harsh inner city accents cryin out the price o their bananas or fresh fish, shawls on their heads and their faces weathered and furrowed. It's the centre o the new Dublin now, though – the oul stalls are still there but they're surrounded by Chinese or Polish food stores and African hairdressers, brightly coloured and festooned with wild drapery and strange symbols, and everywhere a mad hubbub of duelling accent and language. Probably symbolic o how some Irish people feel – like they're surrounded by outsiders in their own land. But things change though, don't they? I suppose Ireland's just been slower to realise that. I mean, we're an island and we're right out at the edge o Europe; even the Romans never made it this far. If yeh thought Japan was a closed society then think again, Ireland was yer quintessential cut-off island – up till I was about twelve I'd never even seen a black person in real life. The only non-white person I knew as a kid was a little fella from Vietnam and everyone, even the older kids on the estate, was afraid of him cos they assumed he was some kind o martial arts killin machine. He couldn't throw a karate chop to save his life, though; all he was interested in was Transformers.

Anyway, Ned's rubbin his hands together feverishly. This isn't usually Ned's style, he's more into coldcallin with dodgy, probably-robbed-somewhere-along-the-line-but-now-untraceable vacuum cleaners or mobiles phones. And he's usually one for shirts and shoes, as well. But not today. Here he is, in a tracksuit and a roughed-up leather jacket, huddled under a red and blue tarpaulin and grinnin from ear to ear. There's boxes and boxes o chocolate, Twixes and Mars Bars, Bountys and Curly-Wurlys, piled up in front of him. And a load o selection boxes under the table as well.

—Where'd yeh get all this?

Ned winks.

—Never divulge yer sources Denny. Not good for business.

—What's wrong with it then? Dog chocolate or wha?

—Nah. Turns yeh into a zombie.

—Voodoo chocolate. Quality.

—That's it.

I get in under the stall. Ned's beanie is pulled down over his ears and a few blond curls are stickin out. His eyes are a clear, cold-lookin blue. His beard's grown out a bit and he looks like yer man off Aston Villa, Olof Mellberg.

—Yeh doin alright? I say.

He pats his pocket. —Tidy sum in here, mo chara. Tidy oul sum.

—When yeh knockin off?

Ned looks at his watch.

—An hour or so. Yeh up to anythin?

—I've to meet Maggit. Supposed to be droppin into Bernadette's with him.

Ned makes a face. —Wouldn't fancy that.

—Yeah, well. It's little Anthony's birthday.

—That's right.

—Yeah. Maggit doesn't wanna drop in on his own, so . . . I said I'd go, like.

—More fool you, Den.

A woman and a little youngfella wander over to the stall. The youngfella's wearin a huge pair o glasses. Fuckin titanic things. His eyes are like poached eggs behind the lenses.

—How much are the selection boxes? says yer woman.

—Three for ten euro love, says Ned.

—Wha ones are they? Are they good ones?

—Cadbury's, says Ned. —A Dairy Milk, Dairy Milk Buttons, Curly-Wurly, them little animal ones, a Fudge and a Crunchie.

—Is there no Toffee Crisp? she says.

—That's Nestlé love.

The woman looks like she's makin a hard decision. Tryin to psych Ned out, like. She kind o twists her mouth and looks over at the side entrance to the Ilac Centre, as much as to say, I dunno, I could probably get a better deal in there.

—The Ilac Centre, says Ned, just that and nothin else, but the way he says it it's like the woman'd be a gobshite to go in there. Crafty fuck, like.

—Ah go on, then, she says, turnin back. —I'll have the three.

Ned sticks the boxes in a plastic bag and takes yer woman's money and hands her the change.

—Wha yeh gettin off Santy? I say to the youngfella.

—A Playstation 2 and games and two joypads, says the youngfella. Rattles it off. Must be sayin it to himself before he goes to bed or somethin, like a prayer or a mantra. I used to do that meself.

—Deadly, says Ned. —Yeh must o been very good, so.

Then somethin occurs to Ned. If yeh squint yeh can nearly see the cartoon lightbulb over his head. He looks up at the woman.

—If yer lookin for a few games for the youngfella I'll be here on Stephen's Day. All the top titles. The new Grand Theft Auto and FIFA, everythin. Just gettin them off me hands, like. Brand new.

—We'll be alright, says the woman, wrinklin up her nose. —Santy's gettin him loads o games. She takes the youngfella's hand and walks off. The bottoms of her pink tracksuit are soakin and dirty-lookin from the rain. Ned looks at me.

—That sounded a bit ropy didn't it? Fuckin FIFA. Shite. Need to work on me technique. Haven't been on a stall in ages. This is fuckin below me, man. Fuckin Curly-Wurlys.

—Yeh were grand.

—Fuckin demeanin though. A man o my talents.

He spits and tugs his beanie down a bit further.

—Ah sure fuck it anyway, he says. And then he smiles. —Sure them selection boxes aren't worth a shite. They're all out o date, lookit.

He shows me one o the boxes. Points at the date.

—Yeh cheeky bastard, I say, but I laugh as well.

Ned winks.

—I was gonna ask yeh, I say. —D'yeh fancy poppin round the house in a week or so for somethin to eat? You and Sinead.

—Yeah, sound.

—I'm makin a dinner. A Christmas kind of a dinner. I'll ask the rest o them as well.

—Yeah, sounds cool Denny. I'll say it to Sinead.

I pick up one o the selection boxes. —That's Maggit's dessert sorted, anyway.

Ned laughs. A couple with bulgin shoppin bags stop at the stall for a few seconds and Ned's just about to start his spiel when they turn and head off. I'm startin to cramp his style now, so I better run. I dunno why, but I feel compelled to mention the séance before I go. Ned's fairly balanced compared to most o me mates, like.

—Did yeh hear about this séance thing?

Ned looks at me for a sec, eyebrows furrowed. —Séance?

—Yeah. Pajo's gonna be doin one at the house. For Paula, like. She says the place is haunted.

—Haunted?

—Yeah. A ghost house, she calls it.

Ned shakes his head.

—Tell me about it, I say. —Expect a shout from Pajo, anyway. He said he wants to get a few of us together. So there yeh go, yiv a dinner and a séance to look forward to.

—Never a dull moment, wha?

—No fuckin chance, Ned.

★

59

—Don't tell me. Yeh robbed it, didn't yeh?

Maggit shrugs, closes his Nike bag and looks at his watch. We're waitin for the 78a out o town. Been here fuckin ages, like, standin outside the Boots on Aston Quay. Least it's stopped rainin. There's a stale chemical smell comin up off the Liffey across the road and some mentalcase Cork chap's rantin and ravin about eternal damnation and all sorts o shite down near O'Connell Bridge. He's a good hundred yards away and I can still hear him. Psychos, those fellas. Wired to the fuckin moon, like, spittin and splutterin and wreckin everyone's head. Where do they get the neck? Well, from God, I suppose. Or that's wha they'd say, anyway. Divine gift o the Hard Neck or some other shite. Must be weird to have that kind o faith. Like a suit of armour, yeh know? Yer bulletproof, like. Or yeh think yeh are, which I suppose brings its own dangers.

I turn back to Maggit. He's diggin a finger into his ear and workin it round in sharp little circles.

—I betcha yeh did, didn't yeh? I say.

Maggit inspects the greasy brown smudge on his finger, then sniffs it.

—And yer point is? he says.

There are loads o potential answers to this, o course. The first would be that accordin to the Bible and all that bollix, robbin is inherently and soul-compromisinly wrong. Hell and damnation awaits. Pitchforks, worms for yer dinner, Whitney Houston on the radio twenty-four seven, the lot. Another more practical reason would be the couple years in Mount Joy Maggit could end up with, given his previous. He did a few months for bein caught with a shitload o Tommy Power's hash while Tommy was in Venezuela a couple years ago. I remember visitin him and some cunts from Mayo had given him a hidin after a hurlin game on the telly. His eye was out like a rotten golf ball.

—Yeh don't give your only son a robbed fuckin . . . wha is it?

—Some kind o . . . hang on . . .

He looks into his bag.

—Some computer yokeybob. Playstation is it? Lookit.

He pulls apart the lips o the bag and sticks it under me nose. There's some grey box thingy with wires and buttons inside. I've never bothered with computer games and that kind o thing, really.

—Wharrever, I say. —It's robbed. That kid looks up to yeh. Which leaves him fucked if yeh ask me.

Maggit clutches the bag closer to him and knits up his eyebrows. He fiddles with the little silver cross hangin from his ample left ear.

—Sure Ned was just sayin about games and that, I say.

—Yeh could o got one off him instead.

—They'd still be robbed.

—Not always. Sometimes he just gets them cheap.

—Wouldn't be beholden to that cunt, says Maggit.

—Wha d'yeh mean beholden? He's a mate for fuck sake.

Maggit spits. I shake me head and lean back against the wall. There's a gaggle o bus drivers to our left, on their tea breaks. Standin in the middle o them there's this mad fella I always see around here. He's kind o like a silent counterbalance to the ranter by the bridge. He looks like Dustin Hoffman in Rain Man and he's always wearin the same shabby suit. I reckon he's obsessed with buses and bus drivers. Every time I've ever waited for a bus he's been here, smilin, hangin out with the drivers. I wonder where he lives? Probably in some sort o care home or wharrever, yeh know, one o these houses where loads o mad people live and they're watched over by nurses and that? Hope he doesn't, though. Hope he has some sort of independence, some little flat say, filled with bus timetables and notebooks packed with odd insights into the secret codes o bus routes. It's mad, isn't it, the weird obsessions people have?

—You bought that dodgy mountain bike off Tommy Power so you can say fuck all, says Maggit.

I shrug. I'm not lookin for an argument, like. And I'm not tryin to paint meself as some saintly character anyway. It's just like I said, foolish thing to do given his criminal record. And he's got a son and I don't.

—Yeh sound like Bernadette, says Maggit, goaded by me silence. —Where'd yeh get this, where'd yeh get that? Fuck sake. Rather chop me bleedin ears off. It's only a bleedin computer, Denny. He won't even know it's robbed.

—Without a box? No even manuals or anythin?

—I'll say it was on display or wharrever. The last one in the shop.

—Gerra grip. Anybody'd know that was robbed. Sure it's got fuckin stickers on it and everythin.

—I'll peel them off.

—And wha about the kid who owned it? Is he not gonna miss it?

Maggit thinks about this. He looks into the bag again, like he might o robbed the answer as well by accident.

—Fuckim, says Maggit. —Why should my son have to do without?

The bus lurches round the corner towards us.

—Cos yiv no fuckin job and no intention o gettin one, ever?

Which is rich comin from me. Maggit surprisinly avoids the obvious comeback and instead just points at his arse. Maggit was shot by a Triad marksman in London a few years ago. Well, so he tells people, anyway. I was there and in reality it was the ancient fuckin owner of a Chinese takeaway that shot him, with an antique musket or a blunderbuss or somethin, in Liverpool, after that crappy Spurs game at the end o the season where Gustavo Poyet scored against us and ruined any chance we had o catchin Arsenal. Still finished ahead o United, like, but anyway, Maggit broke into the place after we were thrown out earlier that day for actin rowdy. Well, it was Maggit and Tommy Power who were actin rowdy, me and Ned were just standin there, waitin on our beef curries and chicken balls. The fella that shot him was about fuckin ninety and we had to make a nappy for Maggit out o tea towels to stop him bleedin all over the place on the ferry home.

—I'm fuckin disabled, he says.

The bus pulls up to the kerb and the doors open. The driver's a woman. Youngish, about me own age and . . . actually, she looks dead familiar . . . the small features, the slightly pointy chin. I think I might o gone to school with her. Can't remember her name though. Sonia, was it? Susan? Sarah? Fuck, it's gone.

—Great to see a few colleens behind the wheel, says Maggit, who obviously hasn't recognised her at all. He winks at her and she gives what must be the most tired and practised smile in Dublin. I drop me change into the machine and try not to make eye contact. I hate forgettin people's names, needless embarrassment for all concerned, like. Me ticket peels out o the machine and I take it and head upstairs, feelin slightly grubby, and we grab the seats at the back, which are me least favourite but almost ritually significant with Maggit.

After a couple o stops the bus is practically full. A gang o people in shirts and ties take their seats, starin blankly ahead or out the windows, off from work and stuck in traffic, heads full o numbers that won't go and the prices o laptops. A few seats up a Chinese student-type is talkin dead loud and quick into a tiny mobile phone. Crazy language Chinese, harsh and singsong at the same time. Makes me think o yer man that shot Maggit; that clangy, bell chime quality. A handful of oldies get on as well, faces aged and lined, the grannies speakin quick and clipped, the oulfellas winkin and laughin deep, and then a couple o local Neilstown bogies hop on and sit across from us. I know them to see but not by name. The fuckin head on yer man, the one at the window, like; spudheaded, bald and battered. Big puffy red and blue jackets. They're mates o that mentalcase racist freakjob Slaughter, I think; yer man that battered the Nigerian student outside Trinity College. Left him spittin teeth or so the story goes. The bus kicks into life again outside Frawley's on Thomas Street and yer man with the head turns for some reason and his small eyes are on mine and he's seein a gangly ghoul, I suppose, a state scrounger wallowin in his labour and in his mind's eye I'm battered, bloodpumpin, and then his mate nudges him and whoop-laughs and I turn me head away. Maggit has the Nike bag on his lap. He picks absentmindedly at a 'No Smoking' sticker on the window as the bus trundles on.

—I'll get him one at some stage, he says.

—Wha?

He turns to me. —Buy him one, like. When I've a few quid.

—Yer foolin yerself, Maggit.

He looks at the bag and then stares out the window again, at town passin by, the cars and bikes and people with bags o shoppin. People I'll never know, I'll never see again.

★

Maggit rings the bell and a little youngfella in a stripy Dennis the Menace-style jumper answers the door. There's cake mashed all over his face and into his hair, makin it stand up in little jammy tufts and spikes.

—Wha? he says.

Maggit hunkers down. —Is Anto's mammy in? he says.

—Wha?

—Anto's mammy, Bernadette. Is she in?

The youngfella looks over his shoulder and back down the hall. I can hear music and laughin from inside. The little fella's obviously dyin to get back in.

—Who's Anto? he says.

Maggit rolls his eyes.

—Ant'ny, he says. —Me son. The little blondy fella; Anto. I've a present for him.

The youngfella picks his nose. —Ant'ny, he says. —It's Ant'ny's birthday today.

Maggit shakes his head. He stands up and looks at me.

—Fuckin hell, he says, under his breath. —Dense, wha?

—He's only a kid.

I ring the doorbell again, and look down at Cakeface.

—Yiv a bit of jam on yeh there, I say.

He looks up at me and starts wipin at his forehead, mashin the cake all over the place.

—Birthday cake, he says, grinnin.

I'm about to ring the bell again when Bernadette comes walkin down the hall and the little fella legs it back inside, squealin. Bernadette's wearing a pair o faded jeans and a pink strappy vest. There's a party hat on her head, perched lopsidedly on her blonde braids. A fierce, righteous look comes into her eyes when she sees Maggit. She stops in the doorway, plants one hand on her hip and lifts the other to her lips, takin a long pull on her cigarette.

—Yer late, Colm, she says, lookin at Maggit. —As per usual. If yid left it any later he'd be seven.

—I know, I know, says Maggit.

He sniffs, then looks at the ground and scratches his ear.

—Sorry, he says.

Maggit looks at me.

—The bus took ages, didn't it?

—Yonks.

Bernadette shoots me a look and I feel like a fuckin beetle or somethin. Somethin small and nasty. Which is fair enough, in a way: if yid got a kid with Maggit yid tend to have a fairly poor perception o men in general. Fuck all to do with me, like, the ins and outs o their relationship, but I feel dead bad for Bernadette sometimes. Ah well.

—He didn't think yeh were comin, says Bernadette. —This is the only sixth birthday he's gonna have, by the way. Yeh do know that, don't yeh? They don't do a repeat

on the weekend, fuckin omnibus edition, it's only once a
year and all yeh have –

—Sorry, Maggit says, again.

I don't know why I came up here with him. Ned was
right; this is fuckin embarrassin, and me bein here seems
kind o inappropriate.

I can hear children whoopin and laughin inside. I look
up and down the rows o bare, unhappy gardens and put
me hands in me pockets. There's a little park across the
road, but yeh wouldn't want yer kids to play there, it's
junkie city, like. Yeh can tell Bernadette wants to tell us to
fuck off but she won't.

Maggit pats the Nike bag slung over his shoulder.

—Here, I got him a computer game thing, he says. —A
dear one, like.

He looks at me again.

—It's a good dear one, isn't it Denny?

I shrug, then look at Bernadette lookin at Maggit
and Maggit lookin at me. Such moments man, brief and
forever, fuckin intolerable. I just nod.

—He'll love it, says Maggit. —Can I come in? I'm
sorry I'm late. Fuckin Dublin Bus like.

Bernadette takes another drag.

—Yeah, she says, and stands aside. —Right. I suppose
so.

★

There's kids runnin all over the place in the kitchen,
bangin spoons off pots and jumpin off chairs, one swoopin
past us with his arms out, makin spluttery machinegun
noises. There's a big sheet o paper thumbtacked to the

wall (actually it's loads o small sheets taped together) with HAPPY BIRTHDAY ANTHONY written in red and blue and yellow marker. Balloons as well, and scrunched up wrappin paper in piles by the sink. The remains o the cake are on the drainin board, next to a pile o plates. Three young, Bernadette-aged women are sittin by the open back porch, smokin, their legs crossed and chins raised just far enough that they can eye me and Maggit down the lengths o their noses. Again, I know the faces but not their names. I must be sufferin the fuckin early onset o senile dementia or somethin. The women are all wearin party hats as well but they don't look too happy, although to be fair me and Maggit probably have a lot to do with that. Bernadette taps her cigarette into a Bob the Builder mug.

—Where is he? says Maggit, scannin the horde o demented kids.

—He's up in the toilet, says Bernadette. —He has the runs.

There's brief eye contact between the mothers, some kind o secret signal unreadable to males. They look at us again, heads still tilted. We hover in the kitchen doorway and the youngfella with cake on his face and another fella with big glasses and ginger hair walk over to us. They start jerkin their shoulders and heads, and kickin out their feet. They both have these serious, set expressions.

I look at Maggit, then back at the kids.

—What's that? I say to them. —A dance?

Redser nods his head. The two o them start makin choppy movements with their hands.

—Are yiz havin a fit? says Maggit. —Spazzos, are yiz? He elbows me and laughs.

—Breakdancin, says Cakeface, lookin up at the ceilin, his shoulders jerkin up and down.

—That's very good, I say.

I can hear the toilet flushin. Then there's a flurry o footsteps on the stairs and little Anthony skids into the kitchen. He's wearin a mini Liverpool jersey and he's got Maggit's Champions League trophy ears and Bernadette's green eyes. He looks up at his da.

—Howayeh Anto, says Maggit, a big grin on his face. He drops down to his knees and holds out his arms. Anthony jumps up and into him.

—His name's Ant'ny, Bernadette calls over. The other women shake their heads, clearly disgusted.

— Ant'ny, says Maggit. —Happy birthday son.

Cakeface and Redser are still breakdancin beside us.

—He's my da, Anthony says to them. They stop and look at Maggit.

—Are you his da, mister?

—Yeah, he says.

Maggit looks dead proud. It's mad seein him like this. Nice, though. He pats the Nike bag and unslings it, then puts it on the lino.

—Wait and yeh see this, Anto.

—Ant'ny, says Bernadette.

—Ant'ny, says Maggit. He looks at Anthony. —Go on so, he says. —Open it.

Anthony takes hold o the zipper and pulls it back. Bernadette arches her head for a better view. Cakeface and Redser peep over Anthony's shoulders and Anthony reaches into the bag. He pulls out the jumble o plastic and wires and plugs and joypads. I can see now that the stickers are them football ones yeh collect for the sticker books.

One o them's Damien Duff, from when he used to play for Blackburn Rovers.

—Playstation, says Anthony.

Maggit nods his head. —Yeah, he says. —The Playstation. That's a great one that, isn't it? Isn't that the one all the big boys have?

Cakeface and Redser and Anthony look at each other.

—Playstations are stupid, says Anthony.

—Wha? says Maggit.

Anthony's turnin one o the joypads in his little hands. —They're gank, da. Playstation 2s are good.

He holds up the joypad and Maggit takes it, lookin at it like it's some unfathomable fossil, alien and infinitely strange.

—That's the old one da, says Anthony. —That's Playstation 1.

Maggit stands up. He looks crumpled or somethin, dead deflated. He places the joypad on the drainin board.

—Jaysis. Is that one no good then? It still plays games and that doesn't it?

—It's no use, says Cakeface.

—No use? says Maggit. He looks at the kid and the sensitive Maggit disappears instantly. —Wash yer fuckin face you, will yeh?

—Don't talk to my son like that, says one o the single mothers, standin up. She flicks her floppy pink fringe and stubs out her cigarette. —He's only a bleedin child. C'mere to me Kyle.

Kyle starts to cry.

—Yeh alright? I say, and reach out to rub his head. Me palm comes back sticky with cream and jam.

—Fuck.

Kyle runs over to his mother.

—Don't fuckin curse in front o my son, says Pink Fringe. —Don't mind them Kyle, she says, huggin the bawlin child.

—Wha did I do?

Pink Fringe kisses Kyle's sweetened head.

—I think yiz better go, says Bernadette.

—I'm only here two fuckin minutes, says Maggit.

—Yeah, and yiv worked fuckin wonders. Gerrout.

Maggit scoops up his empty bag.

—I'm entitled to see me own son, Bernadette, he says.

Bernadette walks over, picks up the Playstation and shoves it into Maggit's arms.

—Yeah, yeh are. And if yeh bring robbed stuff into this house again I'm entitled to phone the fuckin police. That fair?

—It's not robbed. Is it Denny?

I'm sayin fuck all. Last time I'm ever comin over here, I swear. Fuckin nightmare.

—I'll get yeh somethin better durin the week, Anto. Yeah? An Action Man jeep or one o them other Playstations. The new ones.

Anthony nods.

—With Tekken 3? he says.

—Yeah, no probs. Anythin yeh want. Tekman 3 and loads o other ones.

—Tekken, not Tekman, Cakeface shouts over, between sobs.

—Tekken, yeah. That's wha I said. Right.

He leans down and hugs Anthony.

—See yeh son, he says. —And happy birthday.

★

71

—That went well.

—Don't start Denny.

We're cuttin through the Lawns. Well, cuttin through an under 11s five-a-side, to be exact. The kids stop and look at us. One o them picks up the ball.

—That's a free, says a kid on the other team. —Handball.

—There's people on the pitch yeh sap, says the fella with the ball. He's small, with a snotty, runny nose.

I look at Maggit.

—Wha d'yeh mean, don't start? Don't start wha?

—Yeh know wha I mean Denny. Just don't fuckin start.

The kids are gettin indignant now.

—Gerroff the pitch!

—We're in extra time yiz pricks!

There are ten mucked-up faces glarin at us. Most o them are wearin Liverpool or United jerseys. One o them's hopped on the bandwagon early and he's wearin a Chelsea jersey. The biggest kid is in United's white away kit, a big number 7 on the back with CUNZER above it.

—Wha are we walkin through their game for?

—Fuck them, says Maggit. —It's a public park.

—We could o walked round just as easy.

A clump o wet muck, little blades o grass stickin out of it, sails through the air and lands on Maggit's shoulder.

Maggit turns round.

—Who the fuck threw that?

None o the kids answer. Maggit grabs up a handful o muck and hurls it indiscriminately at the group o kids. They part ranks and the muckball splats in the middle o one o the goals.

72

—Gunner eye, says Cunzer.

—Wha did you say?

—Spanner eye, says a different kid.

Maggit looks livid, like he's gonna lose it completely.

—Calm the fuck down you, will yeh? I say. I put me hand on his elbow. —They're only kids yeh fuckin lunatic.

Maggit shrugs me off and runs back a few feet. The kids scarper all over the place, stoppin when they're safely out o range o Maggit's temporary madness. Maggit stands there, fists balled, soakin up their taunts:

—I'll get me da after you!

—Big ears!

—Wanker!

—Giz a chase!

Fuck this.

I turn and start walkin. He's a mental fuckin bastard, Maggit is. I know he's a mate but he's mad as fuck and he wrecks me head sometimes. I head for the gate at the bottom o the park, the one straight across from where me nanny Cullen used to live. The steel's bent and rusty. I squeeze through the half-fucked turnstile and turn back on the other side o the railins. Maggit's a hundred feet or so behind me. The kids are standin in a bunch, hurlin abuse and muckballs at him. I wanna wait for him but yeh have to draw the fuckin line. Need a drink man, too fuckin right. I'll give Maggit a buzz when I get to the pub. I'll get the drinks in like, so no fuckin change there. It's still too cold for Bulmers so it's two pints o Guinness and the rickety table by the window. Fuck, when did things get this predictable? Need a change, man. Need fuckin somethin, yeh know?

THE STILETTO IN THE GHETTO

The anointed day. Stupid fuckin séance, like. Why I'm goin along with this I don't fuckin know. We're standin underneath the Spire. Another one o Bertie's deadly ideas. What a fuckin waste o money. I mean, I'm all for culture and that but, given Dublin's troubles with heroin, spendin millions on somethin that looks exactly like a four hundred foot tall syringe in the middle of O'Connell Street is a bit fuckin thick. And I don't think Bertie and his mates are streetwise enough for it to have been ironic.

—I'll meet yiz here at six, yeah? I say. —Don't be late. Pajo wants to get started by about eight.

—The stiffy by the Liffey, says Maggit, pattin the Spire and winkin.

—The nail in the Pale, says Ned.

—Yeah. The poker near Croker, I say.

Ned and Maggit laugh. —Never heard that one, says Ned. —Ever hear that one, Maggit?

—Nah.

Maggit and Ned don't seem bothered about the séance at all. Although there's no reason they should be, really – I'm the one who has to live with the consequences. I still think Paula would be better off just givin up the drink for a while, gettin her head together. But at the same time the whole situation still bothers me; it kind o gnaws away at me. Ghosts and drink and madness. Which causes which, like? In what order do they come? Gives me the creeps.

I take out me mobile and have a look. It's ten to five. Loads o time. We cross O'Connell Street to the GPO. There's two women and an oulfella standin to our left, a table in front o them covered with leaflets and forms. There's a load o posters behind them, stuck to the wall o the GPO. Horrible pictures o slimy dead foetuses. They look like tiny, semi-translucent aliens. I fuckin hate that – people pushin their beliefs onto yeh, tryin to shock yeh into submission.

—Make sure yeh get a proper bunch, Maggit, I say.
—Fresh.

Maggit nods.

—Make sure, I say.
—Yeah, fuck sake. I will.
—Right. I'll meet yiz in an hour, yeah?

Ned and Maggit nod. I take a last look at the strange and gory pictures behind the pro-lifers and hurry along O'Connell Street. Next stop Trinity College. I cross at Bachelor's Walk, the dyin sun glintin orange off the Liffey as I cross O'Connell Bridge. Town's still packed so I have to weave in and out o the crowd. Exhaust fumes and the wordless drone o hundreds o voices. Tacky traditional Irish music spills from the open shop front o Carrolls, the Polish workers behind the tills smilin and noddin to American tourists, and a huge black security guard mumblin into his walkie-talkie. There's fuck all Irish people workin in shops these days. It's pretty much all foreigners. Polish especially. There's loads and loads o them. There's even a Polish supplement in the *Evening Herald* – the *Polski Herald*. The thing that seems maddest to me, though, is that I've never even spoken to a Polish person. Ever. No one's integrated here. When I was over in Wales that time it wasn't too bad, yeh got to talk to people from all over. Well, in Cardiff, anyway – the Valleys were backwards as fuck, worse than here. I reckon there's somethin nasty brewin in Ireland, though; yeh can feel it. People gettin angry, lookin for someone to blame for their woes. Mad bastards like Slaughter stewin over it, formulatin their twisted theories; the worst o them honin their arguments with broken logic and fucked up economics.

Ah, fuck it anyway. Does me head in thinkin about it; it's fuckin embarrassin to be honest. Although it's helped the journey pass at least; I'm nearly at the Bank of Ireland when I clock one o them charity workers in front o me. A short, slightly plump girl with blonde hair and a bright yellow bib. I'll have to make sure I don't –

Bollix. Too late, I'm after makin eye contact. Shite. I don't have time for this. Or the money. Head down, Denny; look away. Just keep goin, look like yeh have a purpose, somewhere to be. Fuck that, I do have somewhere to be. I have an –

—Hi, can I talk to you for a minute?

I'm still a few feet away when she says it. Just keep walkin, Denny.

—I like your hair.

Me hair? I look up and make eye contact again and that's it, game over, I'm fucked. I stop.

—Thank you, the girl says. She has an accent. One o these hard-to-place European ones. She tucks her hair behind her ear and smiles.

—Do you have a couple of minutes?

—Ehh well, I kind o –

—Just a couple of minutes? Please?

She tilts her head and smiles. It says BODIL on a tag on her bib.

—It'll only take a couple of minutes, I swear. She smiles again and raises her eyebrows. I glance over at Trinity and back at the girl.

—Are you a student?

—Me? Ah no, no.

—Oh, OK. You look like a student.

Do I? I don't know whether that's a good or bad thing. Bad, I'm inclined to think. Ah well.

—I'm with Enable Ireland. Do you know anything about Enable Ireland?

I shake me head. It sounds familiar, but no, I don't know anythin about Enable Ireland. Course, I'm about to find out, even though I'm late and, worse, when we get to the end of her spiel it's gonna be embarrassin for both of us cos I don't have anywhere near enough money to open a direct debit or a standin order or wharrever.

—Well, we're a charity that helps with the education of young people in Ireland with difficulties of all kinds, including Down syndrome. We do really good work. Really good. Do you know that Ireland is the richest country in Europe per head of capita?

—Ehh –

I kind o shrug me shoulders. I'm not unaware of Ireland's wealth, I'm just not party to it.

—Oh it is, it is. There's a lot of money in this country. And I mean a lot. I'm from Sweden and we have a lot of money floating around in Sweden but nothing to what we've got over here.

I nod. Bodil, if that's her name, which I assume it is, is beamin. She's really into this. Fair play, like. Fuck, I wish I had the money to give but I don't, I'm pure broke; penniless, brassic, near fuckin destitute if truth be told. If Bodil was some pushy student-type from Blackrock it'd be easier to break the news, but she's not; she seems dead nice, dead genuine. And from Sweden, as well: a Swedish girl miles from home workin away for an Irish charity while I'm a native and on the dole, no good to anyone. It pops into me head to ask her about the gjengangers Pajo mentioned, just for somethin to say, but I decide against it.

—The problem is, says Bodil, —not a lot of that money is being set aside for the people who need it most. It's a really bad system, really unfair. I mean, education is not only there for people with money, or people who just happen to have been born without any difficulties.

Me mobile briefly buzzes in me pocket; a text.

—Enable Ireland is really trying hard to take up the slack. It organises all kinds of events and offers all kinds of support to the families of people with learning difficulties. It's –

—Sorry, emm . . . I'm gonna have to go. Sorry.

Bodil blinks, then kind o nods her head. She clutches her clipboard to her chest.

—Oh, OK, she says. —You're in a hurry?

—Yeah. Well, like, I don't have much, emm . . .

Why am I even explainin all this? All I have to do is say I'm late and fuck off.

—Like, I'm not workin at the moment, so . . .

Bodil smiles. —That's OK, that's fine. Thanks for listening.

I stick me hand into me pocket and fish around for change.

—Do yiz take donations, like? I can –

—No, sorry. It has to be a bank thing, like a debit or something like that. It's a pain in the butt, I know. That's OK though, thank you.

I stand there for a second, not knowin wha to say. I feel like a gobshite.

—You'd better go, she says, and winks.

—Yeah.

I take a few steps sideways and then hurry on. Behind me I hear Bodil tellin someone they have cool shoes and in front o me the sun is settin over the walls o Trinity. Better get a move on.

★

The main courtyard o Trinity is cobbled and I like the feel o the smooth bumps through the soles o me runners. There aren't that many people about. I feel weird about that whole Bodil thing. It's crap bein broke all the time. But that's not it, really. It's more to do with . . . I dunno, like . . . bein broke's one thing but bein on yer own's worse really. In a relationship sense, I mean. I . . . well, it's not as if I've always been with someone anyway, like I've stumbled from one relationship to the next. I dunno though. Sometimes I'm just not bothered. Or I think I'm not. I am really. I think some part o me head's broken. It's like I'm waitin for everythin to fall into place; some mad, impossible story to unfold. It's dead easy for other people. Ned and that. Even fuckin Maggit.

I turn right and cut through the courtyard, through the little narrow alley and walk up the steps to the arts block. The automatic doors pull back and I step inside. There's a security guard so yeh have to be careful. He looks up from his little glass-walled booth and then looks back down at his *Evening Herald*.

There are still a few students millin around. They all have that semi-American, well-to-do, Bob Geldof-style accent. I walk up and down the wide corridor, lookin for . . . what's the name of it? Shit. Emm . . . oh yeah, the Edmund Burke lecture hall. I take a left turn and, aha, I have it. I peek in through the glass in the door and the room's full. Sound; the lecture must o run over or somethin. I sit on one o the weird, uncomfortable, square seats in the corridor and wait for a few minutes. A cleanin lady with huge, hoopy earrings is pickin up crisp packets and apple cores and wha have yeh, and dumpin them into a black plastic bag. I nod at her as she passes and she nods back.

I pull the phone out o me pocket. Forgot about the text I got while I was squirmin in front o Bodil. I click on MESSAGING, then INBOX. It's from Pajo.

DONT FORGET THE OTHER THING, C U AFTER. P.

The other thing? What's he on about? I don't have any credit so I can't ring him. Can't even text him back. Ah well, it's his own fault; Pajo's texts are notoriously oblique: he doesn't send messages like, he sends fuckin clues.

The phone buzzes again and another message comes through. From Ned this time. Here we go again, MESSAGING, INBOX.

THE STILETTO IN THE GHETTO

Yet another name for the Spire. That's a new one to me. I stick the phone back in me pocket. Then the door to the Edmund Burke lecture hall opens and students start pourin out. I sit and watch the crowd pass me by. After a few seconds I spot a familiar face. There he is, the very man, Kasey Cassidy.

I wave and Kasey ambles over to me, grinnin. Every time I've ever seen him he's been wearin a leather jacket and a T-shirt with the logo o some hicky metal band like Iron Maiden but today he's wearin a suit. A fuckin suit. The fuck's that all about?

I haven't seen Kasey around for a while. He's a good mate o Pajo's, a junkie occultist. He's funny, like, and harmless. Pajo and Kasey used to be shootin buddies when he was on the gear. Kasey's still usin as far as I know. He's a fair few years older than me. I remember him and Paj havin a drink in Bruxelles, that bar off Grafton Street, for his thirtieth, and that was a year or two ago. His brown, greasy, shoulder-length hair is tucked behind his ears.

—What's the story Den Quixote? says Kasey. —How yeh keepin?

—Grand. Yerself?

—Very well indeed. Tip top me man.

We sit down on the square things and Kasey sniffs and blinks and yawns, a frazzled smile on his face.

—What's with the tin o fruit?

—Ah, just a tryin to keep up with the Joneses, yeh know?

81

This is a bit of a sketchy explanation but fuck it, it's probably better just to let it slide; don't wanna end up implicated in anythin. Kasey's known to be a bit of a scammer.

—Fair enough, I say. —Lecture any good?

Kasey shrugs. —OK, Denzel, OK. It wasn't wha I'd call a spectacular affair now. Good though. So so. Bit above mediocre. Sure yeh know yerself.

Kasey's been doin this for years, smugglin himself into lectures all over the city. He was in UCD last week for a talk on banshees. Or *bean sídhe*, to be precise. No one clocked him. It's all about havin the balls, apparently; yeh walk in actin like yeh belong and no one says a word. Kasey reckons he has a few degrees stored in his head at this stage, even if he doesn't have them on paper.

—Wha was the lecture about?

—Bram Stoker Society ran it, says Kasey. —So it was quite decent. So so. Vampire myths in different cultures kind o thing. Interestin. Wasn't mad on the angle, though.

—No?

—Nah. Bit wishy-washy. So here, have yeh got me stuff? I don't mean to seem rude Denver but, like, I've a bit of a cravin on me, yeh know?

—Yeah, that's alright. I have it here. Were yeh talkin to Pajo?

—Yep. He rang me this mornin. Very rare object he was after.

—Yeah?

Kasey nods.

—Sound, I say. —So d'yeh wanna . . .

—Get outside first. Don't wanna blow me cover Dennicus, they're showin some rare film about demonic

82

possession next week. Catholic Church was down on it in the seventies.

—C'mon then.

We get up and head back outside. Kasey chats away about all kinds o mad stuff while we're walkin, gesticulatin wildly, everythin from ghosts to the CIA's shady dealins in Nicaragua. When we get to Temple Bar we find a seat outside the Bank of Ireland HQ, beside the huge bronze sculpture thingy.

—So yeah, as I was sayin, says Kasey. —The CIA were in it up to their necks. Them and Reagan. Never trust an ex-filmstar US president, Denville. Take it from me.

I smile and nod.

—Serious Denzig.

—I know, yeah.

I surreptitiously pass Pajo's bottle o methadone into Kasey's jacket pocket.

—Sure he wasn't even that good of an actor, says Kasey, winkin hugely as he passes the short, thick candle into me own jacket pocket. —If I had to pick an ex-filmstar for a US president I'd go for Clint Eastwood meself.

Kasey pats his pocket, smilin.

—They got up to all sorts over there, Denly. Terrible stuff altogether. Blew up a pharmaceutical plant. All them drugs. Wha a waste. But sure they'll get their just desserts on the other side, wha? The lake o fire.

I stand up and so does Kasey.

—Yep, I say.

Kasey slaps me on the shoulder and winks again.

—What's so special about this candle? I ask.

—Baby goat fat.

—Yeh serious?

—Yep.

—Baby goat fat? How the fuck d'yeh get baby goat fat?

Kasey taps his nose. —Goat babbies are mortal like the rest of us, Dendelion. Be a sin to let them go to waste.

—Yer mad.

—True. He grins. —D'yeh wanna lift?

—Yeh in the van?

—I am indeed.

—I've to meet Ned and Maggit at the Spire.

—The pin in the bin, says Kasey.

I laugh and we make our way back across the river.

★

Everyone's in the kitchen. It's like a weird three wise kings scenario; I bring in Kasey's baby goat fat candle, followed by Paula with a bottle o Jack Daniel's she picked up in Super Valu, followed in turn by a scowlin Maggit with a bunch o daffodils from the garage in Cherry Orchard. Pajo's sittin at the head o the kitchen table, a sombre look on his thin face, the recipient of our strange gifts. The curtains are drawn and the doors to the sittin room are pulled over. Ned and Teresa are already sittin. Teresa's just in from work and she looks knackered. She did a twelve-hour shift at the factory and her eyes look bleary. Her thick brown hair's tied back in a short ponytail, revealin the half dozen or so little rings in her ear.

—Where d'yeh want these? says Maggit.

—Emm, put them, like, in a vase, says Pajo. —Yeah? In the middle o the table, if yeh can.

Maggit shakes his head, lookin annoyed and uncomfortable with the flowers in his hand. —Have yiz a vase for these? he says.

—Just leave them there, says Paula. —I'll get somethin.

Maggit tosses the flowers onto the table beside Ned. Ned's grinnin.

—Don't say a word, you, says Maggit.

—Wasn't gonna, says Ned, still grinnin away.

—Wha about the baby goat candle? I ask.

—Light it and, like, put it in the middle as well, says Pajo. —And open the whiskey and put it beside it.

Paula's rummagin under the sink. She turns and looks back over her shoulder. —Are we not drinkin the whiskey?

Pajo shakes his head. Paula stands up with a pint glass in her hand. She fills it with water and comes back over, placin the glass on the table. She takes the daffodils and pulls off the paper and cellophane wrappin and puts them in the pint glass.

—We not havin a shot even, no? says Paula.

—No, says Pajo. —It's, like, for them. Yeh know?

Maggit shakes his head again.

—Can we not have a drink at all? says Paula. —There's absinthe in the fridge.

We've had the absinthe ages, which is a bit of a minor miracle. Paula's been savin it up — she got it cheap when her and Teresa were in Turkey. A good while ago, this was. Before ma died.

Pajo bites at his thumbnail and thinks for a second. —Emm, yeah, OK, he says. Then he seems to warm to Paula's misplaced assumption and nods, smilin. —Yeah, like, we'll all have a shot, he says. —One each. That'll start us off, yeah? No more after that, though.

Paula goes and gets the absinthe from the fridge.

—I'm grand for a drink, love, says Teresa. —Seriously, I'm shattered.

Pajo shakes his head. —No, if it's part o the ritual, like, we all have to do it. Just have a little one, Teresa.

Teresa rolls her eyes. —G'wan, so.

—I'll only do yeh a small one, says Paula.

Paula winks at her and she sets down a tray with six shot glasses and the bottle of absinthe. She fills out the shots, Teresa's noticeably smaller than the others. I light Kasey's candle and open the whiskey, then sit back down, between Paula and Maggit. I look at me watch; it's half ten. I feel a little bit nervous. Dunno why, like. Fuckin ghosts, it's all bullshit.

—Right, emm, thanks for comin, says Pajo.

—It's not a fuckin weddin reception, Pajo, says Maggit.

—Shhh, says Paula.

Paula looks a bit . . . I dunno . . . fraught or somethin. I can tell by lookin at her that she's . . . I dunno, edgy, maybe. Or a combination of edginess and excitement. She's not afraid, anyway, put it that way. It's mad but I've never known Paula to be afraid. Not properly afraid, anyway.

—OK so, says Pajo. —Emm. First off, I think . . . well, oh yeah, yiz'll have to turn off yer mobiles. Yeah? Like, no distractions and that.

Everyone fumbles for their phones and there's a couple o seconds where the room's filled with mingled ditties as the phones shut down.

Pajo has the same kind o look as Paula, nervous and kind o hopefully expectant at the same time. He runs a thin hand through his hair and then places his palms flat on the table.

—Right, before we start we should go through some stuff, yeah? Just to, like, make sure everyone's kosher.

Everyone nods and mumbles.

—OK. Emm. Right. First off, no one's to be afraid, yeah? Bad vibes can attract bad spirits. So everyone should like, chill. Emm, actually, the shots'll be good coz they'll loosen us up.

—Will we have them now then? says Paula.

—Eh, yeah. Yeah, might as well.

Each of us lifts our shot glass, the green liquid glintin in the light o the bulb overhead.

—Do we do a toast or wha? says Ned.

—Emm, nah, says Pajo. —OK so, down we go.

We knock back the absinthe. Teresa makes a face and shakes her head.

—Hate that stuff, she says.

Paula rubs Teresa's shoulder.

—OK, says Pajo. —Right, so yeah, like I said, everyone just chill, yeah? OK. And, emm . . . Pajo looks at me. —Should I say about the flowers and the candle and that, Denny?

—I don't even know wha the flowers and candle are for, Pajo. You're the expert.

Ned smiles.

—Yeah, yeah, says Pajo. —Emm, right. Yeah, so, the flowers help to attract the spirit. They can smell them, I think. Or they like it, anyway. It's good. It's good for the vibe. Especially daffodils, they love daffodils.

—And the whiskey's in case the ghost's Oliver Reed? says Ned.

—Yeah. It's . . . no. I mean . . . no. It's like, it's another strong smell, just. It's somethin they might remember. Yeah? So they can, like, home in or wharrever. Em. And the candle's for –

—Spookiness?

—No. It's the light, spirits are attracted to it. They can see it, yeh know? It's like the light o the other side, o the spirit world. That kind o thing. It burns a special kind o colour, cos o the baby goat fat. We can't really see it like, but they can. Yeah? Yiz OK?

Pajo runs his finger round the inside of his shot glass and sucks on it, then continues.

—So, it's like, it's about communication. We wanna talk to whoever it is that's here. Yeh know? Pajo turns to Paula. —Wha do yeh wanna know, Paula? D'yeh think, like, d'yeh know who it might be?

Paula looks at me and then back at Pajo. She's told me about this before but it's still fuckin freaky.

—There's someone under me bed, she says. She looks at me again. —It's a man but it's pretendin to be a woman. Or a girl, really.

Ned raises an eyebrow; he hasn't heard this before and he looks a bit bemused. Teresa has but she still looks concerned.

—I don't really wanna say anymore about it, says Paula. —It's weird. It's a bit mad, I know. Just . . . I'd rather just see wha happens. Is that alright?

—Yeah, OK, says Pajo. —That's fine. It's just that, no one should get afraid and that, yeah?

—Yeah.

—Yep.

—Alright then. OK. Let's, emm . . . will yeh turn off the light there, Denny?

I nod and stand and, after a second's hesitation, flick off the light. It goes dead dark. I reach for the chair and sit back down. The flame o Kasey's ritual candle is dancin slightly, bobbin in some unfelt draught. It doesn't give off much light and I don't think the actual flame looks any different to any other I've seen. It smells fuckin rank, though; horrible, like our chip pan but ten times worse. I can just about see everyone round the table, their jumpy shadows loomin behind them.

—Everyone put their hands flat on the table, says Pajo. —Yeah? We need to be dead quiet, like. Total silence.

No one says a word. We sit there for about a minute.

—My name is Patrick, says Pajo, finally. I can see Pajo's face floatin in the gloom. His eyes are closed.

—And this is Colm, Denny, Teresa, Edward and Paula. We'd really like to hear from yeh. It's, emm . . . well especially Paula would. She'd like to know, like, who yeh are.

Pajo falls silent again. Paula shifts slightly beside me. There isn't a sound in the whole house, cept the pops and creaks o the place settlin for the night. I watch the candle flame flickerin, and the reflection o the flame in the whiskey bottle. Ned's eyes are closed, and so are Teresa's. Maggit's lookin at his hands on the table. I'm startin to feel like –

—Did yeh hear that?

I turn me head and look at Paula, then Pajo. His eyes are open again; I think he's noticed it. He nods at me.

—Can yiz hear that? says Ned, eyes still closed.

—Shh, says Paula.

—Emm, thank you, says Pajo. —Thanks for gettin in touch.

I can see Ned smilin at that.

—We'd like to ask a few questions. Emm. Like, who . . . who are yeh?

Nothin. Just a low down noise. Jesus, there is a voice though, definitely. Or voices. There's words, it's language. I have to strain but there's a weak voice comin through. Fuck. Somewhere above, it sounds like. Or am I imaginin things here? Am I –

—What's yer name? says Pajo.

There's silence for a few seconds more.

—Who are yeh?

Then Ned bursts out laughin. —It's Simon fuckin Cowell, he says, openin his eyes.

—Wha?

—That's the fuckin X-Factor. Listen.

Everyone strains, silently.

—It's Louis Walsh now. Listen.

—For fuck sake, says Paula. —Did someone leave the telly on upstairs?

—Oh shite, I did, yeah, says Teresa. —Sorry.

—Jesus, I was gettin fuckin worried there, says Ned. —Fuckin hell. Imagine if Louis Walsh was hauntin the place? Fate worse than fuckin death.

Pajo bites his thumbnail again. —Emm, yeh wouldn't be able to, like, go up and –

—I'm not goin up on me own, says Teresa.

—I'll go with yeh, says Paula.

Paula stands up and Teresa does likewise. I can hear them talkin on the stairs on the way up. Maggit fills himself out another shot and downs it. He looks at Pajo with a kind o disdainful smirk.

—It's not my fault, says Pajo.

—Don't worry about it, Paj, I say. Jesus, I feel dead fuckin relieved. I fill meself out a shot as well, and gulp it back. It sounds stupid but me nerve ends are buzzin. I was startin to get a bit windy there for a sec, started doubtin meself. A few seconds later Paula and Teresa come back in and take their seats.

—Sorry Pajo, says Teresa.

—Yer OK.

—Are we alright to go on? says Paula.

—Yeah, says Pajo. —Emm. OK. Pajo takes a long, deep breath. —Right. Sorry about that, he says, not so much to us but to whoever or whatever might be out there. —If yeh could let us know yer there, that'd be cool. Emm. Like, if . . . yeah. Who are yeh?

Again, there's nothin. I can hear the wind outside and the breathin o me fellow would-be spiritualists.

—Let us know yer here.

—I need another drink, says Maggit. He reaches across the table and takes a swig from the bottle. —Anyone else?

There's general noddin, includin from Pajo. The bottle gets passed around and everyone takes a mouthful, even Teresa. We had a few scoops in town already and I can feel a slight buzz.

—I want to know who yeh are, says Paula, suddenly. She looks determined. Pajo looks up. Paula looks at him and Pajo nods.

—Are yeh happy? says Paula —I don't mind sharin me room with yeh but I need to know who yeh are.

—Just give us some kind o sign, says Pajo.

—I know yer not me mother, says Paula.

I get a little chill up me spine when she says that.

—Yeh can, like, speak through me if yeh want, says
Pajo. —Like, if yeh don't want to –

The baby goat fat candle sputters out. Fuckin hell.

It's pitch black.

—Jesus, says Teresa.

—Must be an oul cheapo candle, says Ned.

—Have you a lighter, Denny?

—No, says Pajo. —No, leave it. See wha happens.

I can't see a fuckin thing. It's completely, utterly, deep
space black.

—Yeh alright? says Paula. I'm not sure who she's talkin
to, me or Teresa or someone else.

—Get in touch.

Someone laughs. Ned I think.

—Get in touch.

—Is this an ad for Vodafone?

—Shhh.

—Who are yeh?

. . .

. . .

—Are yeh there?

. . .

—Is that your hand down me jeans, Denny?

—Shhh!

—Who is it?

—Speak to us.

—We're here to help.

. . .

—Use the force, Luke.

—Will you shurrup?

—Yeah, shurrup you, will yeh?

—Jesus. Sorry.

. . .

—Speak.

—Did somethin happen here?

. . .

—Somethin bad?

—Are yeh stuck?

—We can help.

. . .

. . .

. . .

—Do yeh want to move on?

—Where's the absinthe?

—We're here to help yeh.

—We're listenin.

. . .

—Fuck, that's strong stuff isn't it?

—Shh!

. . .

. . .

. . .

—Yeh OK there, Pajo?

. . .

—I won't stay for long.

—Pajo?

—I'm only passing through.

—Pajo?

. . .

. . .

. . .

—Pajo?

. . .

. . .

—My name is Paula. Who are you?

—It doesn't matter.

—Is this for real?

—Shh!

—Why are yeh here?

—I'm a wanderer. I'm always somewhere. Now I'm here.

—Wha d'yeh want?

—Is that not just Pajo talkin?

—Just shurrup will yeh? For fuck sake.

—Why are yeh here, though?

—I've been here before. You remind me of someone from long ago.

. . .

—Who?

. . .

—Who do I remind yeh of?

—A woman.

—Who?

—Emer.

—Emer?

—A long time ago.

—Who are yeh?

. . .

. . .

—Did yeh die here?

—I died in the North.

—North Clondalkin?

—Shh.

...
—The North.
—Wha d'yeh want here?
—Nothing.
—Why are yeh here then?
...
—Yeh still here?
...
...
—Ask him somethin. Quick.
—Ehh, do yeh want us to do somethin?
...
—Yeh still here?
...
...
...
—Death is nothing much.
—Wha?
...
...
...
—Why are yeh pretendin to be a fuckin girl?
—I have no time for tricksters.
—Wha d'yeh mean?
—I moved him on.
—It's gone? The thing under the bed?
—I cast him out.
—Why?
—Because you look like her.
...
...
—Are yeh still there?

. . .

. . .

. . .

. . .

—I'm turnin the light on.

—No, leave it.

—Fuck this.

Someone stands up. There's a commotion and then the light flicks on. Me eyes burn. Everyone looks at Pajo. He's sittin with his eyes closed.

—Oh Jesus. Givvim a shake, says Teresa.

Maggit pours himself another shot.

—Was that for real? says Ned.

—Betcha he's on somethin, says Maggit. —A fuckin load o pills, watch. Fuckin clown is off his head.

Teresa puts her hand on Pajo's shoulder and shakes him. He makes a snortin noise and then opens his eyes.

—Yeh OK? I ask.

—Ehhh . . . grand, says Pajo. —Did I fall asleep?

—Yeh fuckin goofed off, says Maggit.

—D'yeh not remember? says Paula.

—Wha?

—All that stuff. Yeh said I was like some woman from years ago. D'yeh not remember?

Pajo shakes his head.

—That's a load o me fuckin bollix, says Maggit.

Paula looks at Maggit. —Will you shut up? Eejit.

Maggit holds up his hands and wriggles his fingers in mock offence.

Paula hunkers down beside Pajo.

—D'yeh really not remember any o that?

96

—I remember, like, askin was there someone there and all that.

Pajo looks ashen. He's shakin a bit, as well. So am fuckin I. Paula looks at me.

—Wha did yeh think o that, Denny?

I shrug. —I dunno, I say. And fuck, I really don't, other than the fact that I'm freaked out. I grab the absinthe and pour meself a good measure. I down it and then pour another one.

—I think we made contact, says Paula.

—With who? says Pajo.

—Some ghostly pervo who thinks Paula looks like his old girlfriend, some queen from ages ago, says Ned. Ned blows out a breath and looks at me. He shrugs, clearly undecided.

—He said the other thing's gone, though, says Paula.
Pajo nods.

—Fuckin mad, wha? says Ned.

—Yeah.

—Fill us a shot there, Denny, says Paula.
I do.

—Thanks.

—Well yeh can tell yer man that yer already taken, says Teresa. She puts her hand on Paula's forearm. Maggit looks at Paula and Teresa and shakes his head.

—Bollix, he says. —Yiz are all fuckin mad. Yiz are –

—Shhh! says Paula. —Listen.
We go quiet.

—Wha?

—Listen. The dogs.

She's right. Every dog in the estate must be barkin, a cacophony o hounds growlin and whinin and barkin like mad.

—God. I'm sleepin with the light on, says Teresa.

GRIFFINSHIT

I'm sittin at the foot o the stairs, a cup o tea at me feet and I'm just about to cancel the call when Ned finally picks up.

—Denny, man, what's the story?

—Took yer time.

—I was playin that new Pro Evolution. Pretty good, like. They've still got stupid fake jerseys but it's better than FIFA. Yid wanna see the head on Rooney in it, Shrekfuckintastic. I've a suitcase o them here. They're —

—Nah thanks, I'm grand. Here, d'yeh know of anyone who's lookin to sell a car?

—Yeh after a set o wheels?

—Yeah. Wouldn't mind, like.

—Wha brought this on?

—Just . . . dunno, sick walkin everywhere. And I'm twenty fuckin six, yeh know? I was sayin it to meself in the mountains. Fuckin hours we were walkin that day.

—Em, well, Chockie from Shancastle could do yeh one, I suppose.

—No, not robbed or anythin. Jesus. Secondhand, like. Someone sellin on or wharrever.

—Bit more difficult, that. I mean, I know loads lookin to offload motors, legit like, but they'd be out o your price range. Unless yer after winnin the bingo or somethin.

—Nah, I've about a hundred euro.

—Won't get much for that.

—I could get another hundred or so off Maggit as well.

—Sounds like hassle, man, co-ownership.

—It'll be grand. Fuckim.

—Actually, isn't yer brother sellin a car?

Goes to show how close me family are these days when I have to hear about stuff like this off o Ned.

—Which one?

—Gino. It's only an oul banger, like. An '89 Fiat I think. Yeh won't be able to get a piece o shite like that taxed and insured, though. Yill be reefed off the road if any guards see yeh.

—It'll be grand, I say.

Fuck the tax and insurance. Don't have anywhere near the money to get the car sorted properly. I just fancy the bit o freedom; it's been on me mind for a while, like. I learned to drive ages ago, when I was about sixteen or seventeen, in the industrial estate out by Palmerstown. Got the lessons off o me cousin Martin.

—Up to you, says Ned. —Can't think of anythin else for that money, though. At the end o the days it's – actually, look man I'm gonna have to go, Sinead's at the door.

—Right, thanks Ned. See yeh after anyway.

—Slan go foill Denny.

★

Delapidated's a good word but it doesn't do justice to me brother Gino's front garden. Place is a fuckin kip, like, an eternal tipsite and the subject o countless ignored council warnins. The grass is long and crabby and dandruffed with empty milk cartons and crisp packets and currytrays from the Chinese up the road and there's a big pile o bashed pallets beside the front window. The cracked and webby porch door is out o the frame and leanin against the wall. Gino's Jack Russell is sittin on the welcome mat and he starts pantin and waggin his stumpy tail when he sees me. There's a black satellite dish stickin from the side o the house. Gino used to have NTL but he got rid of it and got Sky instead cos, as his wife pointed out, with NTL yeh just get a little box that yeh put with yer video and that, under the telly, whereas with Sky yeh get a dish, which is more conspicuous; she didn't want people assumin she hadn't the money for cable TV.

I walk up to the door and hunch down and scratch the dog behind the ear. Pajo rings the doorbell. Maggit plonks his arse down on the wall, smokin, a scowly look on his face. He wasn't mad on the whole car idea, but he's after agreein to give somethin off it anyway, so I'm not bothered.

—Ring again there Pajo, I say.

Pajo steps forward and is about to push the doorbell when there's a crash from inside, followed by a deep bellow. There's an argument goin on upstairs.

—Yeh mad fuckin bitch, yeh!

—How dare yeh, Eugene. How fuckin dare yeh! You're the one foolin around.

—Foolin around? With fuckin who, Tracy? With who?

—That slag Nuala Dunne!

I stand up and look up at the bedroom windows.

—Jaysis, says Pajo. —Bit of a domestic there. Should we come back after?

—Fuck it, says Maggit. —We're here now. Maggit looks up at the window, then back at me. —Gino and Nuala Dunne, wha? Yid wanna be desperate.

—She's alright, Nuala, I say.

—Alright? She has a face like a full fuckin skip, Denny.

And then the front door flies open and Maggit nearly falls off the wall. I instinctively hop away from the porch and me heel skids in a smooth swirl o dogshite. I'm expectin a pickaxe handle in the skull . . . but it's not Gino. It's his eight year-old son Jason and he storms past me to the gate, strugglin into a blue Nike jacket as he goes. He stops at the end o the garden and turns round, his eyes big and full o tears.

—Wha d'youse want?

—I was just lookin for yer da, Jay. Are yeh alright?

—Fuck off, he says. Then he looks up at the big upstairs window. —Da, here's the eejits to see yeh! he shouts, and turns and stomps away up the street.

—I think we should just, like, leave it for the moment, says Pajo. —Come back after.

—Yeah, probably, I say. —We'll head down the 79 and have a few jars, wha? No point in discommodin Angry fuckin Dad in there. Sure we'll –

It takes me a few seconds to realise Maggit and Pajo aren't lookin at me, they're lookin over me shoulder. I turn around and Gino's standin there, his yellow Liverpool jersey slightly ripped at the collar and a bead o sweat tricklin down the blasted bridge of his nose. His recedin hairline looks more severe than the last time I saw it. He's the image o me da, Gino is: the same harsh-lookin mouth and the same twinklin eyes. He's growin a beard as well, which, coupled with the dodgy hairdo, makes him look a lot older than thirty-four. He spits into the garden next door and draws his thick forearm across his glistenin forehead.

—Wha? he says.

★

I haven't seen Gino since the funeral. I think we're both happier when we exist on the edges of each other's radars. We've never been close, not even when we were younger. Gino and Shane were thick as thieves though. The two o them, they were lunatics. Always in fights and out actin the maggot, robbin, all sorts. They were mad into horses as well. Kept them in the fields down near the canal. They loved their horses but they were a status symbol as well. They made names for themselves as harchaws, like me da did as a younger man. They got on well, the three o them, when they were drunk especially; that's when the wild and proud and stupid bonds they shared came out, the fighters and carousers. The big men. It's like there's a part o them that doesn't fit with the time they live in.

Me da used to be in mad moods after he'd come home at night from the pub. He'd go from tellin stories to sittin there dead sullen and quiet in the armchair. I came downstairs one night for a drink o water and saw him sittin in his chair, dead still, the only light comin from the streetlight outside the house. I looked at him for a few seconds. I thought he was dead at first, then asleep. And then me eyes got used to the dark and I realised he was wide awake, his eyes open. I asked him was he alright but he said nothin back.

Anyway, we pass through the hall and the kitchen. I can hear Tracy stompin around upstairs. Me and Maggit and Pajo stand by the sink while Gino rummages around in the fridge. He pulls out a can o Budweiser and cracks it open.

I don't know wha to say to him. Our ma's dead. All of a sudden I'm in the collective shoes of all the people who've bumped into me in the past few months; neighbours and old people I vaguely know from pubs, concerned looks on their faces.

Sorry for yer loss.

Terrible sad news about yer ma.

Sure time's a great healer, son.

Fuckin hell.

I take out me phone and look at it for no reason. Gino takes a sup from the can.

—Em . . . how yeh keepin? I say.

Gino nods and turns and opens the back door.

★

The wooden fencin round Gino's back garden is warped and collapsin in on itself and the grass is dark and long and peppered with the bobbin white heads o Jinny Joes. There's a narrow concrete pathway through the middle and two archin trees at the back framin a paintpeelin and shitestreaked pigeon loft that looks like it was lifted from the set o The Texas Chainsaw Massacre. In front o the loft and half obscured by the grass is the car. How the fuck did Gino get the car out here? Oul Blind Robbie is sittin on a kitchen chair under the pigeonloft's overhang, his beard tangly and his shoulderlength hair stickin out from under a tatty Coca-Cola baseball cap. Robbie's an old mate o me da's. They used to buy pigeons off each other. Me and Paula were terrified of him when we were younger; we used to say that he could see into the future with his mad, sightless eyes – he could tell yeh how yid die. Robbie's strokin a sleek and exotic-lookin pigeon on his lap and there's two kids, one freckly and redheaded, the other pale and fairhaired, standin on either side of him like bizarre underage sentinels. The kids are both wearin identical green tracksuits with their zippers tight under their chins. Yeh always see them round the place with Robbie. They're not related to him or anythin, or I don't think they are, anyway – they're like his squires or apprentices or somethin, pigeon fanciers in the makin.

—The car's up here, says Gino.

—Cool, I say.

Robbie says somethin under his breath to the kids and they laugh into their tracksuit collars and look at each other knowinly. Pajo trails his hands through the grass and wild flowers.

—They're lovely, he says. —Are they geraniums?

No one answers him.

—Anythin strange? I say.

Gino shrugs and sniffs and picks at the edge of his wide nostril. —So so. I hear yer havin a great time up there in ma's, wreckin the place.

—No. It's –

—Yiz are, Denny. I heard off Shane. Off o fuckin everyone. That Paula one'd wanna get her fuckin act together. Tell her I said that. And if all this I'm hearin about fuckin junkies and all sorts is true . . . won't be happy, Denny, that's all I'll say.

—Yeah, fair enough.

Gino stares dead ahead while he's sayin this but he turns round when we're a few feet from the car and he's smilin, ready to do business. The smile looks anythin but comfortin on his battered face. Looks predatory, like the kind o smile he'd wear before loafin someone. Or bitin their nose off, which he's done before. John Sweeney, that was. He got it sorted out, like; got it fixed up, but yeh can still see where Gino bit. It's all misshapen and lumpy. Gino fuckin Cullen, wha? That fuckin smile, on a face that's somethin like mine but older and remodelled by other people's fists. He slaps the car's bonnet and the car makes a weird, birdlike sound.

—There she is ladies, he says.

It doesn't look like much. Looks like a pile o fuckin shite, to be honest. But I suppose I can't complain with the money I'm offerin. In a way it's –

Fuckin hell.

The car's full o chickens.

I don't believe this: a dozen or so fat white chickens huddled on the seats, cluckin and blinkin away in their scruffy straw beds. Shite all over the place as well and a heavy, concentrated farmyard smell. I look at Pajo and Maggit and then at Gino, who's on his haunches and pullin up handfuls o grass. He picks out single blades and lets them fall and then he looks up at me, eyes squinted against the glare o the sun.

—Yeh OK? he says.

—Are they chickens?

—No. They're fuckin griffins.

Robbie and the two kids laugh. So does Maggit.

—Ah here, I say. —If I wanted a chickencoop I could o got one down the pet shop.

—Wash the thing out and it'll be grand. Bit o fuckin elbow grease, Denny. There's not a brack on it.

—Could o been worse, says Blind Robbie. —Usually dead bodies in Gino's motors. Yid wanna check the boot. Robbie laughs to himself and his small eyes roll and tumble randomly in their sockets like two bluish egg yolks in shallow bowls, and it actually does occur to me to check the boot there and then, just in case, like. But I don't. I take a step back and Pajo hops forward eagerly and sticks his head through the passenger seat window and starts cluckin and cooin. Maggit looks at me and shakes his head. There's a slight smile on his face, though.

—How the fuck am I gonna get the thing out? I say.

—Crane, says Gino.

—And how am I gonna get a crane?

—A mate o mine's workin on that site down the road.

—He'll lift it out?

—Yeah. I'd say so. I'll givvim a buzz.

—Will he want money?

—Few quid probly.

—And who's payin him?

—Who d'yeh think?

—This is . . . I didn't think it was gonna be –

—Denny, yeh told me yeh wanted it. I have the money spent already. It'll be a few quid only. Although yer man's off on his holliers so yill have to wait. Think he'll be back next week.

—Look . . . it'd be one thing if it was somethin off Top Gear but –

—It's grand. Yid wanna see the roll cage in it, that car's been rallied by fuckin pros.

—Yeah, it looks like it has as well. State of it.

—Yeh could roll that car all the way to Wicklow and it'd be grand. Solid as a rock.

—Yeah, but . . . yeh know? Yeh can't just –

—Wha?

I look at Maggit. —Wha d'you think?

—Don't give a bollix Denny, he says. —You're the one wanted a car. I'm happy walkin.

—Yeah, yer givin the few quid still though aren't yeh? Off it?

Maggit looks at the car and shakes his head again, lettin out a long, exaggerated sigh. Tryin to ingratiate himself with Gino, like. —Yeah, he says. —Wharrever Denny.

—I'll give a hundred for it, I say to Gino.

—We said one fifty.

—Yeah, it's fuckin diabolical lookin though. And I've to pay to get it out o here, which is a fuckin –

—One thirty.

—One twenty. And that's a rip off.

—Alright. One twenty.

I look at the car. It's red with a big thick bumper. I know fuck all about cars, really. I mean, makes and that – I don't have a clue. Pajo's nearly halfway in the window, his denim jacket ridin up and a few inches of his pale, skinny back showin. Maggit's diggin in his pocket for the fifty euro with an unimpressed look on his face.

—I'll have to owe yeh the score, I say. After the shock o seein the car I need a few scoops, like.

Gino nods. Maggit hands him the fifty and I give him me scrunched up ball o tens and twenties. Gino sticks

Maggit's money into his pocket and hands my fifty to Robbie. Robbie hands the fancy pigeon to the blond kid, who receives it with reverence, and him and his redheaded mate carefully pick their way up the steps to the pigeonloft door. The redhead unhooks the latch and they disappear inside.

—That's grand, says Robbie, stickin the fifty into his jeans pocket, and, to be honest, I'm already experiencin a severe dose o buyer's remorse. I look over the car again and Pajo finally pulls his head out o the window.

—Do we get the chickens as well? he says, a dirty white feather stuck to his face and grinnin from ear to ear.

ROCK N ROLL

A foreign, Borat-lookin fella wearin a shabby suit and with glasses balancin on the tip of his nose finishes up at hatch three and the queue shuffles forward. It's like a penniless version o the United Nations in here, Eastern Europeans, Asians, Africans . . . representatives of every shoddy, goin-nowhere-but-down country on earth. We're a shoddy country ourselves too, full o guilt and doubt and hidden nastiness. It's just that, given a possibly brief period o financial well-bein, we happen to scrub up well.

Have to sort this rent allowance shite out. I've been puttin it off, like. Fuckin Shane. I dread comin into places like this. Officialdom, Jesus. I break out in sweats and all sorts, makes me look dead dodgy. It's a gift that I only have to come here once a month to sign on.

Gonna pick up a chicken after I'm done here. I've invited all the heads round for an early Christmas dinner tonight. I didn't ask them to come around on Christmas day cos they'd probably rather do their own thing. It'd be a bit embarrassin askin them; I don't want them to come out o pity or wharrever.

There's a couple o young, presumably Polish fellas behind me chattin in, well, Polish, and in front of me there's a tall, slim African woman with her little girl. The woman's back is gorgeous. I know that sounds like a weird thing to say but it is, it's lovely. Her jacket's under her arm and she's wearin a loose, wide-necked yellow and orange blouse that falls away from her neck in a swathe o soft, silky cloth and reveals a huge slab of her back. Her skin's a deep coffee colour and completely smooth cept for the little nobs o vertebrae and her hair's pinned up, enhancin the view. Yeh never used to see black people in Dublin so a close-up like this still has a bit o novelty value. Plus it's all yiv got to look at in places like these, people from odd angles, lost in their own thoughts. The little girl's holdin the woman's hand and she looks up at me with huge, dark eyes and smiles, then half hides behind the woman's leg. I give her a wink and she giggles, clappin her hand to her mouth. She's dead cute, her hair stickin up in little stiff braids and tied off with beads and ribbons. She giggles again and I make a face, then her mother turns and puts her hand on the girl's head and says somethin in ... well, I don't really know wha language, they've loads, don't they, Africans? All these different tribal tongues. She has a nice profile as well, yer woman. I catch her eye and give her a smile but she turns back round without a change in her poised expression, her eyes still and unfathomable and her head tilted slightly upwards. She says somethin to the kid again, a bit of anger in her voice this time, and roughly jerks her closer to her. Proper yanks her arm.

Fuck. Bit embarrassin that, like. I mean, I wasn't tryin to come on to yer woman or anythin. Just bein friendly, yeh know? Doin me best like, nice to be nice and all that.

The little girl peeks up at me again, half her face obscured by her mother and the other half mostly hid behind her hand. I give her a quick, self-conscious smile and she makes this gleeful squealin noise before her mother jerks her forward again, pullin her completely out o view.

I peek at me watch, quarter to ten. I might ramble up to Boss Hogs after I'm done here, grab a breakfast roll or somethin before startin on the shoppin.

Me mobile bleeps. Text message. From Pajo.

HOWS THINGS DENNY. STORY WITH THE GHOST? STILL GONE? P.

Fuckin hell.

I thumb in a reply.

I HAVE ENOUGH TROUBLE BELIEVING YOU EXIST PAJO, NEVER MIND FUCKING GHOSTS. I'M AT THE DOLE. I'LL TEXT YA AFTER.

A skinny fella wearin a FCUK jumper vacates the chair at hatch three, noddin as he passes me, identifyin with me, I suppose, as a fellow native Dubliner, and the African woman steps forward, the little girl now timid and joyless as her mother takes yer man's place in front o the hatch. She pokes round in her handbag for her social welfare card. I stick me hand into me pocket and run me fingers over the little raised numbers and me name, printed in block capitals on me card. DENNY CULLEN – STATE SCROUNGER. Well, not really, like, but it might as well say that, the way some o the people behind the glass carry on in here. Yid think I was a criminal.

Bzzzz. Another text.

HAVE FAITH. P.

There we go, that word again: faith. Pajo fuckin loves it. I fuckin hate it. I hate it cos there's no way o trickin yerself into it, no amount o thinkin about it can get yeh there – yeh have it or yeh don't. And I don't. The African woman stands up, gatherin her purse and her sparkly, sequinned

112

shoulder bag. That was quick. She's a stunner from the front as well. She looks at me through slightly narrowed eyes, her cheekbones high and her mouth tightly shut. She takes a step forward and there's an impatient cough from the hatch so I step forward meself, passin her with inches between us, and despite the fuckin craziness of it all, the ineffable, yawnin fuckin difference, I have this brief image in me head o me sittin beside her on Bray beach on a big towel with the Liverpool crest woven into it and she's wearin a yellow bikini, lookin ludicrously lovely, dark and long-limbed, her kid makin sandcastles in the distance and the two of us chattin about Undertaker's latest match, sayin how deadly he looks for a forty-odd year old, how agile he is for a big guy, how cool and evocative his entrance music is.

Jesus, get a grip, Denny.

I take a seat on the bolted-down plastic swivel chair in the middle o the woman's still-lingerin perfume and slide me social welfare card under the window, smilin at the fella opposite me. He's wearin an eye-patch. He's got a beard as well so he looks a bit like a slightly fat, middle-class pirate.

—Howayeh?

Yer man nods vaguely. No messin about in these places.

—Name and address of most recent employer? he says.

—LISK, I say. —That was over a year ago, though. They're a construction company.

—Yes, I'm aware. Address?

—I dunno. I was never in the offices, like. I was on a site in Wicklow, near Powerscourt.

—Right. We'll need the address. Reason for termination of previous employment?

—Eh, I was sacked like. That was donkeys ago though, like I said.

—That's unimportant. Sacked?

—Yeah.

Bit of an embarrassin story that. We were workin on a hotel in Wicklow, in the middle of a wood, lovely spot, and I got caught pissin in one o the en-suite bathrooms. Thing was, the jax weren't hooked up yet and there were no pipes or anythin so I was just pissin onto the floor, really. I was dyin though and the prefab jax were five storeys below and a few minutes' walk away. And anyway, it was Markus, this skinny German fella who was supposed to be me supervisor, who told me to do it; all the Germans on site did it, apparently. Manky fucks. Trust me to get clocked by one o the visitin suits. Ah well.

—Hmmm, yes. Do you have your P45?

—Yeah, here.

I push it under the glass.

—Have you claimed for assistance with rent this tax year, Mr Cullen?

—No.

—No?

Jesus mate. Don't sound so surprised. —No, I say again.

—I was over in Wales for a while as well, so it was –

—What was the purpose of the visit?

—I was studyin there. Or I was gonna. In the end I . . .

—Mm hm?

—Yeah . . . I had to come back. I wasn't over for long.

—I see. What was your position with LISK?

114

—Just a labourer, like. A general op or wharrever. I was with the fireproofers.

—You're aware that your current unemployment benefit payments are contingent on you seeking and eventually securing new employment? And that you need to be receiving unemployment benefit to receive a rent allowance?

—Yeah, that's grand. I'm after ringin round loads o places. Stuff in papers and that.

—We will seek to verify this.

—OK.

—Address?

—Wha? Em, I don't know it like. I was never –

—Home address, Mr Cullen.

—Oh right, sorry. Yeah, it's 26 Glennonfield Park, Clondalkin.

—Phone number?

—We've no phone.

—No landline?

—It's cut off.

Thanks to big-gob Paula, o course.

—No phone.

—Yeah.

—OK. No phone. You have a bank account, Mr Cullen?

—Yeah, Bank of Ireland.

—Details.

—Em, I don't have them with me. It's the O'Connell Street branch.

The phone buzzes in me pocket again, another text. From Pajo I assume. I'll have to wait to check it.

—We'll need the details.

—Yeah, sound. I'll sort that, no probs.

—Mm hm. OK. A letter from your parents.

—Wha?

—To verify your tenancy.

—A letter?

—Yes.

—Like, typed?

—Hand-written will do. Make sure it's legible, signed by both your parents.

—Me da doesn't live with us, he left years ago. I don't see him.

—Your mother's signature will be fine.

—Well, actually . . . me brother owns the house. It's in his name.

—Your brother? I see. He's the landlord?

—Well, kind o, yeah. It's me ma's house though, yeh know? Me da left ages ago and Shane paid off the mortgage. Me ma's . . . em . . .

—Your brother legally owns the house?

—Yeah. I think so, anyway.

—You'll need a letter from him then. Whoever owns the house.

—OK.

—Are you living alone?

—No. Em, me sister lives with me. And her, eh . . .

—Hmm?

Jesus. I hesitate over the word 'girlfriend'.

—Well, her mate, like. A lodger or wharrever.

—OK. If you can get all that back to us this day next week please. Otherwise any prospective payments may be compromised.

—Right. Em, see yeh.

Yer man nods and flips through a cardboard box o files.

—Thanks, I say.

Fuckin hell. I stand up. I'm actually sweatin. Can yeh believe that? Fuckin grill yeh to death, these pricks. I squeeze out past the thrummin, impatient crowd o local single mothers, Poles and Slovakians, Africans, Dublin desperadoes in jeans and tracksuits and men of indeterminate Eastern European ethnicity and heave in a huge gulp of air when I get outside. A 76 zooms past. Don't know how I didn't notice it before but the side wall o the Mill shoppin centre is sprayed with VICTORY TO THE IRAQI INTIFADA in huge letters. Deadly, wha? All them dry-shite dole office workers havin to stare at pro-insurgency propaganda all day.

I start towards Boss Hogs and then I remember the text from Pajo. I lean against the wall and thumb through me messages.

FELL DOWN THE STAIRS. QUADRICEPS DESTROYED. CAN YOU PICK US UP SOME BANDAGES AND ICE OR PEAS. THANKS. :(P.

★

I pull open the greasy oven door and have a peek inside and, fair enough, I'm no expert or anythin, but there's definitely somethin weird lookin about that chicken. Too wrinkly or somethin. It looks like the head of a baldy oulfella, if he'd no face or ears or anythin, and he was roasted up and blistered and –

Fuck, that's a bit of a weird thing to think, isn't it? Intrusive thoughts, them. That's wha me ma used to say. I remember sittin beside her on the 78a, comin home from me nanny Cullen's. I was about fifteen; I was playin for Ballyfermot United and I dropped into me nanny's after trainin and me ma was there as well, the room wreathed in cigarette smoke. Maggit played for Ballyfermot as well but he wasn't there that night, he was off with Bernadette. Me and me ma hopped on the bus outside the Gala. I was still in me football shorts. When the bus pulled up outside Cherry Orchard hospital a few stops later there was an oulfella with a cane standin there, his trousers too small for him and his skinny hairy ankles showin.

—Imagine he just flew up into the air, me ma said. —Up into the sky like a rocket.

I loved when she said things like that. Mental, out o the blue things.

—Or imagine he was flyin alongside the bus, I said. —He was right beside the window and he was flyin like he was sittin down, but he had no chair or anythin.

—And then he got sucked under the wheels and he was killed, me ma said. She looked at me and she was holdin in the laughter. —Jesus that's terrible isn't it? she said. —That's intrusive thoughts.

We looked at each other for a few seconds and then we laughed, the two of us, like fuckin lunatics. I couldn't stop meself. I laugh now, thinkin of it, lookin at me freaky, baldy-headed roast.

The chickens on the telly don't look like that. But fuck it, it's not like this is Master Chef. I asked Maggit and Pajo and me mate Ned and his new girlfriend Sinead over. We're havin chicken instead o turkey though cos turkey's a bit dear. Paula said she'd give me a hand but I told her it's cool, I can handle it. Course, I'm startin to regret that now, but . . . ah, so wha. They're all in the front room, laughin and singin. Ned brought over a stack o dodgy Christmas compilation CDs he's tryin to shift and I can hear Cliff Richard croonin about mistletoe and wine in the front room, much to everyone's approval. I mean, I fuckin hate Sir Cliff, sanctimonious prick that he is, but at Christmas . . . well, it's cool, like. Or as cool as it can be, since ma's not here. Meself and Paula got the decorations down from the attic this mornin and did the place up proper. Old cards, decades old, some o them, sent by friends and relatives long dead, hangin in chains on the walls, tinsel tacked to the shelves and the doors. The tree's up and everythin, and that sparkly snowman Mrs Cunningham next-door got me ma last year, jiggin and jivin on top o the microwave. Maggit said it was a bit Father Ted-lookin when he saw it, a bit tacky like.

I'm pokin at the bubblin mass of anaemic-lookin sprouts when Paula sticks her head round the door. Cigarette smoke and whooped laughter tumbles in behind her and she smiles at me.

—Yeh OK in here? she says. —D'yeh need a hand?

—I'm grand.

I look in the oven again.

—Here, is that chicken a bit weird lookin to you?

Paula comes in. She takes off her paper crown, sets her cigarette on the edge o the table and has a look.

—Ehmmm . . . no. No, it's grand.

She looks up and smiles. I must look worried or unconvinced or somethin cos she says:

—It's fine, Denny.

—Cool. Are yeh sure?

—Yeah. Definitely. Here, have yeh been bastin it, though?

—Bastin it?

I take a drag from her cigarette and blow the smoke sideways from me mouth. There's a cheer from inside and the CD's switched off. Then the telly's volume is pumped and that high-pitched Walkin in the Air song starts to blare.

—The Snowman's on, Denny, Pajo shouts from the livin room. He sounds dead excited. His leg's wrapped up after his fall. I believe Pajo when he says he took a spill, but I reckon the only reason he said his quadriceps is fucked is that Triple H, the wrestler, had that injury a while ago, and it's stuck in his mind – Pajo's bruised leg therefore becomin a blown quadriceps.

—I'll be in in a minute, I say, over me shoulder, then turn back to Paula and the wrinkly bastard of a chicken.

—What should I o been doin? I say.

Paula sticks her crown back on. —Yeh get the juices out o the tray and squeeze it onto the back o the chicken, she says, mimin the suckin up and splurgin out o fatty juices. —To keep it moist and that. And for the flavour.

—Shite. I didn't know yid to do that.

I'm a bit ragin, now. I want this to go well.

—Is it fucked or wha?

It is. I know it is. Fuckin old man's head.

—Ah no, says Paula. She grabs her cigarette and heads back for the livin room. —Might be a bit dry, that's all. But sure they're used to nothin in there. She jerks a thumb at the rest o them in the livin room. —They'd eat a baby's arse through the rungs of a fuckin cot.

Fuck it, man. It'll be the best dinner that pack o delinquents have had in donkeys. Well, cept for Sinead who's got money, but there yeh go.

—Are yeh nearly done, then? she says. —What'll I say to them?

—Em . . .

I look at the chicken again. The bones where his feet used to be are gone black. But besides that, and the wrinkliness, it looks nice enough. Well, not un-nice, anyway. Fuckin do, like. I switch off the oven.

★

Maggit's holdin his bottle o wine by the neck, a chickenleg in his other hand. He's back on his detox, apparently. His selection box from Ned's stall is on the window ledge, waitin to be scoffed.

—So anyway, says Maggit, a runner o red dribblin from his chin. Dunno if it's wine or chicken juice or wha. Looks a bit like blood, actually. —Me da used to have this thing where if yeh went down too early for yer presents he'd storm down and bate yeh and send yeh back to bed. Which was fuckin crap cos then yid seen yer presents but they'd be robbed back off yeh and yid a raw arse to lie on for another few hours. Fuckin prick he was.

I top up me glass with the wine Sinead brought over. Nice stuff, actually. Fruity, like. Don't usually like red wine. Sinead's nice as well. She's quiet, like, and a bit posh, but she's sound. Her hair's black and it's done in braids. Ned's sittin beside her. He's mad into her, yeh can tell to look at him.

—Mad random fucker, like, says Maggit. —When he'd a few drinks especially, the fuckin dipso bastard.

A bit o rain spatters against the kitchen window. Ned drapes his arm around Sinead's shoulders. Paula's up sortin out the crackers, her head angled back towards us, grinnin. Teresa had to work late so she's not here. I'll save her somethin for when she gets back, though.

—So anyway, says Maggit —This one year me and Pajo scouted the whole house out before the big day. Reconnaissance, like. Every dodgy floorboard and stair, we marked it down in Pajo's homework copy. We even put an oul sock in the bedroom door so it wouldn't close all the way and then make a load o noise when we opened it again. So come one o' clock me and Pajo sneak out o bed and creep down the stairs. Not a sound, like. Fuckin James Bond job. We didn't have the copybook with all the plans in it cos we'd lost it a few days before but fuck that like, we knew every fuckin inch off by heart at that stage. So we got into the sittin room and it's deadly. Yeh know how it is when yer small. All the presents and that, it's the best fuckin day o yer life. I got this big Manta Force yokeybob and Pajo had some . . . wha was it?

—Wrestlin stuff, says Pajo. —Bret Hart and Hulk Hogan and all. The big rubbery ones. And a deadly ring for them. The proper WWF one.

—And Jake the Snake, I say. —Didn't yiz used to have him?

Pajo nods. —Yeah. I lost his snake though. It fell down the shore. I was ragin.

—Yeah so anyway, says Maggit. —There we were playin away, the tree all sparkly and the cards everywhere and wrappin paper on Pajo's head and wha happens? Me da comes in — fuckin sneaks in like; we never heard a fuckin sound, the sleeveen fuckin shite — and he whacks me full force in the back o the head with the bleedin leg o ham for the Christmas dinner. The leg o fuckin ham!

Ned whoops.

—Jesus, says Sinead. —That's horrible.

—Tell me about it, says Maggit, rubbin the back of his neck like it's still sore, twenty years later. —And then he pulls out Pajo's copybook and says thanks for the tips, lads, gives Pajo an almighty smack in the arse and chases us back up the stairs, the two of us roarin cryin.

We burst into hysterics. Pajo makes that funny hissin noise he makes instead o laughin, his shoulders shuckin up and down. We all look at each other, eyes glintin, happy. I cut off another slice o wrinkly-lookin but quite-nice-actually chicken and everythin's grand until Sinead says:

—That's child abuse, that is.

Pajo coughs. We all look at Sinead.

Silence.

—No, I'm serious, she says. —You could get done for that. Should get done for it, actually. If everyone just —

—Ah no, says Maggit. —It was only me da, like.

—That doesn't make it right, says Sinead.

We stop lookin at Sinead and look at each other instead, and then closely inspect our peas and beans or half-empty wine glasses. Child abuse? That's a bit much, like. When it's yer own da . . .

I fork a roastie and Bing Crosby's dreamin of a white Christmas and I reckon we're all thinkin o smacked arses and whacked necks, and how it all meant fuck all in the end. Par for the course really, isn't it?

No one says anythin for a few seconds, then Ned says:

—Ye of the un-smacked arse, wha? Me middle-class darlin.

He grins at her, then puts on a husky Darth Vader voice:

—Welcome to the dark side, Sinead.

DENZERINO

I tilt me head and smile a big unnatural smile and . . . sweet fuck all. I wait a few more seconds . . . still nothin.

I glance down at the pair o fluffy granny boots shufflin on the other side o the curtain, then look back at the screen, me reflection in the glass still grinnin its now strained, slightly mental-lookin grin. Me hair's gettin a bit long, it's curly and it grows up more than down. It's startin to look a bit like an afro. I don't know where I get that from, both me ma and da have straight hair. Well, they did have straight hair; me da's gone baldy. I push me hair back from me forehead and inspect me hairline. It's still grand. For now.

A shock o white sears me eyes and when I open them there's two pulsin globes bobbin in me vision. I slowly stand up and pull aside the greasy curtain and stumble back into the world. Which is to say, the fruit and vegetable aisle in the new Tesco on Ballyfermot Road. The picture booth in Liffey Valley is broke so I ran the car up to Ballyfermot. Gino's mate shifted it a couple o days ago. Took a whole day to clean the shite and straw out and yeh can still smell it. Pajo's got the chickens out his and Maggit's back garden. He's delighted with them. And me, as well, I'm delighted – tellin yeh, it's deadly just bein able to jump in the car. No more fuckin 78a.

Class.

Gettin on, yeh know. Gettin ahead. Feel in a deadly mood today. I need two passport photos to register with this agency I dropped into yesterday, in Clondalkin village. I'm startin to consider gainful employment. Well, I'll fill out the forms and see how it goes.

There's two grannies chattin to each other across the aisle, one gesticulatin at the other with a bent and hairy lookin carrot, like she's some mental, geriatric conductor. There's an earthy tang o dirt and both o the grannies are speakin quick and clipped, the old school Dublin inner-city machinegun twang me nanny Cullen used to have. The carrot-less granny turns and looks at me, smilin.

—Ah, she says. —Gettindoulpassportpichers.

I nod and smile back, blinkin hard; me eyes are still a bit fucked. I glance back at the oul photo booth. I know the pictures are gonna be useless but I'm after spendin a fiver on them so I'm not leavin them there.

—Gosomewherefoddin, son, says the granny with the carrot, and she points the wonky vegetable vaguely (I assume) in the direction o some foreign hotspot.

—Somewherewirrabirrasunshine, says the other one.

—Not actually goin anywhere like, I say. —Just gettin the photos done.

They look at each other and nod sagely, eyes closin slowly and openin again.

—Forrajob, says the granny with the carrot, and the two o them nod again. —Teddiblehardtogerrajobthesedays.

—Ohgodyeahjaysis, speciallywirralldemfoddiners.

The carrot-less granny reaches to her left without turnin her head and scrabbles at a pile of apples, her wrinkly hand lightin quickly on one apple and then another. The old, spotty hand closes round an unlucky yellow and she plucks it up and drops it into a cellophane bag, then expertly flips it and twists it and places it into her otherwise empty trolley.

—Millionsodempolishaswell. Neverseendalikes.

There's a clunk from the booth, followed by a whirrin sound. The photos are warm and slightly sticky. Most o me face is obscured by me hand and the one visible eye is red and demonic lookin. Not as bad as I'd thought they'd be, but still crap. I stuff them into me jeans pocket.

—See yiz, I say to the grannies, and head for the booze aisle.

—Enjoydaholliers, one o them says.

★

Cheerios, multivitamins, potatoes (small bag), steak and kidney pie (x2), three-for-two Chicago Town pepperoni pizzas, marked down toffee cheesecake (has to be eaten tonight), packet o digestives, family pack o Monster Munch, tray o frozen chicken fillets, milk (two litres, semi-skimmed – Paula won't drink the full fat stuff), bag o Granny Smiths, huge box o Lyons tea bags, king prawns for Teresa (they have the faces on, and their legs and everythin; I reckon if yeh eat something's whole body like that yeh gain their memories – no prawns for me, so), two bottles o cheapo red wine, Guinness six-pack (cans), Budweiser six-pack (bottles), a large bottle o Smirnoff and four Christmas tree-shaped air freshener things for the car. I know I shouldn't really be gettin all this drink in (usin mostly Teresa's money, as well) but wha can yeh do? Sit in and stare at the telly all night? Yeh need the option o drink, even just as a fallback.

There's a woman in the queue in front o me, oldish but with a nice figure, her trolley filled with things I'd never buy. It's mad when yeh see that, stuff other people buy at supermarkets. Tinned pears, a tub o Elmlea whole cream. Things I'd never think o buyin.

While she's payin for her stuff I keep lookin at her hands: they're dead elegant lookin, the skin milky pale and the nails red and immaculate. The mad thing is that facewise (and I'm not slaggin here, just sayin) she's in rag order, all clown style make-up and hairy moles and saggy skin. Why lavish all that attention on yer hands and none on yer face? The mug of a sixty-year-old prostitute and the hands of a faerie queen. The people yeh see. She pays with a card and steers her bagged shoppin towards the exit.

The fella on the till is young and snatches up each item and scans it without lookin. A little bleep. Monster Munch. Bleep-bleep. The milk, the cheesecake. Bleep. Sometimes it takes two scans. The packet o digestives takes three.

—How do Denwaldo?

I turn round. It's Kasey, noddin his head and grinnin his big stoner's grin.

—Heya Kasey. What's the story?

—Here, will yeh get us twenty Blue?

Kasey splats a crisp fifty euro note onto me box of Cheerios. Then he looks at me and grins and hurries out into the foyer where he plonks his arse down on a miniature version o Postman Pat's delivery van. He shoots me a big thumbs-up.

★

Me and Kasey stand under the Tesco's awnin, smokin his cigarettes with me shoppin bags round me ankles. There's a line o bristlin cars and buses stuck in traffic across the car park, the shitty 78a like a weird mobile zoo; a woman with a nose ring and green hair, a double-chinned man with a red potato for a nose, a teenager with a mobile phone glued to his ear. A taxi pulls up in front of us and a woman in a trouser suit clutchin a plastic container o pasta salad ducks in. The taxi pulls away, stoppin about fifteen feet up the road, the lights still red.

I haven't seen Kasey since that day in Trinity. Although that's nothin new, I suppose; always off on his travels, Kasey. He's back in his usual attire, as well: the oul leather jacket and the near threadbare Anthrax T-shirt. He takes a huge drag on his cigarette, his dark green eyes on the slow-movin traffic. He taps his ash and looks at me, smilin slightly.

—Keepin OK so, Denstable? he says.

—Not too bad. After gettin a car.

—Yeah?

—Yeah. It's only an oul banger I got off Gino but it does the job, like.

—That'll do. So how'd the séance go?

Another big drag on me cigarette. —Dunno, really. Pajo went a bit . . . well, hard to say, like.

—Did yiz make contact?

—I wouldn't wanna say, Kasey. Pajo started sayin all this mad shite but . . . I dunno. I reckon he was just . . .

—Puttin it on?

—Well, no. Not puttin it on. He wouldn't lie. But he might o convinced himself.

—And is the ghost still there?

—Paula says it's not. So . . . happy days, I suppose.

Kasey takes another drag from his cigarette, lookin thoughtful. I shrug and take a good drag meself, blowin the smoke out in front o me, the bluish-grey ribbons like spectral fingers.

—Yeh in the money or wha? I ask him, handin over his forty odd euro change.

Kasey shrugs and taps the side of his nose. —Well, yeh could say that, I suppose.

—Yeh workin?

Kasey laughs. —In a manner o speakin, Denethor. I've managed to come across certain substances that are much in demand in today's affluent Ireland.

—Yer not fuckin dealin are yeh?

Kasey shrugs.

—In wha? I say.

He winks.

—Fair enough, I say. —Yid wanna be careful, though. Less I know, wha?

—You said it, compadre.

We stand and smoke for a bit. The sky's turnin a bit dark, the clouds huge and sluggish.

—Wha had yeh up at a culchie doctor's? I say. —Maggit was tellin me.

Kasey looks at the ground and shrugs. He scrapes the back of one runner against the front o the other, then shrugs again, lookin sideways at me.

—Boys in blue dropped me off, he says.

—How come?

Kasey takes another, final, gargantuan drag. It looks like the cigarette's sucked into him, like some stage magician's trick. The tip turns orange and smoulders and a pair o thin smoke trails tumble from his nostrils.

—Well, he says. —Long story short Denver, I was on me way to Donegal to see me sisters. Drivin up. I was drinkin and that, yeh know? Off me face on cider and pills. Wasn't feelin the peachiest that week, yeh know? Can I be honest with yeh?

He drops the butt of his cigarette and looks at me. I nod.

—Pure bummed out I was. Rock bottom, as they say. And halfway there I just says to meself, out o the bleedin blue like – fuck this shite. I was drivin alongside some river and Gerry Ryan was on the radio talkin to this culchie farmer about bleedin irrigation of all the wide world's subjects and I just ran the bleedin van into the river.

—Fuckin hell Kasey.

—Have yeh ever heard Gerry Ryan's show?

Oul halfmad Kasey. A new unlit cigarette hangin slantways from the corner of his mouth. One hand in his jeans pocket, the other makin a fist and slowly openin again.

—Yeh alright Kasey?

—Grand, Denno. Grand. He laughs again. —Bleedin van only went halfway in, sure. I thought it'd be like the films, yeh know? The way they just go flyin off the road and the car sinks and that's that. End o story. Trust bleedin me though. I was left sittin on the bank with freezin bleedin water pourin in over me runners. Stayed there for ages, like. Listenin to Gerry Ryan and drinkin me cider.

—Wha, and the police saw yeh?

—Yeah. A squad car pulled up on the motorway and these two coppers came down. They thought I robbed the van. They pulled me out and dragged me up the embankment. This pig hits me a smack in the head and then I was in the back o the car. They said they were sick o the likes o me comin up from Dublin, wreckin the place. I told them it was me own van and that I was tryin to kill meself and me ma was from Donegal. I thought I was in for a night in the cells and a bop in the head, yeh know? Bate the brass monkey or wharrever. But wha did they do only bring me to a fuckin mental hospital. Said I was a sadcase and a bleedin waste o time and they'd other things to be dealin with.

—Fuck.

I can't think of anythin else to say. It may sound a bit mad, like, but the casual admittance of attempted suicide isn't that much of a shock to me. Not when yeh know people like Kasey. I wouldn't say it happens every five minutes or anythin but it's not earth shatterin, either.

—Fuck is right. It took me another day to come down, I'd popped that many pills on the drive. I was away with the bleedin fairies Del. That's when this culchie doctor tells me I'm unwell. He should know I suppose, with all these certs he had on the wall. He said I needed help. All I need's a valium and a shite, I says to him. Ran off that night. Hitched back to Dublin with this truck driver from the Liberties, slept in Stephen's Green and got the bus home. The gardaí towed me van out o the water for me. They rang me ma. I've to go up and collect it. It'll probably cost a few bob but –

—Kasey. Yer alright though, yeah? I mean, yer –

—Sound, Dennicus. Sound as a pound. Or sound as a euro. Sure yeh can probably claim somethin for bein mad. Off the council or the government or somethin.

132

He points up at the sky.

—Silver linin, he says. —Always, Den. There's always a silver linin. Anyway I'd better head. Stay cool Denzerino. Don't let the bastardos bring yeh down.

THE EXISTENCE OF
MONSTERS

The steam's puffin up from the kettle and it's like a parade
o spooky jellyfish or somethin, chuggin up and out, each
puff gettin bigger and hazier the nearer it gets to the smoke-
stained ceilin and then it's gone, exorcised or absorbed
although there's always more behind, pushin on the one
in front, a puffin procession ghostly and never-endin. And
the way it billows as well, it's –

The kettle clicks and the little red light goes off. They
say a watched kettle never boils but it just takes fuckin
ages.

I take up the kettle and pull open the greasy press with
me other hand. Grab a cup. And two more. Have to put
the kettle back down cos it's gettin heavy. Put too much
water in, which me mate Pajo wouldn't approve of cos
it's a waste o energy and wha have yeh, which is right I
suppose. I burrow me hand past the digestives and Bisto
and Pringles and fish a couple teabags from the battered
blue tin in the corner o the press.

—Growin the tea leaves yerself in there?

That's Paula. Watchin EastEnders in the front room
with Teresa. Well for her, like. Talk about women o leisure.
Yid have to surgically remove them two from the fuckin

sofa. Actually, nah, I take that back – Teresa works so I can't say anythin, really. All the nice plants round the house are hers, as well; they're the only healthy-lookin things in the place. Paula has no excuse, though; fuckin bone idle, she is.

—Wha did yer last servant die of? I say.

—Overwork, says Paula. The two o them laughin. Phil Mitchell's threatenin someone in his gravelly, gobshitey voice on the telly. Hate that prick.

I pull at the fridge door handle and there's that suck and give as the door pops open. Hardly anythin in it cept drink for Paula's party. Paula and Teresa went to Kilkenny for the weekend, saw Falter Ego play, and now that they're back Paula wants to celebrate the house's new ghost-free status. She said the party's gonna be massive, which means a massive fuckin headache. Shane's deffo gonna hear about it. Symbolic or not, I think this party's a bad idea. I should just fuck off, really, for the night, wash me hands of it.

Ah, I dunno. Seems like –

Fuckin hell, lookit this. Must be four dozen cans in here, at least. Heaven forbid anyone put food in the bleedin fridge, like. Bottles o wine as well, alcopops, a bottle o Baileys. Fuck. Foodwise, there's a brick o rockhard butter squeezed between two six packs o Bulmers and a few carrots wrapped in misted cellophane on the bottom shelf. That's it for solids. I take out the milk. Check the sell-by date.

Grand.

Pour it in and stir. Let the mini-whirlpools settle. Grab the jar o coffee from the top o the fridge. It's beside the fruit bowl which to be honest has seen better days: the two apples in it are covered in them horrible squashy

135

pulpy brown bits and the less said about the shrunk, multicoloured orange the better. Fuckin hell. Me ma would never o let the place get like this; she was dead house proud. When me ma was cleanin up – say, doin the hooverin, or washin up or wharrever – she'd blast Rod Stewart on the stereo, and kind o dance around the place as she went. Paula used to love that when she was younger – she'd be up and dancin with me ma, soapin up the plates. Me ma'd said it was borin cleanin the place without a few choons, then sing along to Maggie May. Me da used to look at her like she was mad. Before he fucked off, like. Even after that, though, me ma never let things get on top of her. She was dead strong, she got on with things. She kept the place spotless and played her Rod Stewart albums. The house was alive back then.

I spoon the coffee into the last cup, Teresa's cracked Thundercats one. Pour in the hot water and stir. The sun's settin over the back garden. It's dead overgrown out there now, all wild and webby. Grass to yer arse and nettles and stingers and lowhangin branches. Can't even get into the shed anymore. Could be a witch livin out there, mutterin her nasty incantations in the gloom, hook-nosed and gammy-eyed, hair thick with spiders and grease. Layin curses on the house. Some foul, evil oul hag, a consort o the ghost.

Yer milk soured.

Yer Cornflakes chewy.

Probably why I can't get a job, some witch's hex. Well, that or the fact I never filled out them forms at the FAS office. Still though. Imagine. A witch surrounded by ancient rusty saws and bollixed hammers and shufflin in the dark, a wizened jaloppy-boned crone half-lost under a mound o shiftin rags. Her eyes cat-like in the dark. A hiss and –

Jesus Denny. Fuckin give it a rest will yeh? I freak meself out, sometimes.

—D'yeh need a hand or somethin?

Paula.

—No, I'm grand. I'm comin.

I hook the handles o the teacups with me index finger and grab the coffee with me free hand. Push open the front room door with me arse and shuffle in backwards. The place is messy and stale and sad-lookin. Reeks o cigarettes. There's kids still playin on the road outside. Heads n volleys or somethin. Paula's head on Teresa's shoulder, their feet tucked under them on the sofa, Teresa's socks white and Paula's mismatched pink and blue.

—Thanks, Denny, says Teresa.

—That's lovely, says Paula.

—No prob. Your turn next.

I can see Pajo strugglin at the front gate as I set the cups on the coffee table. First o the guests, unsurprisinly. Ever eager to kiss sobriety goodbye, our Pajo. He's jugglin a packed Spar bag and tryin to reach the lock, a deep and serious look on his face.

—Go out and help him, says Paula, eyes still on the telly, cup o tea clasped two-handed below her chin. The drums start thumpin on the telly. Phil Mitchell looks vaguely befuddled or angry or both and the map o London fades in.

★

—Dance music?

—It is a party, Denny, says Paula.

A thumpin beat's poundin from the speakers and Paula straightens up from the CD player. She waves an empty CD sleeve in front o me. SUMMA CHOONZ 4 WINTA BLOOZ, it says. Free with the *Daily Star*.

—Yeah. Dance, though?

—Yes. Dance music. For dancin to. There's no way The Clash or The Ramones or fuckin Johnny Cash is goin on tonight.

—Wha about Mastodon? I say, just messin, like.

—Them with the mad fuckin demon singin? Supposed to be singin, anyway.

—It's progressive metal.

—Bit o Leonard Cohen, says Ned from the armchair, winkin at me, his hands danglin over the six-pack between his feet. —Just in case we start feelin too happy.

—No way, says Paula, roundin on Ned. —No chance. Don't even mention Leonard Cohen tonight. He's banned. Fella'd put bleedin years on yeh.

Synths kick in. Bit o bass and a stream o sampled YEAHS. Hate that stuff. I knock back the last o me Guinness and set the empty on the CD player. I can't get me head round music with no guitars in it. Ned shrugs his shoulders and mock sighs.

—Ah we'll be grand, Den. Get enough o that Guinness down yeh and she can stick the bleedin Spice Girls on. He sinks back into the armchair and knits his hands behind his head. —Fuck it like. Sure it's all relevant art isn't it? I mean, Famous Blue Raincoat on one hand, Spice Up Yer Life on the other. Can't fault it man. All good stuff.

—Well when yeh put it like that. Is Sinead comin up?

—Should be, he says. He pulls one hand free and looks at his big, colourful watch. Presses a few buttons. —Depends wha time she can clock off college at. Exams like.

—Cool.

—Yeh heard from Maggit?

—Yeah, I say. —He said he'll drop up later.

—Sound. The old gang, wha?

Yep. The old gang. Some things never change, man. Never.

★

The place is startin to fill up. Paula and Teresa are throwin shapes and tossin their heads beside the fireplace, cans miraculously still in the maelstrom. Pajo's standin in the doorway, face set and serious, shuckin his shoulders and wrigglin his fingers as he spews some no doubt half-mad tale at Kasey, hunched and longhaired on his haunches below him. Kasey's head's tilted and noddin sagely, a can o cheapo Dutch Gold hooked and danglin from his index finger. Two urban seanchaí deep in their impenetrable musins. Or a couple o half-drunk wasters, take yer pick. Four o Paula's mates are squashed onto the sofa, gigglin and pawin each other and jiggin up and down in time with the beat, drinks held up and out in front o them. Three girls and a fella. One o them's Charly, who lives not far from us. Just round the corner from The Steerin Wheel, actually, which is dead handy. She's gay as well, most o Paula's girl friends are, and she's black but she was brought up in Dublin and she has a stronger Irish accent than me. Paula introduced the other two but I'm after forgettin their names already. Bollix. The chap has a feminine look and voice, and his legs are crossed kind o girlishly. Donal or Donald or somethin, I think Paula said. Proper, expensive-lookin haircut as well.

The girls are all pretty in their own way but the one on the end's an absolute stunner. Curly, liquorice-black hair and a darkish complexion. Her Adidas tracksuit isn't exactly doin anythin for her, like, but not even that can do her much damage. Does she look foreign or somethin? Spanish, maybe. Or Italian. Eyes cool and pennydark. Donald or Donal leans and whispers somethin into her ear. She smiles and ducks her chin, laughs with her bottom lip between her teeth.

I squash past Pajo and Kasey and into the kitchen, catchin Pajo mutterin somethin about ectoplasm on the way. Kasey says, check under the beds. For fuck sake. There's two more female unknowns leanin against the kitchen table and chattin to Rochey from up the road. He's like a fuckin shark for this kind o thing, Rochey is; he can taste any perfume in the air in a five-mile radius. He smiles and winks as I pass him, his arms thick and veined. Proper gym rat, Rochey, mad into that MMA stuff and on the juice and everythin, chest bulgin beneath the show-offy pink T-shirt. I pull open the fridge and grab another can and out the open front door I can see a big red van pull up across the road. Scatters the kids. The door slides back and that new fella ducks out. Dunno where he's from. He looks Middle Eastern or somethin, his tanned face and arms pokin out from his shiny yellow high-vis vest. He leans in and says somethin to whoever's still hid in the dark o the van before it pulls off. I snap open me can and take a swig. The two girls Rochey was chattin to walk past me and head upstairs.

—Denny, says Rochey, grinnin.

—Wha?

—C'mere. Check out the talent. Her there. She's a fine thing, isn't she?

Rochey points surreptitiously through the door and I amble over. He's pointin at the girl in the Adidas tracksuit. She's sittin on the edge o the sofa now, cigarette in one hand, can o lager in the other, laughin raucously at Pajo, who's performin a skittery jig somewhere between breakdance and epileptic fit. Everyone else is standin round, clappin and breakin their shite laughin.

—Isn't she? Her there. Savage bit of arse. They'd have to dig me out of her.

—She's nice, yeah, I say, feelin annoyed at his fuckin terminology. I mean, she's nice, but . . . I dunno. The way fuckin fellas go on. I mean, I'm a fella as well, like, but . . . ah, wharrever. No point in sayin anythin to Rochey, anyway. Not unless I want me brains sprayed all over the wallpaper. Probably go all fuckin roid rage on me, the malletheaded prick. And anyway, she's probably gay, the Adidas girl, so Rochey'll be in for a knockback if he tries anythin.

I gulp at me can and Rochey whacks me on the back and saunters into the front room, towards the Adidas girl. She's just lookin up at him and the beginnins of a smile or howayeh are twitchin on her lips when I turn back into the kitchen. Ned pushes past me and into the hall, natterin into his mobile. I'm feelin the first effect o the drink now, a slight, nice wooziness. Quick glance at the clock and it's twenty past ten, and a new, hundred mile an hour tune blasts from the stereo inside. Laughin and screechin from Paula and her mates. I grab another can from the fridge and Tommy Power comes shufflin up the garden with his girlfriend and a UN relief package-sized tray o lager. He nods at me and winks and eases the tray onto the kitchen table. Rochey pops his head into the kitchen and him and Tommy whoop and shake hands. Tommy's girlfriend pulls out a chair and sits miserably.

—Yeh alright, Denny?

It's Ned.

—Yeah, cool.

—Yeh look distracted.

—Wha?

—Isn't that wha they say in films?

—I'm grand. I'm not distracted-lookin am I?

—Right then. Yiv a big sour puss on yeh. Ned takes a sup from his can. —Might never happen, Denny.

—D'you know half o these people?

Ned shrugs. —No. Well, you and Paula and Pajo. And Kasey.

—And Rochey.

—Yeah. Who let the steroid machine in?

—Invited himself. Like most o the rest o them, probably.

—D'yeh wanna head off somewhere else, Denny? I don't mind.

—Nah. Well, I wouldn't mind headin but . . . yeh know? Wouldn't know wha the fuck'd happen. No use leavin Paula in charge cos the place'll be in fuckin ruins.

—Fair enough. Look, just get a few drinks down yeh and yill be grand. It's that bleedin hash and the pills, Denny. Has yeh paranoid. Best thing yill ever do is give that shite up.

—I've done pills about twice or somethin, Ned. I'm not a pillhead.

Ned knocks his head with his knuckles.

—Yeah, but yiv got fuckin hash plants growin in yer lungs. Clear head, Denny. That's wha yeh want. Won't get anywhere when yer hepped up on fuckin goofballs half the time. Need proof?

—G'wan.

—Stick yer head round the door there. One word and two syllables.

—Pajo?

—Fuckin Blockbusters, Mr Cullen.

★

Darkness over the estate and the streetlights are on, givin everythin that weird, washed-out quality. Shadows deep and dark and freakishly long. Place is absolutely packed, now. Had to get out, felt a fuckin panic attack comin on. I'm leanin against the garden wall, Guinness in hand, stressed out. Hate when I get like this. Although it's probably due to the hash, to be honest. I never used to smoke the stuff until I came back from Wales. I just tried it and it does calm yeh down. But it gives me the creeps sometimes as well. Ned's right, I have to knock it on the head. And fuck it as well, I still can't remember that girl's name. Typical o me, that. I mean, it's not that I forget names, exactly, it's more that I forget to remember them. Although to be fair I probably wouldn't even say anythin to her if I could remember her name, I'd be . . . I dunno, maybe I would say somethin. Actually, I'm probably subconsciously forgettin her name so I have an excuse to stay away. Wouldn't surprise me. And then again, she could be an alco or a junkie or somethin. Or she could be spoken for. Or, like I said before, gay.

I haven't even so much as kissed a girl in, like . . . dunno how long. Back in Wales, anyway. Months ago. Wha d'yeh do, though? I mean, the whole approachin girls thing, it doesn't sit right with me. I just keep thinkin to meself, it must annoy them. It's all dead transparent. The chase, the lines, the buyin drinks. It's a load o shite. It'd be nice, alright, to be with someone, but sometimes . . . I don't see it happenin. Not to me. I feel like I was born in the wrong time or something; I wish I lived in Middle fuckin Earth.

There's a wave o raucous laughter and clappin and stampin o feet from inside. Ned must o managed to wrangle his 'musical compromise' cos The Pogues are pumpin from the open front room window and into the night. Streams of Whiskey, one o their up tempo ditties. The dance stuff'll be back on soon enough so maybe I should head back in. Although, big crowds, yeh know? Specially when yeh hardly know anyone.

Kasey's slumped to me right, propped up against the wall by his elbows. Kasey's always like this, up and then down. He'll be fuckin manic in half an hour. Pajo's swayin slightly in front of us, a joint juttin upwards from his lower lip. He draws deep and passes it to Kasey who takes it and regards it and guides it carefully to his scabby lips. Another long, deep drag. Me next and I hesitate before takin a quick toke, savourin the soothin mellow rush. That'll do for now. Gettin a bit wrecked, like.

—Wha were yiz talkin about in there, Paj? I say.

Pajo looks up at me, slow-blinkin jelly-boned stoner.
—Spirits, he says.

—Vodka, I say, just windin him up, like. And to steer the conversation away from Paula and this ghost bollix.

—Ah no, no, says Pajo, shakin his head. —Ghost spirits. The paranormal.

Kasey nods, eyes still closed. —Afterlife, he mumbles.

They're obsessed, these two.

—Any conclusions then? I say.

—Hard to say, says Pajo.

Kasey nods. —Other than they do exist. The proof's there, Dendrite. It's incontrovertible.

—Thing is, says Pajo. —Wha are they though?

Kasey nods again.

—That's the, like, the real question, says Pajo.

—Wha are the options? I ask.

—Loads, says Pajo. —Could be, like, dead people stuck. Like for a bad death, so they can't get away. Could be psychic energy. Where someone died and there's all this . . . wha is it?

—Like a stain, says Kasey.

—Yeah. Left there. That's not real, though. I mean, like, with that option, it's not a soul, not a real ghost. It's just like a replay. Yeh know? A psychic replay. So that's just one option. Pajo shakes his head. —The world is so big. It's mad, isn't it?

—Wha?

—Dyin.

—How d'yeh mean?

—That yeh can die. That, like, yer not alive anymore, yeh know? There has to be somethin. There is somethin. I think so anyway. Pajo looks at the ground and then back up at me. —D'you?

—I dunno man.

Really I wanna say, no, there's fuck all after yeh die. Yer gone, obliterated. But I can't.

—Be shite if there wasn't anythin, I suppose, I say.

Pajo looks pleased enough with this vague wisdom. He smiles and draws on the joint.

—Any word from Maggit, Paj?

—He said he'd drop up. After. I think he was callin up to Bernadette's.

A battered mini chugs past the garden, headlights briefly illuminatin the street. It turns at the top o the road and disappears, the lilac dark closin round it. Yeh can almost hear the whoosh as the dark sucks back in. The Sickbed of Cúchulainn kicks in, all wild fiddlin and Shane MacGowan's drink-ravaged voice. Shapes flashin behind the front room curtains, bobbin heads and flailin arms.

There's a gust o cool and clean wind. A fella and girl wobble down the garden path towards us, cuttin through our smoke and conversation. Become a fuckin Mecca for wasters and drunks and druggies, this place has. Night after fuckin night, like; the house that never fuckin sleeps. There's loads o people squeezed out into the hallway, drinks clutched to their chests. Laughin and whoopin. Ned's the only one I recognise, sittin at the bottom o the stairs with a mobile stuck to his ear, noddin his head and knittin his eyebrows.

I should go back in there, shouldn't I? If I'd a set o balls I'd go up and talk to that girl, the one in the Adidas tracksuit. Before Rochey or some other shitebag has a chance to work their magic, if they haven't already.

I look at Pajo. Right, fuck it. I'm goin in. —Did you catch the name o that girl in there? The one in the Adidas tracksuit?

—I think it –

There's a loud yeow! from up the road and Pajo stops midsentence, turnin his head slowly, lighthouse-style. I can see two figures weavin through the bollards at the top o the street. Scratch that, three figures, actually: Dave

Dempsey pushin Dommo Power, Tommy's brother, along in his wheelchair. Slaughter's alongside them, laughin and throwin shapes and clappin and stompin in time to The Pogues. Bollix. Hope these pricks aren't thinkin o stoppin. They're closer now, Slaughter in his patched denim jacket, his shaven head grey-lookin in the dark. Dave's guidin Dommo along, the legs o Dommo's jeans tucked up under his stumps and a half-gone six-pack on his lap. Used to be a mate o mine, Dommo. Donkeys ago, when we were kids. Fell drunk on the tracks five or six years ago and a train ran over his legs. Sliced the fuckers right off. Dead fuckin bitter, like. He's one o the biggest dealers in Clondalkin now. Keeps a stash of every kind o drug yeh can think of in a little compartment under the seat of his wheelchair, for emergency sales and personal use. That him and Slaughter are in cahoots these days is bad news.

They stop at the gate.

—Party? says Dommo.

—Yeah. Well . . . yeah.

—Tommy in there?

Slaughter's starin at me dead-eyed, machine-gunnin his head to the song's frantic beat with a big mentalcase grin on his face.

—He popped out about half an hour ago. Said he'll be back though.

—Fuck it, I'll wait for him.

Dommo spits and Dave swivels the chair and pushes Dommo into the garden and along the path. Slaughter stomps along behind but doesn't follow them into the house. Fuckin hell. This is gettin worse by the minute. Slaughter was tellin me a while ago about this Irish white power website, and how Ireland needs to be claimed back from immigrants and all this. Why he thought I'd wanna hear that is beyond me; I think in some ways he just assumes your allegiance as a white Irish male. He said Samantha Mumba should be sent back to Africa and that him and his mates were gonna saw the head off the Phil Lynott statue outside Bruxelles in town. Thank fuck Charly and yer man Donal are already gone.

Slaughter winks at me. —How yeh doin, boy?

—Grand. Yerself?

—A fuckin 1, boy. Not a fuckin bother.

—Good to be out, yeah?

I'm referrin to the few months he did a while ago for bottlin some fella outside Eamonn Doran's. Did it in full view o two gardaí and then tried to take them on as well.

—Fuckin deadly, he says. —Borin in there. Still celebratin. Haven't slept in four days, boy. Fuckin Colombian marchin powder, wha?

—Cool.

—Cool is not the word.

Slaughter slaps his hands together and rubs them.

—Any decent colleens in there? The fuckin Slaughter's back in business, boy.

I don't know wha to say so I just open me mouth and make a noise and nod me head vaguely.

—Sound boy, sound. Here, did yeh see yer man across the road?

—Who?

—Fuckin Iraqi or somethin. Sandnigger anyway.

—The new fella?

—Yeah, him across the road there. Prick. Need to have words there, boy.

—He seems alright.

—Alright?

—He's quiet. I think he's a builder or somethin.

—Fuckin builder. They'll be buildin him a new set o knees. Slaughter guffaws and twitches his shoulders. —New set o knees, boy.

—Chill, says Pajo.

Slaughter looks at Pajo. —Wha?

—It's a party, man. Relax. Cool yer boots.

Slaughter rubs his bristly head. —D'you fuckin want somethin? Was I talkin to you?

—Just go on in, Slaughter, I say. —There's loads o drink and that in the fridge. Rochey's in there as well.

—That queer? He's never out o that pink fuckin T-shirt, is he?

Another noncommittal head movement. Best way o dealin with Slaughter; don't have too much of an opinion, like. Keep it vague.

—Sure yer sister's a fuckin dyke as well, isn't she? No fuckin thanks, boy. Bent fuckin city in there. Tell Dommo I'm headin into town. I'll see yiz so, girls.

—Bye, says Pajo.

Slaughter stomps out o the garden and looks quickly back over his shoulder at us as he passes the gate. I stand and watch him go, a hunched and hurryin silhouette bristlin with pent-up fury. After a few hundred yards he's lost in the huge and poolin dark.

*

—Get out! Get the fuck out o here!

The early hours and Paula's screechin like a demented banshee at Shane, her voice jagged and high-pitched and

149

meldin weirdly with the trance music pumpin from the stereo. Shane's backin off, face slack and pale and shakin with anger or disgust, edgin with little stumbly steps out o the hall and into the garden. Surprised he hasn't decked Paula, to be honest. Seen it happen before. Probably too many people around. He steps out o the porch and into the garden. His car's parked across the road, the engine still runnin.

—Fuck off, you! Paula screams.—This isn't your fuckin home!

Shane turns his back on her and walks to the gate, then turns around and looks at her. His sister. His only sister.

—Yeh demented bitch, Paula, he says and reaches behind him, pullin open the door o the car. —We'll fuckin see tomorrow, alright? We'll fuckin see tomorrow. He shakes his head and crumples into the seat. The car pulls away, cuttin through the dark.

—Prick! Fuckin poxy fuckin prick!

I put me hand on Paula's shoulder. —Leave it, Paula. C'mon.

Paula wheels round on me, lip quiverin and her eyes dazed and wanderin. Totally pissed, like. Stoned as well, probably. She shakes her head, her face contorted, and pushes past me and back into the front room. It didn't even look like she recognised me.

Fuck, man, I hate this shite. Feels like we're . . . ah, I dunno. Fuck it. Shane came bargin into the house sayin the Cunninghams next-door rang him and were givin out about the noise. Which is fair enough I suppose cos they're gettin on a bit, Mr and Mrs Cunningham. Knew this'd happen. And Paula did as well. But there's no way Shane was goin to get any kind o compromise out o Paula. Specially

150

when he's roarin his fat fuckin head off and double fuckin specially when Paula's drunk. And Slaughter's back as well, sittin at the kitchen table, a bottle o Jägermeister in front of him, grindin his teeth, his jaw protrudin. Must o popped a load o pills or somethin. Freaks me out, Slaughter does. Wha mad fuckin thoughts must run through his mind. When I think of his head I see a lopsided gothic church full o bats and shadows.

I slump down onto the bottom stair. The toilet flushes above and a few seconds later Pajo's stoned face hovers into view.

—What's up?

I look up at him. —Here, man, I say. —Sort me out Paj.

—Yeh OK?

—Cool, man. Just . . . give us somethin, yeah?

—To calm down, like?

—Yeah. Actually, no. Fuck it. An upper.

Pajo bites his lip and scratches his head. —Yeh sure, Denny? I mean, that's not really your thing –

—Pajo, yer not me ma.

—Well. I –

—Pajo. If yeh have somethin just gimme it. I'll give yeh the bleedin money.

Pajo reaches into his back pocket and pulls out a little wad o newspaper, unwraps it carefully.

—What's that?

—Just pills. Got them at that trad festival last week.

—Cool. Yeah, wharrever. That'll do.

Pajo puts a small white pill between his front teeth and snaps it in two.

—I'll have the other half, he says. —Yeah?

—Grand. I won't die of a fuckin heart attack now, will I?

Pajo's right; pills aren't me thing, like. Bit suspicious o them.

—Ah no Denny. Just drink a bit o water. Keep yerself hydrated.

—Right. Water.

—Yeah.

I pop the crumbly crescent into me mouth.

★

Fuckin hell this is deadly. A few more pills popped and I'm boppin away like a mentalcase. I usually hate dancin. I feel dead self-conscious and lame but I don't give a bollix how stupid I look now. And I do look stupid, sure I can see meself in the mirror and I look like a total spazzo with me arms pumpin and me legs kickin and faces spinnin round me laughin and whoopin and clappin but everyone else is dancin as well, a meaty thudthudthud from the speakers, total tuneless bollix but fuck that as well, who gives a fuck? Pajo with his mad breakdancin routine beside me, his badges clackin away and Paula weaves through the faces towards me and grabs me hand and twirls me and laughs, her eyes weird and floaty and then she's gone and into the kitchen. Fuckin hell, this buzzin energy. I'm dancin away and starin at the ancient teary-eyed harlequin me uncle Victor found in a field in Germany and gave to me ma one Christmas, the tiny fine-boned black and white face sat on top of a ruffle o monochrome frills and a black tear on her cheek that must o been hand-painted by some Bavarian sprite it's that small. Tiny foreign weepin clown that's sat on the mantelpiece for years and years unnumbered and someone slips their hand into mine and I turn and it's the Adidas girl her hair and skin and eyes so dark so fuckin fantastic. Her teeth white and her lips turned back in a slight and gorgeous smile and she winks at me and I wink back and then we dance, her like the girls on Ibiza Uncovered with her arms thrown over her head and me like a court jester all floppin limbs and shufflin feet but sure who cares? Thudthudthud o the stereo and shadows hoppin and flailin on the walls, Rochey stiff and angry-lookin in the corner but fuck him as well, Ned ruined drunk stood on the armchair reelin off old Irish poetry his eyes half-closed and hand on heart and the Adidas girl's face so close to mine, the tiny lines at her eyes and her lips shapin strange underwater words I can't hear, can't fathom at this immeasurable blissful depth and we dance and dance with each tune bleedin into the next, ages and ages we're here, hours, time tickin slow-motion and backwards, her warm breath on me ear and the lacquered crispness of her hair against me neck and she drags me through the faces and into the kitchen past Paula and Teresa kissin by the table and the army o empty cans on the window ledge and the throng of arms and feet and voices and laughter and drunk faces and thudthudthud in the hall and up the stairs stumblin and laughin, her hand on her mouth and onto the landin and her embrace, the two of us rollin together along the banisters, towels fallin on revellers below and her warm body against me, her back to the wall now and the zipper of her tracksuit top a tiny stiff pinprick against me bony chest as her hand twists the door handle and pushes it open and we half-fall into the blackened room thudthudthud through the floorboards and I pat the wall for the light switch, I dunno why but I do, there could be monsters I used to think, slaverin long-toothed freaks under the bed. Me palm hits the switch and the bedroom is summoned up in front o me and me skin crawls cos fuckin hell monsters do exist, a clan o thin and slowly peddlin wraiths with white eyes on the bed and on the floor, Slaughter lyin beside one o them, a girl, his hand down the front of her jeans. There's a small spike protrudin from her arm, a belt lashed round her thin bicep and she's completely out of it. Slaughter looks up at me, eyes amphibious and a grin on his face.

—Get the fuck out o here yiz pricks! I scream at him. —Get fuckin out!

Slaughter laughs, the sound all warped and gloopy as he pulls his hand free and it's black with blood. One o the wraiths stirs, his chin wet with drool I can see it glisten and his milky eyes flicker and I pick up someone's battered runner and hurl it at Slaughter and it thuds against the wardrobe by his head. The Adidas girl's arm is on me shoulder and her bubbly underwater words around me ears but I just turn and crash down the stairs wall to banister and through the floatin faces and into the front room.

—What's up with yeh? Calm the fuck down.

Rochey's wide and acned face in front o mine.

—He's in me ma's room the mad fuckin prick.

—Calm down for fuck sake.

—Fuck off.

—Wha?

—I said fuck off –

And a fantastic white flash explodes inside me eyes and I stumble back with a searin pain in me temple. Rochey comes at me again and his fist whacks into me stomach and I bend over heavin for air and people are screamin and shoutin over the thudthudthud and a big meaty thump on the spine sends me to me knees and I stick me palms flat in front o me on the beer-soaked floor like a fuckin dog. I feel like shit I feel like death I feel like there's a fuckin tumor in me head, a fuckin scorpion scuttlin on me brain. I tuck me chin towards me chest and wait for the next smack and there's a huge crash and I look up and Rochey's fallin back against the mantelpiece and Maggit grabs his pink T-shirt by the scruff and pulls him up and hits him full in the face with his head and a forest of arms curls round him and pulls him away and into the kitchen and I crawl forwards hands and knees and me ma's sad clown is smashed on the floor into half a hundred tiny useless splintered bits.

★

Jesus, it's fuckin freezin. Me arms and face all scratched from the thorns. I stomp down the nettles. Take that yiz cunts. Want me fuckin bike, man, wanna be fuckin out o here. Trust me to make a fuckin holy show o meself. And that horrible fuckin image, man; Slaughter in me ma's room with that girl. Jesus.

—Denny, just get back inside, will yeh?

Maggit's hand on me shoulder. I turn round and look at him, his dark eyes and gaunt face. Three big splots o blood on his grey fleece. Over his shoulder I can see a girl lookin out the kitchen window, with long, straight black hair, her arms folded. She looks like a nymph. I don't remember seein her inside. She can't be older than sixteen. I shake me head and scrabble at the lock on the shed, the paint peelin and the wood rotted to fuck.

Maggit spits. —Wha are yeh lookin for?

—Me bike.

—Bit fuckin early in the mornin, isn't it?

—Fuck it.

—Wha about the witch?

—Who?

—In the shed.

—Fuck her as well.

—Say she'd fuckin love that. And you as well yeh dirty prick.

I pull open the door to a deeper dark. Musty fuckin tomb. I stumble in and fall on me knees.

—Bollix.

Maggit takes me under the arms and hauls me up. I scramble round the shed. Old damp cloth, sharp corners and rust. Whack the back o me hand against somethin. Grab it. Handlebars and brakes. I pull the bike away from the wall. Lift up a rug and drop it on the table. Where I think the table is. A soft collapse. Drag the bike out the door. Maggit's standin there, lookin at me. Behind him the nymph's eyes flash in the dark. He lifts a Corona bottle to his lips and takes a swig, holds it out to me. I shake me head and he shrugs.

—How d'yeh know about the witch? I say.

—I saw her at the window. Big gammy eye on her.

—Wha?

—Yeh told me about her yeh sap. Have yeh any idea how much yeh fuckin shitetalk, Denny? Specially when yer fuckin drunk.

—I have to get out o here.

—Yer drunk. Fuckin pissed. Go to bed. She wasn't laughin at yeh if that's wha yer worried about, that girl.

I shake me head.

—Fair enough. Don't say I didn't warn yeh. Watch yeh don't get a smack of a fuckin bus or anythin yeh big sap.

I wave Maggit away and there's a big ball o sadness hot in me throat. Jesus. I feel like cryin cos fuckin hell, nothin, ever, changes. I haul the bike up the path, bashin the stingers aside. Which way's which? Fuckin hell I can't even see straight. Pedals snagged in the weeds. I reef the bike up and out and stumble forward and there it is, the back wall. I pull up the latch and push open the gate. Sodium-lit alley. Bins and all manner o bollix. Stinkin fuckin refuse and a skinny white cat shootin off between heaped cardboard boxes. I hop on the bike and weave through the alley.

★

Been here hours, sittin on me bench by the canal with the buckled mountain bike beside me, shivered and half-slept then woke and watched the bleary sun creep over the trees, me addled brain slowly movin backwards through stages o stoned drunkenness and back to head-thumpin sobriety. There's a massive, cold puke-patch a few feet down from me and I can still smell it. There's a little bird peckin at it. Me arm's a bit sore and the ribs on me left-hand side are throbbin dully. Head's in bits as well. Fuckin sucker punched again. I didn't feel cold durin the night but I do now. The kind o cold I imagine old people feel in their draughty lonely flats, a cold that gets into yer marrow and hurts. Not that I'm complainin. Well, I am complainin a bit I suppose. I love it here by the oul canal though. Always have. I can see the top o the factories over the trees, a red slanted corrugated roof with a platoon o crows standin there in line, tiny black shapes nuzzlin themselves against the mornin sky.

The canal's a lot less deep than yid think, actually. Lookit. A few feet only. The mossed and wavy skeleton of a bike and a fat brown fish dartin from a clump o weeds, everythin lookin flat and wide below the surface. It doesn't really seem to be movin, either. Near still, flat and scummed and trollied. There's a pallet floatin near the bank with an old paint bucket and a crumpled lager can and a one-legged plastic doll onboard, strange passengers on a half-sunk boat, off on their travels. I remember seein a dragonfly around here, last year. Fuckin hell, have yeh ever seen a dragonfly up close? They're huge. Fuckin bird-sized, nearly. Big bulbous faces and giant flashin wings. Legs long and thin trailin behind them. They seem more like animals than insects to me. I know that's a bit mad, but . . . I dunno. I kinda have it in me head that there's a hierarchy o things, like with the rabbits and badgers. I'm not sayin that people are miles above animals, like . . . or that humans aren't animals, it's . . . fuck, dunno. Insects are definitely lower down than birds, anyway. But not dragonflies. Too fuckin big, dragonflies. I know that's linkin size to worthiness and I don't really mean it like that but dragonflies are definitely way further up the ladder than, say, normal flies. Or them ugly little shell-backed scuttlers yeh see under rocks and bits o wood. Nickelbacks, I call them. Like tiny fuckin fossils, or somethin. Shrunk trilobites. Ick. Hate them yokes. Gimme the bleedin willies.

There's a fella about fifty or so feet upstream o me, standin on the little rickety pier. Been here a while. He's probably a hobo or a junkie or somethin. Or both most likely, and definitely a bit doolally into the bargain. He's wearin billowy grey tracksuit bottoms and a multicoloured jacket. A woolly monkey hat. Patchy grey beard although he doesn't look that old. He's mutterin to himself and breakin up bits o bread from a loaf under his arm and tossin them into the water. Big chunky bits. Thing is, there aren't any ducks or swans or anythin around. Nothin. He's just throwin in the breadchunks and they're hittin the canal with a slap and floatin slowly past me and on and up to . . . wherever. Some homeless supplicant makin his offerins to the green gods o the canal, maybe. Prayin for better weather or a good harvest. Or a decent place on the housin lists.

Love it here, have to say. I mean, yeah it's cold and me head's in a jock and me teeth are rattlin like a set o them Halloween chompers but fuck it, there's no Paula losin the plot, no Shane threatenin eviction. No job centre, no filthy house. No chairs that me ma used to sit on, no programmes on the telly that me ma used to watch. Nothin. Feels like yer miles away from the world, even though there's a fuckin highway only twenty-odd feet behind me and a load o poxy factories on the opposite side. Fuck it, though: the canal's penned in by trees and bushes for miles and miles, a thin strip of oldtimes in the middle of a newer, shinier, noisier Dublin. Secluded from all that, yeh know? It might as well be the seventies or wharrever, back when this was all still fields and wildness. Me da used to tell Gino and Shane about how him and his mates had to walk through miles o ditches and empty field to get to the Lough and Quay for a few pints. And back again drunk by moonlight. Back when Clondalkin village was just the old round tower and a few houses and shops. And the canal, o course.

The pathway is all pebbled and uneven with a stripe o grass in the middle and the waterway's never more than a few yards from yeh. No wall or anythin. So easy to fall in.

Loads have over the years. Which is the dark side o this place, I suppose. I mean, the water's not deep here but it is further up, past the lock. Twenty feet deep there. All that still black water. Loads have died there over the years. Fell in drunk or wharrever, which could o happened to me last night, easy. There was a crowd drove a car in about ten years ago and every one o them drowned. Trapped in that horrible freezin blackness as the car filled up. Addicts, they were. Out o their faces on drink and pills and who fuckin knows wha. And then that fella, only a while ago. African fella. Cut up in a bin bag and dumped in the canal. Fuckin hell such fear he must o felt. His head was cut off and everythin and they never found it for ages. In the end this girl, an Irish girl and her ma, admitted to it. They took his head in a schoolbag and brung it to a park and smashed it up with a hammer. Can yeh believe that? Jesus. That such fuckin badness can exist.

Wha a night. God, Slaughter with his hand down that girl's fuckin jeans. And in me ma's room and everythin. Mental fuckin bastard, that Slaughter fella. Epileptic bats and gibberin shadows. How fuckin low and sad and manky this world is.

Always a fuckin dark side, yeh know?

Even to the oul canal.

Bodies. Tears and shite and blood and spunk. Wha do yeh do though? Sit upstream of it all, I suppose. On yer oul half-burnt bench with yer hands in yer pockets and yer chin tucked into yer chest to keep out the cold. Watch the fish and the sad willows.

Wha else can yeh do?

There's always fuckin badness, man. Always.

THE MAN COMES AROUND

Took me two days o shiverin and pukin and starin at the telly to get over that fuckin party. Watched a load o old wrestlin videos; the nineties was the best for wrestlin. Paula's worse than me; she's barely set foot out of her room. She just appears at the top o the stairs sometimes and shouts down to me for a cup o tea. I had a shower this mornin, shaved and that, and ran the car down to the shops. Don't think I'll be botherin with pills for a while.

I pull the last bag o shoppin out o the boot and slam down the door and that's when I notice the two gyppos in the glass behind me. Two gypsies on a horse and cart, one old and one young, the cart's wheels cuttin through the grey, slushy remains o the snow. The older gypsy's broad and redhaired and the younger one's lean and grinnin, me own age or younger and he's wearin a titanic pair o workmen's boots with the leather tongues flopped out like a couple o Beagle's ears. They stop the cart a few feet from the car. The young one winks at me.

—You Denny Cullen?

I look round, the estate emptied by the cold, then back at the gypsies. —Yeah, I say.

There's a huge grin on the younger fella's face. He rubs his palms on his jeans and sniffs. —I know yer brother Gino well, he says. —He's great pals with me brother Paddy.

—Gino doesn't –

—I know. He's up in Ballyer now. I don't want Gino.

I set the shoppin bags down at me ankles and place me hands flat behind me on the bonnet o the car. —Can I do somethin for yiz?

—I dunno, Denny. Maybe yeh can. Yer mates with that Gillespie fella aren't yeh?

—Maggit?

—That's the one. The young guy looks at the older one, winks a huge wink. The older gypsy gives a little half smile and nods his head. —Him with the big ears and supposed to be on the IRA security council. Gerry Adams's right-hand man I believe.

—Well, he's not, but he probably did say that. He's –

—Where would he be now, Denny?

I shrug. —Dunno, man. Haven't seen him for a few days.

Haven't seen him since the party, actually. All of a sudden I remember the girl, the girl in the Adidas tracksuit. Don't really wanna remember her, though, cos it gives me this stupid sense o loss, even though I don't know her and never will. It was nice, though – just that closeness. And then the thought hits me – yer on yer own, Denny, and yeh always will be. No surer thing. The certainty of it nearly knocks me off me feet.

—Yeh sure now, Denny? says the gypsy. —Not seen him at all?

—Yeah. I . . . look, I dunno what's goin on but I haven't seen Maggit in a while and I don't know when I'm likely to. Is there some trouble or somethin?

The older fella picks his nose. His nostrils are huge, cavernous. The younger one scratches his stubbled cheek.

—Well, Denny, yeh could say that alright. Y'see, this oul Maggit fella done somethin on me cousin.

—Right.

—Right indeed. Now bein the fella I am Denny, I can't sit round and scratch me arse all day knowin this. Yeh get me?

—Em. Sorta. Wha did he do?

—Well. I'd rather not get into the details, Denny. All I'll say to yeh is that Niamh is just turned sixteen year old this week. Now. I can do one o two things. I can either bate the absolute bollix out o this Maggit chap. Yeah? And I do mean the absolute bollix Denny when I say that. Or I could take somethin off him instead.

—OK.

—Y'see, Denny, I'm not a violent man.

The older fella gives his little smile again.

—Well fair enough, I'll throw a few digs when I need to but I'd rather do a bit o business, that's the best way, I'd say. That's more civilised. And Niamh, poor confused girl that she is, well, she likes this Maggit gobshite. Sure who could resist a freedom fighter like himself? Great mate o Bobby Sands that he was. God she'd be terrible upset to hear he'd had the face kicked off his head.

—Look, man, wha are yeh tellin me all this for? This is fuck all to do with me. I don't know wha the hell Maggit gets up to. He's a waffler. That's his own thing.

—Don't worry, Denny. Sure I know it's nothin to do with you. Thing is. I'm not lettin this go. It'd be as easy to bate this Maggit chap but I won't. For one thing I don't think he'll be around for a while, cowardly little sleeveen that he is. So I'll tell yeh what I can do for yiz. Y'see, I'll –

—This is nothin to do with me, though.

—Look, Denny. Here's what's happenin, yeah? I'm havin that car offa yiz. Yeah? Now, I know yer mate Maggit owns a share in it so ye two can work out the money he owes yeh.

—Ah here. There's –

—Denny. I'm not a robber. I won't take that car off yeh. You'll bring it up for me, as a peace offerin. Yeah? Just drop it by the haltin site on the Fonthill Road. Then we'll be quits.

I just stand there, lookin up at him. Me feet and hands are freezin.

—I don't believe this, I say.

—Isn't it a tragedy?

The older fella laughs.

—My name's Franno, by the way. Francis Ward. Been nice to meet yeh Denny. And here, I have somethin for yeh. Franno swivels and reaches behind him, pulls at somethin. The older guy farts; it sounds like a wet rumbling. Franno rummages away then turns back round and he's holdin a little black pup by the scruff, its back legs pumpin slow and useless. A weak yap-yap-yap.

—That's a little present from Niamh for our good comrade Maggit, says Franno.

I reach up and take the pup, wha the fuck for I don't know, and pull him in to me chest, all squirmin bones and squashy warmth.

—I'll see yeh soon so, Denny, says Franno, still grinnin his huge grin.

—Gyup! says the giant redhead and he flicks the reins and the horse stomps its front hoofs and flares its nostrils and tosses its head and starts off through the snow.

★

I set the dog down on the floor and he looks up at me for a second and yaps and sniffs the greasy skirtin board. I open the press beside the cooker and dump the old Cornflake box in the bin and replace it with the new Cheerios. Then I rummage in the bread bin and stick a couple slices o Brennan's under the grill and flick on the kettle and sit down at the kitchen table. The little pup's yappin away, big hazel-coloured eyes and a little white tip on his tail. Victor's shabby copy o *Huckleberry Finn* is lyin on the table beside the pepperpot and I open it and look at the same paragraph for a few minutes but I can't concentrate so I get up and look in the front room. The place is in bits. Battered beer cans and curry trays, overflowin ashtrays. Some fat bloke asleep on the sofa under a sheet, two big feet stickin out, one stuffed into a red sock and the other free and hairy. I close the door and pull the tray from under the grill and the toast's half burnt. The pup's standin in a little yellow pool. I grab him and head upstairs and knock on Paula's bedroom door.

—Paula?

No answer. I knock again. —Paula.

I twist the handle and push open the door. Poke me head in. The curtains are pulled and the room is sweaty and messy and dark. A shape shifts under the duvet.

—Paula.

—Wha?

Paula's voice is dry and husky. The bang o sweat and cigarette smoke in here'd knock yeh fuckin out. Empty cans everywhere.

—Who's the manatee downstairs?

—Whose humanity?

—Listen. The manatee. Who's that on the sofa downstairs?

—Is he fat?

—Yeah.

—Frankie.

—What's he doin? I wanna watch the telly.

—Tell him to go home. I don't even like him. Big fat head on him.

—You tell him to go home. I'm fuckin sick o this.

—Just turn on the telly. Don't mind him.

Paula shrugs the duvet up over her head and turns away from me. A thin strip o light from the gap in the curtain's cuttin through the murk. It's Sunday so Teresa's in the bed as well; there's a bit o her hair stickin out from under the duvet.

—Have you heard anythin from Maggit recently? I say.

—No.

—Have we any dogfood?

—No. Dogfood? No.

—They're takin me car on me.

—The gardaí? I'm not fuckin surprised, Denny. Yiv no insurance.

—It's gypsies. Cos o Maggit.

I hold up the pup, like he proves somethin. Like he's evidence o the gravity o what's happenin.

—Lookit, I say.

Paula's wildhaired and bleary-eyed head pops out from under the duvet.

—What's that?

—A dog for fuck sake. Lookit. A puppy. A gyppo told me to give it to Maggit. Is that some kind o mafia thing, would yeh say?

Paula yawns with one eye open. —He's lovely.

166

—I'm not askin yeh if . . . yeah, well. Pajo can look after him. I'm callin round to him now and yer mate better be off the sofa when I get back. Ninja Warrior's on soon.

★

I stick the puppy in under me jacket and hurry out to the car and then hurry back cos I forgot to turn off the grill and then back out again. In and out like a blue-arsed fly, me ma used to say. I hop in the car and cut through the estates to St Marks and pull up outside the house. I leave the puppy yappin on the backseat and haul the bag o Pajo's chickenfeed out o the boot. Weighs a fuckin ton, tellin yeh. I hoist it up into me arms like a fireman carryin some unconscious child (conked out by smoke inhalation, I assume) and take two steps before feelin a shootin pain in me back. The chickenfeed slips out o me arms and hits the ground with a dull whump.

I pull the cigarettes out o me jeans and light one up and stand there like a hunchback at the garden gate, smokin in the lingerin snow and rubbin me spine. Definitely somethin wrong with it. I take a huge drag and flick away me cigarette and hobble to the door and knock.

No answer.

I look at me watch and it's half eleven. A young woman with a red scarf scurries from her garden and across the green, her hands in her pockets and her head down, like somethin from a Christmas card.

I knock again, then stand back and grab a little loose chunk o concrete and lob it carefully at the front bedroom window, a little shootin pain hoppin up me spine. The concrete clumps against the glass and I catch it on the

167

way down and lob it back up. There's a shuffle behind the curtains. I knock again and I can hear footsteps on the stairs and then there's a blurry shape shamblin towards me. The shape fumbles at the door. It's Pajo. His hair's plastered to one side of his head and his eyes are sunk and red. He's topless and scrawny and wearin a pair o Glasgow Rangers shorts. He smiles and yawns and scratches his shoulder.

—Mornin, he says.

—Heya. What's with the shorts?

Pajo shrugs. —Just shorts, Denny.

—Rangers, though?

—Lettin me skin breathe.

—Lettin yer skin breathe?

—Yeah. I saw it, like. On some telly thing. Like, some lifestyle thing or somethin. American I think, on MTV.

—Is Maggit in?

Pajo blinks and rubs his eyes. —No. He's, like, down the country I think. Wanna come in out o the snow?

I point back up at the gate. —Drag that in for us, it's for the chickens. And I have a present for yeh in the car.

Pajo looks at the feed. —Deadly. I only had Monster Munch for them yesterday, Shawn nearly choked.

—I'll stick the kettle on, I say, and squeeze past him and into the hall. Pajo's huggin himself in the doorway, grinnin. He looks dead happy and excited. Easily pleased, Pajo. I hand him the car keys.

—And I have a story and a fuckin half for yeh as well, I say. —Yer not gonna believe it.

★

Maggit and Pajo get their house for free, practically, cos neither o them are workin and Pajo's on some kind o disability thing cos o the methadone programme he's on. They've lived here for a few years now. It's hard to imagine Pajo and Maggit separately, even with all their differences. Their house is actually fairly well kept, which is kind of embarrassin when I think o mine and Paula's. There's a photo o Pajo and Maggit as young kids, their da behind them, on the mantelpiece, back when they were just Patrick and Colm, standin in front o the school. Even then, though, Pajo's smilin and Maggit's scowlin.

Pajo's sittin on the sofa with the puppy on his lap and the day's first joint between his teeth, grinnin away like a big kid. The puppy's sittin still and starin at him, its head tilted, sussin out the skinny greenhaired giant above him. I told him about the gypsies and Maggit and the car but I probably should o waited to give him the puppy till after cos that's all he seems to care about.

—He's deadly, isn't he? he says. —Lookit him, Denny.

—I see him, yeah. He's cool. D'yeh want him so?

—Course I do. Yeah.

I flick through the stations and sip at me tea. It's scaldin, like: not enough milk in it. I leave on Takeshi's Castle cos Ninja Warrior's on after it. I wasn't really into Ninja Warrior when I first seen it but it's grown on me. Not that I'm particularly in the mood for watchin telly now, though; since I actually related the tale to Pajo I'm becomin more and more aware that a gypsy is just after tellin me to hand over me car to him.

—What'll we do, Pajo?

Pajo looks up at me and scratches his wispy beard. Sucks his teeth and says nothin.

—No ideas at all? I say.

—Not really sure, Denny. Em. Yeh should probably, like . . . well . . . should yeh not just give them the car? Yeh can get another one.

—Sure I haven't even given Gino the full whack yet. He'll still want the rest of it so I'll be payin for fresh fuckin air, like. Don't fuckin think so.

—Yeh don't wanna cause trouble, Denny. Yeh –

—I didn't cause any trouble though, did I? Why should I have to give it away, it's stupid.

—Yeah, I know. Pajo strokes the puppy absentmindedly and the puppy chews on his finger. He pushes his flop o hair back over his head. —Wha can yeh do though, Denny? Gypsies, man. That's hardcore. They're, like, a mystical race.

—Mystical Pajo? Gerra grip, will yeh?

—Well. I wouldn't mess with them, anyway. That's bigstyle, Denny. That's . . . like, significantly over our heads.

—I rang Maggit a few times this mornin and all I got was the message box. Will you ring him?

—He won't answer me Denny, yeh know he won't. He'll suss that yer after puttin me up to it.

I sink back into the chair. —This is a joke.

—Chill, Denny. Cool yer boots, man. Don't get stressed.

I sip at me tea again and look at Pajo and the puppy, Pajo small-lookin amongst the big threadbare cushions, the puppy curled up on his lap.

—I know, Pajo. I know it's not the end o the fuckin world or anythin. But I'd be lost without the car now, yeh know? It's cool havin the bit o freedom.

Pajo smiles at me. —It'll be alright, Denny. We'll sort somethin. Then he leans in and winks at the puppy. —I'm gonna call yeh Ignatius, after Doctor Keen, he says, and then squeals as the puppy hops up and bites him on the tip o the nose.

THE GIFT OF FAR SIGHT

I turn into a sheltered patch o gravel at the side o the road and stop the car. Mental fuckin weather today, the trees and bushes at the roadside tossin like mad. It'll be near gale force later on, yer woman on RTE said. I hit the stop button on the tapedeck and Cohen's voice warps and dies mid-sentence. I've had to make a load o mix tapes cos there's no CD player in the car. Dunno why I put Leonard Cohen on this one. The sky is huge above the trees, heavy with fat, throbbin clouds. No rain forecast, although there could be more snow apparently. I grab me beanie and stick it on and slip the whiskey bottle into me pocket and hook me fingers round the strap o me Adidas bag, all bulgy and weighed down with books and teabags and I open the door and duck out o the car. I zip me jacket chin-high and a small white car zooms past, the head of a pudgy baldy bloke barely pokin above the wheel. The car glides round the bend I just turned off and back towards Dublin. I stick me hands in me pockets and head on up the road, me jeans snappin in the wind. There's a rustle in the bushes beside me and a squawk somewhere within the tangle o branch and twig, some tiny secret act o violence I suppose. Somethin dyin to feed somethin else's kids. There's a gate somewhere along here. Can't be too sure with these oul bockedy country back roads. Not that Balbriggan's really in the countryside. Well, not anymore, anyway. It was always in Dublin but now Dublin city's seepin out and suckin all the little villages and fields and hills and back roads into its giant smoky gob. Progress, yeh know? The Celtic Tiger and wha have yeh. Tell yeh wha though, that Celtic fuckin Tiger's the one endangered animal I'd happily put a bullet into. Prosperity me bollix. For Bertie Ahern and his mates, maybe.

The clouds are huge and purple-black. It's only five but it's gettin dark already. A crow squawks and darts overhead and I kick the gravel, pebbles scatterin and clatterin in front o me. Thick smell o country grass and all manner o stale dry animal shite. A gust o icy wind sets me teeth knockin and through a gap in the bushes I can see a wide lumpy field with a cow standin in the middle, its fat arse and swishy tail. It raises its big heavy head towards me but I'm gone already. Where's this gate? Been that long since I've been here, yeh know? I'm probably miles off. Bleedin freezin, as well. Should o worn me combat jacket, not this flimsy little yoke. Dunno wha the fuck I was thinkin. I stop and then step out into the road and look back at the car, small and sheltered in the distance.

Still haven't heard from Maggit. The gyppos haven't been back either though, thank fuck. Yer man Franno was probably just tryin to shit me up. Hope so, anyway.

Have to say, it's great havin the wheels. I mean, yeah, it's an oul banger, barely fuckin roadworthy, but it's nice to be able to hop in and just, like, drive. Get out o the house, yeh know? Been drivin all over Dublin. Have to keep an eye out for the garda, though, cos o the tax and insurance. I was in Skerries yesterday, me and Ned and Sinead. Hadn't been there since I was a kid. Bit cold, like, but it was good.

Saw a seal as well. I think it was a seal, anyway. Ned said it was a dead scuba diver for a laugh and Sinead gave him a look.

Fuck this. I'm goin another five hundred yards and that's that. Don't wanna leave the car too far off, like. Can't have me little jaunt turnin all American Werewolf in Dublin.

Yes. There it is thank fuck. The little bandy wooden gate set back into the wall o bushes. The lock chatterin in the wind, a big black puddle underneath and beyond a wide uneven field o muck and horseshite and crabgrass and set right at the opposite end, smudgy and far off, me uncle Victor's caravan. There's a faint yellow light in the window, a beacon to vagabonds and cold, wanderin nephews. I shoulder the Adidas bag and blow into me hands and rub them together and stick me left one on the top rung o the gate and vault over in one quick and grunty motion.

★

I was about ten and me ma and uncle were sittin outside me uncle's caravan, laughin. I was inside and I remember this gorgeous sunlight streamin in from the windows. That gorgeous sunlight and a cracked yellow mug and a bowl and spoon and oil spittin from the pan on me uncle's stove.

Me ma and uncle talkin:

—I'll tell yeh Kate it was dodgy for a while there but sure I sorted it in the end, no trouble at all.

—And is that it now, Victor? Finished?

A hint of amusement beneath the worry in me ma's voice.

—Ah o course, says Victor. —Finito. They were lucky I didn't lose me temper.

—Blessed, I'd say.

I poked at the sizzlin fishfingers with a fork, teeterin on a low stool. There was a plate to me right and a horsefly was bangin against the window. I had to keep me eye on the horsefly – they were worse than moths for brainlessness.

—. . . you'll be the one to lose out, Victor. Just be careful.

—Me? Sure I'm as careful as they come, Kate.

I forked one o the golden, drippin fishfingers and plonked it on the plate.

—. . . will he be OK in there?

—Ah o course, Kate. Sure it's only fishfingers. A culinary genius like himself.

I cut the fishfinger in half with the fork. The meat was flaky and white. Steam risin. I thought I was deadly; the big man, makin the dinner. I skewered another one and placed it dead carefully beside the first.

—. . . a fierce-lookin fella altogether. Huge hands, he had. Yid wanna see these hands, Kate. Enormous they were, like a troll's . . .

Then it was all fucked. I went for the last fishfinger and a little spot of oil hopped out o the pan and landed on the back o me hand. I hissed and put it to me mouth, suckin the scalded skin. It was burnin the fuck out o me, me eyes welled up and I lost me balance. The stool tipped beneath me and I went flyin, the caravan spinnin upside down and me head crackin against the edge o the little fold-out table.

I was knocked out for a few minutes. Away with the fairies. I had this mad dream, faces and voices and all sorts. I felt like I knew everythin all at once. That was the sensation I had, like I was filled with knowledge. I knew it all, everyone's stories, everyone's lives; how things'd work out, where language came from, what was at the heart o things. It was mad. When I woke up me ma was holdin me in her arms. Her eyes were blue and young and dead relieved. Me uncle Victor was watchin me from the corner. His eyes were hidden behind the glare in his glasses and there was an empty, greasy plate on his lap.

I told them about the dream and Victor sat up in his chair, settin the plate aside.

—Jaysis, he said. —D'yeh know wha, Kate? That's the Salmon o Knowledge all over again. He shook his head and took off his glasses and went on to tell us the old myth; told us how Finnegas the poet had sat by the River Shannon for years and years, hopin to catch and eat the Salmon o Knowledge, the flesh o which was supposed to grant the eater this deep insight and wisdom. And how in the end young Fionn mac Cumhaill bollixed it all up on him; how, one day, Finnegas had to go off somewhere and so handed over the rod to Fionn, tellin him that if the Salmon bit while the old man was away, Fionn was to cook the fish but not to taste it. *Definitely* not to taste it. So Fionn says fair enough and sits by the river and sure enough he catches the Salmon while Finnegas is away. Fionn sets up a spit and cooks the fish and it's all goin grand until Fionn notices this blister bubblin up on the fish. Can't have that, he thinks, and pokes it with his thumb to burst it, which o course scalds the thumb off him and what does he do but stick his thumb in his mouth and suck it and hey presto – he's tasted the fish and he gains all the knowledge and poor oul Finnegas gets fuck all.

176

Me uncle Victor took off his glasses and looked at me.

—The little bastard's after robbin me lore, he said, grinnin and shakin his head. —The Fishfinger o Knowledge!

★

I knock on the flimsy tinplated door and take a step back. I can hear shufflin and bangin inside. After a couple o seconds it goes quiet.

—Who is it?

—Denny.

There's more commotion and then the door flaps open, clangin against the side o the caravan. Me uncle Victor's standin there, tall and skinny in a raggedy housecoat. He squints through his sellotaped glasses and his thinnin black bootpolish hair dances in the wind. The big Village People moustache twitches and a yellowtoothed smile cracks his face.

—Ah Denny me best oul skin, I haven't seen yeh in fuggin donkeys. Come in out o the cold and I'll stick a suppa tay on for yeh. The bollix must be fuggin froze off yeh. Lookit the face on yeh yer blue as the dead.

—I'm grand, Victor. It's not that bad.

Victor sets a slippered foot down onto his warped rubber welcome mat and grabs me by the shoulder and ushers me in.

—Ah no, Denny. That's no weather to be out in. That'd freeze the shite in an Eskimo's arse for Jaysis sake. Get in and I'll stick on a hot suppa tay.

I squeeze past Victor and into the caravan and he slams the door shut and fires the bolt. I slump me bag onto the floor and pull the whiskey bottle out o me pocket.

—Here, I say.

Victor takes off his glasses and I hand him the whiskey. He peers at the label and shakes the bottle and grins. —Ah be Jaysis Denny yer the only man. Yer a grand youngfella Denny let no one tell yeh different. He tightens the cord round his housecoat and stumbles into the dark kitchen area. —I'll get the glasses, he half says, half sings. —Yill have a drop yerself won't yeh?

—Yeah, cool.

—Ah o course yill have a drop with yer oul uncle yid never refuse me.

I'm standin in wha I suppose yid call Victor's front room, if this was a house and his whole caravan wasn't his front room. This end, though, is a small rectangle, lined with built-in sofas and with two long windows on either side and a smaller, round one at the end. Loads o little ornaments and ancient-lookin knickknacks on the windowledges and books in huge leanin piles everywhere. Hundreds o books. I pick up a battered copy of Ondaatje's *Coming Through Slaughter,* a book I loaned Victor a year or two ago, before I went to Wales, and set it on the windowledge beside a brass workhorse and plonk meself down. I have to hunch over to warm me hands at the little glowin gas heater beside the coffee table. Dunno how a stringbean like Victor manages in a place this small.

Victor shuffles back into the light and hands me the glass o whiskey. The thing's near full, glintin and syrup-coloured. Victor takes a sip and sighs and slumps down onto the sofa opposite me, his long legs stretched out.

—Ah that's the very stuff.

I take a little sip meself and it rushes to me head and back down to me belly. I take off me beanie and ruffle me hair and Victor has another sip and then leans forward, his face suddenly serious.

—There's no trouble at all Denny is there? Is there anyone after yeh yid tell me now wouldn't yeh cos they'd rue the day, Denny. Oh Jaysis they'd rue the fuggin day.

I can't help laughin. Victor's wired to the moon. All the stories and the manic mood swings and bouts o bluster. Chap wouldn't harm a fly, though.

—Nah, I'm grand Victor, I say. —Not a bother. I got meself a car, like. I drove up.

—Ah I see, I see. A motor. Very good. Gets yeh where yeh want to go.

—Just about, anyway.

—Beats the bollix out o walkin in this weather all the same, Denny. A fuggin yeti would shun an evenin like this.

I grab me bag and rummage through it. —I got yeh Lyons teabags, I say.

—Ah. A saint.

—And a few books.

—And a scholar as well Denny yeh always were. Did yeh know the library turned me away last week? The bleedin cheek o them I was tha near deckin yer man behind the desk, glasses or no.

—Why?

—Robbin books, he says to me. I says to him are yeh callin me a robber yid better have bleedin proof, buddy. Every book I ever got out o here was stamped officially one hundred per cent.

—Wha did he say?

—He showed me the computer thing and said here, lookit Mr Cullen, some o them books are out near

179

four year, they might as well be robbed as far as we're concerned.

—So yeh decked him, then?

—I did consider it. But violence Denny, it should always be a last resort. I suppose he has a point, anyway. Could be other people wanted them books as well.

I laugh again and take a sip o me whiskey. The wind's howlin outside and the leafless trees are bent and tossin madly. Yeh can hear a hundred tiny creaks at once in the caravan, and feel a hundred tiny tremors. Like bein at sea, almost.

—Yeh gettin on OK yerself, Victor?

—Ah God yeah, Denny. Yeh know me. Not a bother. Love me peace and quietude. Although I must say now it's very good to see yeh Denny, sure it must be five or six year since I saw yeh last.

—I saw yeh at the funeral, Victor.

Victor sinks back slowly and places his whiskey on the coffee table.

—Ah that's right, Denny. Sure didn't I see yeh at yer mother's funeral.

I look out the window and then back at Victor and gulp back the last o the whiskey. Victor's lookin at his glass, runnin his long forefinger round the rim.

—That was a terrible pity, Denny, he says, his head downcast slightly but his eyes still on me. —That was a terrible thing altogether there's no fairness in the world. Sure yer mother was a young woman only when yeh lookit the ages people live today. God that was a terrible shock, I do still think about her. Let me tell yeh son, fambly is very important. Yeh might not know it now but it is, sure yiv not much else in the world if yiv no fambly. Yid think

180

it was only last week yer granny and granda brung yer ma home from St James's. I was eleven year old, I never seen a thing so small.

Victor looks up at me. —Are yeh copin OK yerself, Denny? Loss is a fearful thing.

—Not too bad. I go down the grave sometimes and that.

—D'yeh know I haven't been to the grave since the funeral? Isn't that a mortal sin? I can't bring meself to go, isn't that just a mortal sin against me soul?

I shake me head. —Paula's only been up the once.

—Has she?

—Yeah. It's after hittin her worse than she lets on, I think. She won't talk about it or anythin.

—It's a terrible thing to lose yer mother, Denny. Specially so young.

—I know. She was sayin there's someone in the house and all this.

—Who?

—Paula.

—No, who's in the house?

—I dunno. A ghost or somethin. Not me ma's ghost. She was sayin there was somethin under the beds.

—Well, the best thing to do now Denny is get a bit o holy water and sprinkle it and say to it begone from the house in the name o –

—She's neurotic, Victor. There's nothin in the house. She's out of her head half the time with drink. We had a séance, anyway. Pajo did. D'yeh know Pajo?

—Which one's he?

—The little skinny fella. Green hair. Yeh saw him at the funeral.

—I remember, yeah. Mad fella?

—Yeah.

—And he did a séance?

—Yeah. Don't really believe in that kind o thing.

Victor purses his lips and knits his eyebrows. —Well who's to say, Denny?

—I'm not the one forcin wha I believe on people, Victor.

—Well. Wha happened at the séance, then?

—Well . . . nothin at first, like, then Pajo was sayin this stuff, like he was possessed. The lights were out.

—And yeh don't believe it?

—I dunno. No, I don't think so.

—Wha did he say?

—Pajo?

—Yeah, or the ghost.

—Well, the way I remember it . . . it's a bit sketchy, like. It wasn't the ghost from under Paula's bed that was talkin, it was some other ghost that said it moved the first one on. It was a bit weird, like. A bit freaky. Even though I didn't, like . . .

—Did it say anything in particular?

—Yeah. Well, it said loads o stuff. It said – or Pajo said – that Paula reminded him of a woman from years before.

—Who?

—He said, like, Emer or somethin. I think it was Emer.

—Emer.

—Yeah. I betcha I know wha yer gonna say.

—G'wan.

—Yer gonna say about Emer, Cúchulainn's wife.

—Well Denny to be honest with yeh now it did occur to me.

—So yeh reckon we were in touch with Cúchulainn? D'yeh not think that's a bit mad?

—Well clearly Denny now it occurred to you. I'm sayin nothin o the sort one way or the other.

I finish off me whiskey and pour another. That whole Cúchulainn thing *did* occur to me. Cúchulainn was a hero in ancient Ireland. A mythological hero, like. He got the name Cúchulainn cos he killed the guard dog o this chieftain with his hurley and sliotar when he was only a kid, and to make it up he took the dog's place, patrollin this chieftain's land. Cúchulainn means hound o Cullen in English. Cúchulainn went on to do all sorts o mad stuff, takin on gods and monsters and the enemies of Ulster. I learned all that from the book Victor got me, years ago. Paula does look like Emer in it, and me ma did as well, when she was younger – that was why Victor bought it – but that means fuck all, it's just a coincidence. And Pajo might o just picked up on somethin, subconsciously even. I might o said somethin about Paula lookin like Emer years ago, when we were kids, and it just happened to surface that night.

—That's all just . . . it doesn't help anythin, Victor, yeh know? This is real life, these are real fuckin problems. I don't know wha –

—Did yer ma ever tell yeh about the time she saw a banshee?

—Yeah, I think so, ages ago.

—I'll tell yeh Denny there's more to this world than yeh think. This oulwan keening and brushin her hair, she said it was. An ancient hag, her face all withered. And didn't our own father die not three days later? A heart attack in his bed, sure none of us even knew he was gone till the next day when yer nanny Cullen shook him and found the life all fled from him.

—I just don't believe in ghosts, Victor.

Victor shrugs. —Who knows is all I'm sayin.

I reach across the coffee table and grab the whiskey bottle. Another top up.

—Yeh tryin to give me nerve trouble, Victor?

—Ah no, Denny. Sure it's a sin to be afraid in yer own home.

—Me ma used to say that.

—Never a truer word spoken.

We sit there in silence for a while with the sound o the wind in the trees and sip our whiskey. Was there a banshee for me ma, I wonder? An oul crone wailin by the skip outside the Cunninghams? Bollix. Just put that shite out o yer head, Denny; yill end up like mad Denise, yill be fuckin shittin when yeh get back home, sin or no fuckin sin. Somethin under the bed, Cúchulainn and banshees. For fuck sake.

—D'yeh wanna go down the grave? I say.

—Em . . .

—I can run us up in the car.

Victor bites at his thumbnail, then looks up at me. —Em. I . . . yeah. I mean . . . yeah. I *should* go up. Then he smiles. —Ah sure we'll ramble up the two of us. Will we?

—Yeah, cool. It's not far in the car. Stick on that tea before we go.

Victor pushes himself up off the chair and onto his feet, a big lankylimbed spider unfolded from its web.

—I'll bring the whiskey with us as well, says Victor, smilin. —I know yer mother wouldn't begrudge us a drop or two, Jack fuggin Frost be damned.

★

We pick our way through the darkenin graveyard and I feel like an old-fashioned graverobber apprenticed to his gangly stalkin uncle, the two of us weavin slowly between stones and statues, Victor stoppin now and then to look at the names and dates o the dead and sayin them back to himself softly and makin the sign o the cross. The place is already shut so there's no one else about; we had to squeeze through a gap in the railings to get in.

—It's over here, Victor. Beside that tree. See it there?

Victor nods and follows me, a bunch o white flowers he picked from his field clutched to his chest. A maze o graves of every kind. A small rusty cross at the head of a bed o half-sunk flagstones. A headstone shaped like a teddy bear. And then a gypsy grave, two marble horses risin from solid spray and between them eight small oval-shaped stones engraved with children's words for a dead father.

We crunch our way down a little path and I stop and nod me head at a new plain white marble gravestone. Me ma's stone. Shane bought it. He wouldn't take any money off me or Paula; he wanted to own me ma's death. Not that he had any time for her while she was alive. We stand, Victor and me, and watch the dyin light obscure the letters on the stone and fuck it anyway but I don't know wha to think. It's stupid to say that me ma died on me but that's how I feel sometimes. There was somethin wrong with her heart, the specialist said; it was always goin to happen. The specialist was a Pakistani fella and he was small with huge glasses and a turnip-shaped head. Actually, it seemed like they all were; it was like a clinical and immeasurably fuckin sad version o Willy Wonka and the Chocolate Factory, with Pakistani doctors instead of Oompa-Loompas. There was somethin terrifyin about wha he said – it was always gonna happen. An unhappy fate, predestination. Fuck. She was fifty-five when she died and she was still a gorgeous woman. Up until then it had been me and me ma and Paula in the house. It was a home, things made sense. Then everythin was fuckin obliterated.

I know I was away when it happened but that didn't mean I'd abandoned her. I didn't. I was tryin to do somethin good, tryin to get on. I would've come back. It does me fuckin head in that I wasn't there. And it does me head in that Paula was.

I was in a pub when Paula rang me, The Otley. There was some rugby game on, might o been the Heineken cup or somethin. I'd never usually bother with rugby but the Welsh are mad into it.

—I can't hear yeh, I said to her. —I'm in a pub.

I stood up and headed for the toilets. They smelled o lemon and disinfectant. Yeh could barely notice the piss for once.

—Hello? I said.

—Jesus Denny are yeh there for fuck sake?

—Yeah, I'm here. I'm in a pub, sorry. It's jammers –

—In a fuckin pub? In a fuckin pub when there's –

—What's up?

—Ma's gone. Jesus Denny, yeh have to come home.

Paula made a show of herself at the wake, fallin across the coffin slaughtered drunk. She'd been whackin back the vodka all day. Shane and Gino had to grab the coffin to stop it fallin over. I love Paula but Jesus, her and drink, she's a fuckin lunatic. And at ma's wake and all, that's wrong man. That's seriously un-fuckin-cool.

The wake was awful, that was probably the worst of it. I'm tellin yeh, interminable isn't the fuckin word. Tick fuckin tock. We had to keep the windows open in the front room, the fella at Massey's funeral parlour said so. It was freezin. I remember Maggit in the kitchen, a pile o sandwiches in misted cellophane on the table and the cigarette hangin from his lip, bobbin as he spoke. He had a can o Guinness clutched to his chest and his newly shaved head made his jug ears look more prominent than ever. He was sayin member the time we were kids and we threw eggs at the Flaherty's house and then Mr Flaherty stormed round foamin and rantin, sayin to yer ma yer fuckin son's after peltin me gaff with eggs and yer ma goes back into the kitchen, grabs a handful o raw sausages and rashers and throws them at him, sayin there yeh go, yiv a fuckin breakfast now.

And I do remember.

Jesus, course I do.

I take a deep breath and Victor kneels down slowly and his knees pop and crack. He places the wild white flowers on the grave and pats them but the wind catches them and they go flyin across the neighbourin graves and into the dark.

—Ah Jaysis lookit me flowers. Ah God.

Victor takes a few steps after them and stops.

—Don't worry about it, Victor.

Victor takes another step and then turns back to me.

—They were good flowers.

—I know.

—Snowdrops. Victor looks at the grave and blesses himself and clears his throat. He kneels back down and lays his palm on the little green pebbles.

—I miss yeh very much Kate but sure yer in a better place now and we'll be soon enough to follow yeh, he says, and he turns slightly and looks up at me. He'd be comical-lookin cept for the big sad eyes.

—Sure it's a lovely oul grave anyway, isn't it? he says.
—Very dignified.

I nod me head. —C'mon and we'll go.

Victor stands up.

—Yeh can stay with us tonight if yeh want, I say.

—Ah no, Denny. It's one thing comin to her grave, it's another stayin in her house. Ah no. Sure I'll make me own way back to the caravan.

—Victor, Balbriggan's twenty miles away. Yill be found dead. I'll give yeh a lift.

—Grand so. Yer a great oul skin Denny I'm tellin yeh true. As good a youngfella as there is.

Victor pulls the whiskey bottle from his duffle coat and hands it to me and I unscrew the cap and drink and the first snow flies slantways through the dark.

★

We're back in Victor's. I stick *As I Lay Dying* by William Faulkner and a biography of Eamon De Valera into me bag.

—I wasn't lookin for swaps or anythin, I say. —Them books I brung are just presents, like.

Victor waves his hand. —Ah not at all, Denny. A swap's a swap and I'm happy to do it. Sure that's wha they did in ancient times instead o money. Ten hens for a sheep.

He seems to mull over wha he's just said.

—Or would yeh say a sheep's worth ten hens? That might be a bit too many hens.

I shrug and Victor points at me bag. —That Faulkner one's a bit mad now but stick with it. It's very good. Me mother is a fish and all this.

—Wha?

—Yill see.

—Right. Are yeh sure yeh don't wanna come up to the house for the night? Will yeh be alright here in this weather?

—Ah I'll be grand Denny. Not a bother.

—Well. I'll see yeh so, Victor. I'll drop up again.

—Safe journey home now Denny. Mind yerself on them roads they're treacherous oul things altogether.

I hoist the bag up onto me shoulders and step out into the night. When I turn back Victor's still in the doorway, a tall black shadow in a neat rectangle o lemon yellow light, the sky above the caravan filled with fallin snow.

★

The wipers are shuckin the snow back and forth off the window and the car in front o me's nothin cept two dull red eyes in the wild grey night. Cohen's croakin about bein an ugly hunchback and yeh can picture him on a stool with his guitar, the smart haircut and the well-set face lined with sorrow and unwanted wisdom and –

Jesus this is a depressin fuckin album.

189

I hit stop on the tapedeck and collapse back into the seat. Cohen's class, don't get me wrong, but I suppose Paula's right; time and fuckin place, man. Can't be doin with downer stuff at the moment, sat here with the car bumblin and chuggin in stasis, eager to be home.

God, I miss me ma. I miss her somethin fuckin terrible.

A fella in a high-vis jacket jogs past, head ducked against the snow, and slips into the little toll bridge security hut thingy up ahead.

I reach over into the back seat and rummage through the bag and pull out the De Valera biography. His face is pinched and worried-lookin on the front cover and he's wearin his oul spidery fine-rimmed glasses. An older De Valera, way after he was bombed to fuck in the GPO. He looks dead like Alan Rickman, actually, the actor who played him in Neil Jordan's film. Specially the nose.

I light up a cigarette and take a few puffs and flip open the book on me lap. The pages old and thick and slightly yellow. There's a big red stamp on the inside cover sayin PROPERTY OF BALBRIGGAN LIBRARY. I tease the little ticket out o the pocket and Victor, yeh wily bastard, it's four and a half years overdue.

THE PATH OF THE BUDDHA

This is a joke, man. A fuckin joke. I stare out the window and shake me head . . . I can't believe this . . . I fuckin knew somethin like this was gonna happen.

The car's outside the garden on its roof. It looks like a fucked beetle, wheels and rusty metal guts in the air. It's surrounded by a gang o kids. I drop me Cheerios and squash on the runners Paula got me yesterday and race out o the house and into the light mornin rain. I push past the kids and give the fuckin heap o shite a boot. One o the lads laughs.

—What's so funny? I say.

—You, he says.

Cheeky fuck.

—Did youse do this?

—No. Did you?

His mates snigger.

—D'yiz know who did it, then?

Fuckin desperation here, I know; I've more chance o gettin a straight answer out of a Fianna Fáil councillor than these poxy kids. And anyway I know full well who did it: the gyppos. And that cunt Maggit's still off gallivantin. Wha am I supposed to do, like?

Fuck it. I turn and head back up the garden. I should probably just get rid o the motor. I'll just drive the thing up and be done with it. I mean, it's only a shitty little rustbox anyway and the gyppos don't seem –

—I like yer runners, mister.

I turn round. —Wha?

The lads are laughin, nudgin each other.

—Yer runners are gorgeous.

He makes a floppy-wristed gesture and I look down at me new runners. Actually, now that these little bastards mention it, they're quite sparkly and vaguely effeminate. And there're little hearts on the laces.

I hurry back into the house.

★

On the phone to Pajo:

—Is Maggit back yet?

—No, no sign of him.

—Fuck sake.

—What's wrong? Did somethin happen?

—It's upside down.

—Wha?

—It's upside down . . . on its fuckin roof, like.

—The car?

—No the fuckin house. I'm sittin on the ceilin.

—OK, OK. Chill, man.

—There's a load o kids out lookin at it. Fuckin gawpin, the little saps.

Silence for a few seconds, then:

—Denny, did yeh hear anythin last night?

—No. Why?

Silence again.

—Wha?

—Sounds weird to me, like. Odd. I mean . . . I don't want to add to yer woes, Denny . . .

—Wha are yeh shitein about?

—Well . . . d'yeh think they, like . . . they might o cursed the car or somethin?

—Jaysis, would you stop. Were you smokin somethin this mornin?

—Yeah, but . . . still, I'm just sayin, like. If yeh didn't hear anythin . . .

—Here, can I ring yeh back? I'm callin the X-Files. Yeh fuckin sap.

I end the call and click on the kettle in the kitchen. I need a cup o tea. Wha a load o bollix, like. Nothin ever goes right for me. Never. I mean, I get a car . . . and let's face it, the car's fuckin shite; a total fuckin banger . . . and it gives me a bit o fuckin pleasure, like, a bit o fuckin freedom . . . and wha happens?

It's typical, this. Totally. That shite with the Triads (so-called Triads) was Maggit's fault as well, and so was everythin else, ever. The chap's trouble. And he's turned into a selfish cunt, as well. I mean, there was a time he'd fight for anyone, he was a socialist, an environmentalist, the lot.

But now he's just a big-eared cunt.

★

Pajo's after comin over for the night. It's the wee hours o the mornin and we're havin a stakeout.

—Bags Charlie Sheen, Pajo says.

—He's not in Stakeout, his brother is.

—Are yeh sure?

—Yeah. What's his name . . . Estevez somethin. Emilio Estevez.

—Right. I'm him, then. You can be the oulfella.

—I'd rather be Richard Dreyfuss anyway. He's a better actor.

—Yeah, he's about ninety though.

I shake me head and get up to make another cup o tea. Pajo's sippin his cappuccino, a little drop o whiskey in it. I'd drink coffee as well but I hate the stuff. I keep a packet o cappuccino sachets in the press for Pajo, though, cos he's a fussy bastard with certain things and won't drink tea. Anyway, we're sittin up to keep an eye on the car, we've a good view from me bedroom window. Me room still looks like it did when I was a teenager – Undertaker posters on the walls, a big Che Guevara flag over me bed, rows o books on me shelves. I have the kettle and the milk and that up here, and biscuits and ashtrays and the whiskey bottle for Pajo. Pajo may be a Buddhist but he still drinks like a Catholic. Although, maybe he's better off. I wish we lived in ancient fuckin times, so I could worship the sun or the moon or somethin . . . somethin that's actually there, actually worth-fuckin-while.

I squash me tea bag up against the side o the cup and then scoop it out and flick it into the basket beside me bed.

—I saw Kasey a while ago, I say.

—Yeah?

—Yeah. He was sayin he was after comin into a bit o money.

—Yeah?

The way Pajo says 'yeah' I know he already knows. Pajo's the absolute worst liar on earth.

—What's the story, so? I ask.

—Ehh . . .

—Well, somethin dodgy then, obviously.

—Ehmm . . . like, em . . . drugs and that.

—Doesn't surprise me.

Pajo sips at his cappuccino. —Will yeh·keep this under yer hat, Denny?

—Yeah, course.

—They're Dommo Power's drugs.

—Yeah? Fuck sake. He'd wanna watch himself gettin involved with them. Slaughter's in with them now, they're dodgy as fuck. Dealin for Dommo's like –

—No, he's not dealin for him. He . . . like, he robbed him.

—No fuckin way. Yeh serious? Jesus fuckin Christ.

Pajo nods.

—Fuckin hell. How did he manage that?

—Ah it's complex, Denny. Very, like . . .

—Complex, yeah. G'wan.

—Well, he heard off some posh fella in Trinity after one o these lectures that he goes to that there was a big shipment comin in, for all the Blackrock heads and that, yeh know? Yer man mentioned a fella in a wheelchair so Kasey put two and two together.

—Is it heroin and that?

—Nah, they don't bother with heroin or anythin anymore, Denny, that's all, like, that's old news. It's cocaine now. All the business heads and that are mad into it, and the students and everythin. Heroin's for nothin these days Denny, it's small change.

—So wha did he do? How did he get his hands on it?

—Well, like, he scammed the fella from Trinity, I think. Although, like, this is Kasey sayin this so it's not, em . . . like, corroborated or anythin. So, wha Kasey said was yer man, this Trinity fella, he buys the stuff off the dealers in bulk and sells it on to the, like, business classes and all this. Yeh know the way they all think Kasey's from Dalkey, like, with the posh accent he puts on and the suit and all this? He just, like, got yer man's trust and lifted a load o the stuff from his gaff. Simple as, like. They're not very wide to that sort o thing yet. Kind o naïve, yeh know?

—So no one knows it was him?

—No. Dommo knows the stuff went missin, like. Yer man from Trinity was just holdin it, he hadn't paid anythin for it yet so there's a load o, like, pissed-off people.

—That's fuckin dangerous. What's he doin still hangin round?

—He says it's a Robin Hood thing, steal from Blackrock and give to Clondalkin.

—Jesus Christ. He's not fuckin well.

—They're all lookin for fellas from Dalkey, though, with posh accents.

I shake me head and sip me tea. Fuckin cocaine, wha? The new scourge o Dublin. Fuckin cunt's drug, cocaine is. Heroin was a waster's drug, a desperado's, it was awful but it was all about escape and despair, while cocaine's for overpaid cunts in suits, our supposed betters. Heroin was a trap and cocaine is a choice. It's . . . actually, would yeh fuckin listen to me? Get off yer fuckin soapbox, Denny. Jesus.

—I'm sayin a few prayers for him, says Pajo.

—To who?

—Like, the Supreme Being. For Kasey.

—Is that for real or wha? D'yeh really believe in this Buddhism stuff?

Pajo turns slowly from the window. He takes another sip from his cappuccino and there's a wary look in his eyes. And why wouldn't there be? I mean, he must be well used to bein slagged mercilessly at this stage. God knows he brings a lot of it on himself, but still.

—Honestly, I say. —I was just wonderin.

Another sup. A longer one this time.

—Well, it's just . . . it's kind o complicated, Denny, he says. —Faith and that. Complex, like.

—Yeah, I know that. There's no easy answers and all the rest. But sure we're here all night one way or the other. Nothin else to do.

—Suppose.

Pajo looks out the window and bites his lip, then turns back to me.

—Well . . . I dunno, really, he says. —I dunno wha started it, like. I think it's just cos o all the sufferin and that, yeh know like? I mean, yiv got people killin each other all over the place – lookit Iraq on the telly – and animals dyin in experiments as well and trees chopped down and all the rest and . . . wha can yeh do about it? I know Maggit'd say go out and join the socialists or wharrever, but that's not for me, yeh know? Politics and that. And this was annoyin me, like. Actually, not annoyin . . . kind o like, hurtin me, yeh know? A kind o, emm, like a soul hurt, thinkin about all this stuff. So –

—But where did yeh get the Buddhist stuff from? In particular I mean.

—I had a dream.

—Serious?

—Yeah, serious.

—Wha about?

—Well . . . em . . . OK. Eh, I was wanderin through the fields in the snow, pure freezin, like. I only had a pair o shorts on me, and a T-shirt. Don't know why. Just dreams like, yeh know? It was nighttime, and there was . . . d'yeh know the way the snow kind o glows in the dark? It was like that. I was lost. I was, like, fallin through the snow and I couldn't find me way back when I saw these footprints so I started followin them. Yeah? They went on for ages. But after a while they split into two and I didn't know which ones to follow. I was pure freezin by now, like. Me fingers were like coolpops, I couldn't even bend them. So I fell down on me knees and started cryin, yeah? Big sobs. And then I noticed there was blood, little tiny drops, like, in one set o tracks. So I just stood up and, like, started followin the clean ones and then they split again, in three this time. But I looked and there was blood in two of them so I followed the clean ones again and this kept happenin, like . . . the footprints splittin and the blood and all the rest. I was dead far into the fields . . . and it was huge, like, the way it used to be when we were small.

—So anyway, the tracks started to get more and more filled with blood so even though there were loads o them, dozens, like, hundreds, I was able to find the way dead easy. Actually, d'yeh know wha the blood in the snow was like? It was like the red stuff they put in them slushy drinks, the way it kind o, like, seeps into it, all pink and faded.

—Where did the tracks lead to?

I start rummagin through me drawer for a few skins as he talks.

—To these oul train tracks, says Pajo. —And, emm, that's where I found the way.

—Off who? Did someone tell yeh or did yeh just know?

—Someone told me.

—Who?

—Jack Charlton.

I burst out laughin.

Pajo looks offended. —He was wearin his cap and everythin. It was definitely him.

—Wha did he say to yeh?

—Are yeh, like, just takin the piss now or wha? says Pajo.

—No, seriously. I'm not. Jack Charlton though. That's some dream, Paj.

—If yeh don't want me –

—Seriously, Paj. I'm listenin, like. It's just a bit mad. Wha did he say?

—He said Follow the path of the Buddha.

I have to bite back a laugh.

—Wise man, Jack, I say. —Wha did he sound like?

—The way he did on telly. Northern English, like.

I lick the skins and stick them together. —Wha d'yeh think he was promotin Buddhism for? Is he not a Protestant?

—Yeah, but he probably seen the light on the other side, like.

—On the other side?

—In heaven, like. He probably –

—Yeh do know Jack Charlton's still alive, don't yeh?

—Is he not dead? Are yeh sure?

—Hundred per cent. I saw him in town a few months ago. There's life after the fuckin Irish job yeh know.

Pajo gulps at his can.

—Maybe it was Bobby Charlton?

★

We sit and watch and the minutes and hours creep by unmarked. The car is in a pool o yellow light, right beside the garden gate. A gang o teenagers stumble past and a girl falls against the bonnet and laughs and a youngfella pulls her to her feet. It's not tha late but I can feel me eyes gettin heavy. Me arms and legs feel like they're dead or dyin. I've stayed awake for days on end before like, but I'm fuckin wrecked here, even though I'm doin fuck all. Pajo's head is noddin forward and back, his tongue restin on his lower lip, eyes openin and closin slowly. This tiredness, it's after comin out o nowhere; settlin on me like a duvet, all warm and comfy . . . we were grand a half an hour ago, talkin shite, me tea in me hand, smoke curlin upwards and Johnny Cash on the radio and now I'm –

★

—They cursed us, Denny. I'm tellin yeh!

Fuckin hell.

The car's upside down again.

RED IN TOOTH AND CLAW

I haven't told Paula but we got a letter from Shane today. A notice of eviction. Typed and everythin. He was probably advised by the solicitor. I should probably be indignant that he didn't say it face-to-face but in a way I'm glad – I don't wanna see him. I knew this was comin, anyway. We've got three months' notice, accordin to the letter. Paula'll tear it up if I show it to her, march straight round to Shane's and have fuckin murder on his doorstep, which'll make things ten times worse. I'll tell her about it tomorrow, maybe. Or maybe I'll give Shane a shout meself. I mean, he might come round if I talk to him, try to be reasonable and that. He might just be tryin to scare us, like. One way or another, though, it's the last thing I need.

I rinse me cup under the tap and hang it on the rack, starin out the back window. I don't think Shane's even seen the back garden yet. Should probably pick up a shears or somethin today. I got a text off Ned earlier this mornin though, and it said he saw Maggit this mornin gettin off the 78a at Neilstown so it'll have to wait. I fold up Shane's letter and stick it in me back pocket, turn off the heatin, lock up, then hop in the car and drop by his usual haunts – the doctor's and the clinic, then the shops and outside the community centre, Finches, then the snooker hall and then into Clondalkin village. I find him comin out o The Steerin Wheel.

I beep the horn and he walks over, grinnin, the smell o cider on his breath.

—Wha the fuck were yeh doin with that girl?

—Wha? Nice to see you as well.

—Wha were yeh thinkin?

—I didn't do anythin. Wha girl?

—Some gyppo looper said yeh slept with his cousin. Was that yer woman yeh were with at the party?

Maggit rolls his eyes. —I . . . her? Jaysis. That gyppo one? So wha? Here, giz a lift back to the house.

He pulls open the door on the passenger side and gets in.

—I thought yer man was gonna fuckin stab me or somethin, I say. —Chop me fuckin balls off.

—Wha would he stab yeh for? Twenty years in The Joy for a sap like you?

—Will yeh shurrup for a minute?

Maggit wiggles his fingers and pretends to look offended. He pulls the cigarette from behind his ear and sticks it in his mouth, then looks at me.

—Wha are you so happy about? I say.

—That'd be tellin.

He winks. I start the car and pull into the traffic. Road's fuckin packed at this time o day, yeh never notice these things till yiv some wheels o yer own.

—Yeh didn't take anythin on yer woman, did yeh? Like, yeh didn't rob anythin on her.

—I didn't as a matter o fact. She'd only a few ornaments in the place anyway. She lives in a fuckin caravan Denny, she'd fuck-all there.

—And yeh didn't touch her?

—Wha? O course I touched her. What's the big fuckin deal? And anyway, she touched me first. I wasn't really into her to be honest. She's a bit mental, I think. A bit, yeh know, doolally.

I shake me head. The lights go red and we stop beside the industrial estate.

—Yer a fuckin eejit.

Maggit looks at me. —Wha the fuck is wrong with yeh, Denny? She practically fuckin raped me. She was fuckin mad.

—They want the car.

—Wha?

He stubs out the cigarette on the dashboard.

—They want the car. They said they'd take the car instead o killin yeh and d'yeh know wha? I'd rather they killed yeh, yeh fuckin eejit. Wha were yeh thinkin?

—Cunts.

Maggit runs his palm over his head and scratches his nose. He looks at the lights o the cars in front of us and then at the people at the bus stop and then back at me.

—They can go and fuckin jump, he says.

—Brilliant. Fuckin ingenious. That's the end o the fuckin car, so. And I haven't even given Gino the full whack yet.

—Don't worry about it. Fuck them.

—That's yer plan?

—Yeah. Fuck them. They're only knackers.

—Why are yeh bein such a prick?

—Wha d'yeh mean?

—I just wanted this fuckin car, Maggit. I –

—They won't get the car. Don't worry about it.

—How? Wha are yeh gonna do?

—Nothin. Fuck them.

—Yer a fuckin prick, d'yeh know that? A stupid fuckin big-eared prick.

★

I'm sittin in the front watchin Gone With the Wind with Paula and Teresa. Maggit's flippant bullshit and Shane's letter is runnin round me head though, so I can't really get into it. I'll tell Paula, obviously, eventually. About the letter, like. I remember an episode o The Simpsons where Homer's supposed to sit an exam after he's gone back to college, but he didn't do any studyin or anythin and he's fucked, he knows he's gonna fail. His solution is to hide under a pile o coats and hope everythin turns out OK. That's exactly wha I feel like doin. It actually sounds kind o cosy.

Me phone rings. Paula looks at me, annoyed, like I've planned the timin o the call to interrupt Scarlett's latest strop. I get up and walk out to the hall.

—Hello?

—He's after killin them . . . he's after . . .

It's Pajo. He's stutterin and splutterin and me blood drains down to me toes. Wha the fuck did that Maggit cunt do? Probably after stabbin Franno in the fuckin head.

—Wha happened? I say.

—He just . . . he fuckin killed them, Denny!

—Wha?

—He bit them, like. He savaged them. All o them!

—Bit them?

—There's feathers all over the place, they were –

204

—Feathers? Wha the fuck are yeh talkin about?

—The chickens. He murdered them.

—Maggit did?

—Wha? No, Ignatius.

—Fuckin hell, Pajo. The fuckin dog? Here, I'll drop over in a minute, yeah? Sit tight.

★

Pajo's back garden's a total mess, covered in blood and guts and feathers. The dog is sittin behind the grimy patio doors, oblivious to − or possibly very pleased about − the carnage he's wreaked. There are mangled chicken carcasses strewn around the place.

—We'll bury them, yeah? I say. —Or wharrever Buddhists do. That cool?

Pajo nods, then says:

—Actually, maybe we should, like . . . we should make a pyre, burn them.

—Yeah, cool. Sound.

Pajo hunches down and pets the floppy head o one o the chickens.

—Yeh keepin the dog? I ask.

—Yeah. It's not his fault really, is it? I mean, like, it's . . . in his nature or wharrever. Isn't it?

—Suppose so.

—Like, they're wolves really, aren't they?

—Yeah.

—Domesticated.

—Yep.

Pajo stands up and rubs his palms on his chest.

—Have yeh spoken to Maggit? I say.

—Yeah, says Pajo, his eyes still on the dead chickens.
—Well, a bit. He said he doesn't give a fuck about the gyppos. He said they're a shower o cunts and there's a smell o burnt sticks off them.

I look up and Maggit passes by the kitchen window with a can o Guinness in his hand. He stops at the sink and fiddles with somethin out o view. He doesn't even look at me.

—When d'yeh wanna get rid o the chickens? I ask.
—Today?
—Yeah, suppose. Better to do it soon, isn't it?

Pajo pokes at one o the carcasses with his boot.
—Lookit poor Shawn there. The foot's bit off him.

All of a sudden I'm takin with this massive urge to laugh. I have to turn me head away.
—Shawn?
—Yeah. After Shawn Michaels. I named them all after wrestlers. And Roddy there, lookit him. Roddy Piper. Doesn't he look afraid? Poor Bret's head is gone . . . I think Ignatius ate it.

And then out comes the laugh, belly deep and uncontrollable. Pajo looks at me, uncomprehendin.

★

There's a knock at the door and Paula answers. She's stood there for a few minutes and when she comes back Maggit's with her. Paula gives me a look and heads into the front room. Maggit takes a big sloppy bite from an already half massacred, tinfoil-wrapped breakfast roll.
—See the car?

Maggit nods. —On its roof, yeah.

—It's like that nearly every mornin.

—So I hear.

—Just as well it has that fuckin roll cage cos the thing'd be fucked otherwise. Sick o beatin the fuckin bumps out o the roof.

—It's terrible alright.

—Haven't seen yeh all week.

—Ah, yeh know yerself. Out and about. I took Ant'ny down to Funderland yesterday. Someone robbed me wallet, the bastards.

—Did he like it?

—Ah yeah, fuckin loved it. Wanna see him on the bumpers, fuckin mad he was. He bashed some kid over the barrier. Fuckin deadly like.

I light up me first cigarette o the day. I wouldn't mind a breakfast roll meself, actually – there's nothin in the fridge. Might run the car down the shops, grab somethin nice. After I get it back on its wheels, o course. Me head's done in with the car, to be honest. Maggit chews the mess o fried egg and sausage and red sauce with his mouth open.

—I'm gonna fightim, he says.

—Wha?

—Yer man, Franno. I'm gonna givvim a scrap.

—You for real?

—Yep, he says, wipin a red smudge off of his chin. —I'll knock the shite out of im.

—Yer gonna fightim. That's pure stupid.

Maggit swallows noisily. —Nah. He's only small, fuckim.

—Fuck's sake, Maggit. Yer –

207

—Look, Denny, he says. —I'm late. He takes another huge bite from his roll. I can hear me stomach grumblin. —I have to go. I've to see Bernadette.

Bernadette's face spins past in me mind's eye. Miserable, put-upon Bernadette. Can't imagine she'll be glad to see Maggit at her door, specially not this early. Although . . . maybe that's why Maggit's been in such a good mood recently? Stranger things have happened than Maggit and Bernadette getting back together, I suppose.

A bit of egg flops out o Maggit's mouth. —The weekend, he says. —Up at the haltin site. Just a straight up, like . . . a boxin match or wharrever. Yeh know yerself. Like on the knacker fight videos Gino had.

—Close yer mouth for fuck sake.

He holds up the remains of his roll and wiggles it, droppin more egg and a bit o sausage. He makes a face. This is supposed to mean somethin. Yid have to ask Maggit, really. We look at each other for a second, then he says,

—Look Denny, I have to run.

I blow out a lungful o smoke and tap the lengthenin ash o me cigarette. I can feel it, soft and warm, as it sprinkles onto me bare feet. Maggit looks at me and shrugs.

—Yeh comin up with us? he says.

—Yeah, spose. Fuck sake though, man, this is pure dopey. I mean, fuckin fightin gyppos . . .

—It'll be grand. Look, I'll see yeh, right? We can drive up. The posse.

—Yeah.

He holds up the remains of his roll. —Yeh want the rest o that?

—Fuck off, I say, although it does smell lovely. Pure greasy spoon roll, like, but fuck, yeh know when yer starvin?

Maggit lifts up the bin lid and drops the roll into it. A smell o mouldy bread and rotten fruit wafts up.

—See yeh, he says. —Don't be rootin around for that roll after I'm gone.

—Yeh sap. See yeh after.

—Good luck.

NONE OF THIS HULK
HOGAN SHITE

Besides the splutter o the banjoed exhaust and the general creakin and groanin o the car, we drive to the haltin site in silence. It's a cold, clear day. I still can't believe what's goin on. Pajo's sittin in the passenger seat fiddlin with his nose. He looks worried. Ned's in the back, the *Evening Herald* spread on his lap. He's been on the same page since we left the house. Maggit's beside him, sittin still, watchin Clondalkin bump by. There's no radio to turn on, and the tapedeck's after packin in so I can't even use that to break the silence. I could just talk, like, open me mouth, but it doesn't feel right.

I turn onto the Fonthill Road. There's a tract of land there that, for Dublin, is still relatively free o people. There used to be miles o fields here, a huge green wilderness between Clondalkin and Lucan that all four of us trekked through as kids, our imaginations enflamed, but now it's been squashed down to a tiny green belt as the estates and factories expand. That's where the gyppo camp is. We pass an oulfella in wellies pushin a bike and a pack o mangy dogs savagin each other by the roadside and then the haltin site comes into view. It's set a little bit back from the road and surrounded by mangled bits o fence and pallet and

chicken wire. There's a gravel path leadin into it and I pull
up just short o wha I suppose is the entrance.

I twist and unclip me seat belt.

—Here we are, I say.

★

There are about fifteen caravans on the site and they're
surrounded by half-wrecked cars with their bonnets in the
air and piles o tyres and blown-up fridges. Strings o twine
are tied from one caravan to the next with washin flappin
from them and there's horses, too; big stocky ones with
blankets on their backs and slabs o muscle under their
necks and legs and with big shaggy manes over their eyes.
A couple o skinny greyhounds pad across the gravel in
front of us.

—They used to sacrifice them in the olden days, says
Pajo.

—The dogs? says Ned.

—Yeah.

—Waste, says Ned.

There's a big fire in the middle o the camp, and there's a
group o lads sittin on boxes beside it, listenin to an oulfella
in a battered armchair. I can smell cookin from one o the
caravans; stew, I think. It smells lovely. I scan the place but
I can't see Franno Ward anywhere.

—Go up and ask the oulfella there where he is, Pajo, I
say.

—You ask him.

Fuckin hell.

—There's yer woman, says Maggit.

211

He nods towards one o the caravans. There's a group o three girls standin by the door, lookin over. They've all got dark hair and dark brown eyes. They're smilin and gigglin between themselves. It's her, the girl from the party that night; the nymph.

—Which one's yer bird? says Ned.

—She's not me bird yeh sap, says Maggit. —Niamh's the one in the middle.

—Yeh serious? says Ned. —She's gorgeous.

—Yeah, and fuckin mad as well, says Maggit.

—Well, yiv to take the rough with the smooth, says Ned.

Maggit looks at him.

—I'm just sayin, like, says Ned. —She's a very beautiful woman.

—She's only sixteen, I say. —Sinead'd kill yeh if she heard yeh sayin that.

Ned looks like he's gonna say somethin, but just kind o lifts his eyebrows instead.

—I'll go over and ask her where the heads are, will I? I say.

—I'll go with yeh, says Ned.

★

—He's in the shack, practisin, says one o the girls.

—Practisin?

The girls laugh.

—Colm's the best scrapper in Dublin after all, she says, and they laugh again.

I look at Niamh. She's more beautiful by daylight. She's stunnin, really: dead pale and delicate and willowy.

And very obviously only a kid. Wha she sees in Maggit is anyone's guess. I try to make a plea for sanity.

—I don't know wha Mag . . . wha Colm's after sayin to yeh, but he's gonna be fuckin battered. Will yeh not do somethin? Can yeh not say somethin to Franno?

—I already have, says Niamh. —He won't listen. And anyway, it's only a fistfight. There's no bitin or stabbin or anythin. Sure they'll only be bruised. And I can fix Colm up after.

They laugh. So does Ned, like he's under a fuckin spell or somethin.

—Fantastic, I say. I grab Ned under the elbow. —C'mon, you.

—How's the dog gettin on? says Niamh.

The images o the pup with its muzzle dyed red with blood pops into me head.

—He's grand, I say.

★

Glowin sparks swirl into the air, caught in the updraft o the thick, greasy black smoke billowin from the fire. We're sittin on a row o battered tea boxes listenin to the oulfella. There're a load o gyppos gathered round, women and men and kids and a couple of oulwans with grey hair piled high on their heads. The kids are wearin Nike and Fila tops and the oldest are in ragtag suits or shawls and dresses. The three girls, immensely beautiful, all o them (fuckin sirens, like) are standin near the back, Niamh's eyes glued to Maggit. The oulwans offered us a bowl o stew each and Ned is millin his, the bowl inches below his chin as he scoops the spoonfuls o beef and potato and broth into his mouth.

The oulfella is tellin a story about a troupe o gypsy poets and harpists who were able to capture their music and verse in jars, and make a mint sellin them to the old kings of Ireland. I've never heard this one before and it occurs to me that the oulfella might just be makin it up; that he might be a proper storyteller or wharrever.

—Good idea, that, says Ned, noddin. —Sellin tunes. Very marketable. Like an olden days iPod.

—Wha songs did they do? says one of the kids.

—Old songs, says the oulfella. —Beautiful songs like you've never heard.

—Were they better than Eminem? says the kid, smirkin.

—Fuckin Eminem. D'yeh hear that little rip? They were miles better than Eminem. Yid cry to hear such wonderful songs. None o this –

He stops.

Franno Ward and his mates step up to the fire, five young men with dark hair and dark eyes. The huge redhead from the cart looms up behind them, his massive waistcoat opened up his huge belly spillin out. Franno's stripped to the waist; he looks to be in proper shape, lean and well defined.

—Jaysis. Here's mini fuckin Hercules, says Ned. He looks at Maggit and then me.

—How're yeh doin, Denny? says Franno.

I nod.

—Get the place ready now, childer, says the oulfella, and the kids spring to their feet.

They know wha to do.

★

—Are yeh takin yer top off? I say to Maggit.

—I'll leave me jersey on.

It's the Liverpool jersey from a few seasons ago, with number 7, KEWELL printed on the back. Maggit got the name put on it when Harry Kewell was still good. Looks dopey now.

The big redhead stops beside us. He's rollin a barrel with two big, flat brown hands. He stops beside us, then raises his fists and throws a couple o mock rights at Maggit, then winks and laughs and rolls on by.

★

Four pockmarked metal barrels mark the extent o the ring, and the kids drag their heels from one barrel to the next to show the borders between crowd and fighters. There are about thirty or forty people bunched around the ring, the kids sittin at the front. A little thin-faced youngwan has her arm around one o the greyhounds, his long skinny face level with hers, and the three girls, Niamh among them, are standin behind her. The fire behind the crowd casts dancin shadows across the ring in the failin light. Faces old and young are filled with a kind of expectant glee. Maggit's standin near me and Paj and Ned, beside one o the barrels, his arms hangin by his sides. His scuffed jeans and Doc Marten boots aren't ideal fightin gear. I can see the motley assemblage of Indian ink tattoos on his forearms and the black dots on each knuckle. He's more wasted-lookin than proper skinny – his shoulders are slouched and his belly's startin to get kind o plump, detox or no. Franno Ward is skippin and shufflin on the spot, jabbin at the air with a succession o lefts and rights. He's wearin a pair o grey tracksuit bottoms. He has a tiny crucifix around his neck and he's obviously done this sort o thing before.

—Yeh alright, Maggit? I say.

He nods.

—Yeh sure?

—Yeah, grand.

—Should yeh not be, like . . . shufflin and that, like yer man there? says Pajo.

—Fuck off Pajo, says Maggit.

He steps away from us, into the centre o the ring. The crowd murmurs its appreciation and Franno steps up to meet Maggit. The oulfella is standin off to the side. He's the ref, apparently. Maggit is about a foot taller than Franno but he was never quick on his feet and he's less so now. I've seen him stitch a loaf on a few blokes in pubs and that when the need arose, and he can definitely take a hidin, but he's done fuck-all but drink and smoke and eat in the most erratic fashion possible over the last five or six years; he's a wreck, like. He looks like a half-dead scarecrow.

—Right, lads, says the oulfella. —I want a nice clean fight, yeah? No bitin, no pokin, no loafin and nothin below the belt, yeah? And no kickin, either. This is a boxin match, not fuckin Hulk Hogan shite.

I assume he's sayin all this for Maggit's benefit. Franno looks to be itchin for the fight to start. His head is twitchin and his tongue is flickin over his lips.

—Shake hands, lads, says the oulfella.

Franno offers his hand and Maggit takes it. They shake for fuckin ages, like in a film, each pair of eyes, Maggit's pale blue and Franno's dark brown, starin directly into the other before they finally let go.

And then the oulfella steps back.

—Fight!

Immediately Franno lunges forward and Maggit barely has time to throw up his guard and take the wild right on his forearms. Pajo flinches beside me and closes his eyes and Franno hops backwards, his surprise attack foiled. He shuffles from one foot to the other, his head low and his eyes peerin at Maggit from over his bunched fists. Maggit rubs his arm before liftin his fists to just under his chin. He takes a step towards the centre and Franno flies forward, his feet actually leavin the ground as he launches himself from his half-crouched position. His wide right-hander catches Maggit on the ear and he stumbles back, takin a flurry of rights and lefts to the stomach and chest before he throws his arms around Franno, huggin him to his winded body.

—Fuckin hell, says Ned. —He's gettin battered.

—Will I stop it? I say.

Ned shrugs. I think o Bret Hart wrestlin Bob Backlund, years ago, and Bret's brother Owen gettin his ma to throw in the towel when Bret was caught in the crossface chickenwing. Bret went mad at Owen for doin it, so maybe I should leave it.

Maggit shoves Franno away from him. Shouts and laughter from the crowd.

—He's doin well to stay standin after that, says a fella beside me. —Decent chin on the cunt, I'll credit him that.

—Givvim stitches Franno! a little gyppo kid shouts.

—Bate im Franno! Bate im!

Franno circles Maggit, who's shakin his head from side to side, turnin on the spot to keep the gypsy in front of him. Franno throws a couple o feints and Maggit ducks back, his guard high. Then Franno steps forward quickly and launches a couple o quick left-handed jabs which Maggit partially takes on his arms before Franno fires off another wide right which again gets in, this time thuddin right on Maggit's cheek. His neck snaps back and Franno wades in again, jabs to the body and chest before he connects with another right hook, this time on the chin.

—Watch the fuckin right, Maggit! shouts Ned.

Dazed, Maggit half turns towards Ned and takes another right to the side of the head. Maggit stumbles and falls to one knee.

—Shurrup yeh fuckin eejit, I say to Ned.

—Yer man's after hurtin his hand, says Pajo.

I turn and sure enough, as Maggit pushes himself to his feet Franno is shakin his right hand and flexin his fingers with a grimace. There's a thin trickle o blood runnin from just under Maggit's eye socket and his face is blotchy and red but he comes forward on jelly legs, his fists bobbin in front of him. Franno comes to meet him, head snakin from side to side. He feints again but Maggit keeps his eye on him and when the right hand comes he steps back, then launches forward with a straight right of his own that catches the traveller right in the face. Franno's head whips to the left and blood flies from his face in a red spray.

—Take that yeh cunt, says Ned.

When Franno straightens himself his face is covered in blood, his nose mashed. Maggit follows up immediately with another right which bashes aside Franno's guard, leavin him open for a left to the head. Maggit yowls and grits his teeth as a second left catches Franno on the top of the skull.

—Yer batterin im! C'mon! Ned shouts.

218

Maggit lands a couple o meaty body shots on the reelin gypsy and then pulls his arm back for a massive right. Franno twists out o the way though, takin the blow on the shoulder. Maggit whirls to get him centred again and comes at him with his guard loose.

—Get yer fists up, Maggit!

And a torpedo of a right catches Maggit dead on the chin. It's a fuckin beauty, as perfect a punch as yeh can possibly imagine. Maggit's head shoots back, spit flyin as the crowd roar, and he stumbles and falls, the greyhound howlin as he crashes into the dirt in a plume o dust and that's it, that quick; he's fucked, knocked out, dead, who fuckin knows. The oulfella starts a count. The dog is still howlin.

On five Maggit stirs.

—Stay down, Colm, someone says. I think it's Niamh.

—Fuck the car, says Pajo.

On seven his legs and arms are workin uselessly on the dirt, and on eight his elbows are propped behind him and his head is raised a couple of inches . . .

Then Franno sways and pitches forward, his body thuddin off the ground.

THE MIRACULOUS
TIME-TELLING FOAL

So quiet up here, isn't it? Well, there's the wind, but there's no city sounds like cars and that. I remember someone sayin that if yer still enough yeh can hear the voice o God in places like this. The Dublin Mountains. Even though it's windswept and barren it's a gorgeous place; yeh never really realise that there's such beauty on yer doorstep. I look back over me shoulder to Sinead's car. It's parked off the road, a huge cliff risin behind it, little skeletal trees on top, black against the empty blue. The land falls away on this side. Plummets and then rises up in humps and mounds. Tiny silhouettes o birds wheelin in the sky. Pajo and Paula are sittin on the car's bonnet, Paula with her shoulders hunched up, Pajo with his legs crossed meditation-style and his eyes closed. Teresa's huddled in the back seat, her nose buried in a copy o Heat magazine. Paula's hair is whippin madly in the wind. She keeps tryin to stick it behind her ears but it's no use, not up here, this place o wind and vastness; cold, stingin wind heavy with salt and a patchouli tang.

—Isn't it deadly? I shout over at them.

Paula squints her eyes and smiles and nods.

—Gorgeous, she shouts, the word caught in the wind and flyin past me. She's humourin me, like; Paula hates the outdoors. Even when she was a kid she was a housekatcher, never out of her room. Now the only times she's outdoors are the brief dashes between pubs and clubs, giddy and drunk beneath a fellow waster's jacket or umbrella. I cup me hands round me mouth and shout again.

—Wha d'yeh think Pajo?

He looks at me and grins. Sticks up his thumb.

—Deadly, he says.

—Any sign o the rest o them?

Paula shakes her head. Her hair flies up, likes she's touched one o them electric ball yokes, or she's underwater; a bobbin blonde nimbus round her head. Ned, Sinead, Maggit and little Anto got the bus to Tallaght, and they're gettin a taxi to Johnny Fox's. The plan's to have somethin to eat up there, then get to the Hellfire Club. We had a few people round last night and Sinead wasn't the better of it so she let me drive her car. It's mad drivin a new car; a proper car with power steerin and a massive stereo. After the fight with Franno I left me own car at the haltin site. Technically the fight was probably a draw but since Franno ended up in hospital with a bad concussion I just thought fuck it, it's not worth it, and left it there.

I actually forgot all about Shane's letter for a bit, with all the shite about the car and that, but it's back on me mind now. I've had a few missed calls from Shane today. I'll give him a shout tomorrow, maybe. I'm turnin me phone off, though. I have this horrible feelin gnawin at me. Somethin weird and hard to pin down. Why can't stuff just be straightforward? I had a dream about that girl last night, the one in the Adidas tracksuit, and we were talkin in a bar. Just talkin. I can't remember wha about, but it was nice. Just dead simple and nice. The only mad thing about it was that Steven Gerrard and Jamie Carragher were workin behind the bar, wearin their Liverpool jerseys. When I woke up I was cryin. Mental.

—Yeh alright?

I turn round. Paula's beside me, smilin. She puts her hand on me elbow.

—Yeh OK Denny? Away with the fairies, wha?

—Nah. I'm grand. Just thinkin like.

—Wharrabout?

—Don't know. Nothin.

—Ma?

This surprises me. Dunno why, like. I look at Paula.

—Ma?

—Yeah.

—No. I just . . . just stupid things, like. Nothin.

Paula scrunches up her nose. She grabs a sheaf o hair in each hand and pulls it under her chin like a bonnet. She looks at me.

—D'yeh think about ma much? she says.

—D'you?

—Yeah.

I look back out at the mountains. Then over at Pajo who's still on the bonnet, his eyes closed and hummin, and then back to Paula.

—It's nice up here, isn't it? I say.

—Fuckin fuh-fuh-freezin, she says, grinnin.

—Yeah but yeh know wha I mean. The scenery and that. And the feel o the place. It's nice like.

—If it was a bit warmer. Yid die o hypothermia up here.

—Yeah.

—Yeh hungry?

—A bit.

—We head to Johnny Fox's?

—Sound, yeah.

I press me heel into the ground. It's spongy. I twist it and feel it give. I shout over to Pajo.

—Yeh right Gandhi? Soon as the rest o them get here we're off to the pub.

★

We don't stay in Johnny Fox's – the hidden pub in the mountains, the one Michael Collins and the IRA men were supposed to drink in while they were on the run – for too long. The temptation's there, like, to just sit here all day and drink and make merry. Specially with the thought o Shane's letter on me mind. But in the end we all just have a Sunday roast and a couple o jars each. Cept Anthony, obviously, who's too young for drink and too fussy for a proper dinner.

—Yeh won't grow up fit and strong like yer da if yeh don't eat it all, says Ned, smilin. He winks at us in an over-the-top way. —Did yeh know yer da used to be a wrestler?

—No he didn't.

Ned looks at us. —He did, didn't he?

We all nod, serious and solemn. Maggit took a few wrestlin classes in Birmingham years ago, when he was a teenager. He went through this mad phase where he told everyone he was gonna become a professional wrestler. Never worked out like, but he was serious about it for a while. One o the fellas he trained with is on telly now.

—He battered Hulk Hogan in Wrestlemania III, I say. —The main event.

Really the main event o Wrestlemania III was Hulk Hogan versus André the Giant. Everyone loved Hogan when we were small, but I hated him. I didn't think a world champion should wear yellow trunks, and I thought it was stupid-lookin that, even though he wasn't that old, he was bald. I still remember Undertaker beatin him in 1991 for the belt. Undertaker hit him with a Tombstone piledriver onto a steel chair, which was pretty hardcore at the time. I fuckin loved it; I still thought wrestling was real and I jumped around like a lunatic, spillin me 7-Up all over me.

—Did yeh, da? says Anthony.

Maggit downs his pint. He nods quickly, then says —D'yeh not like cabbage, Anto?

Anthony shakes his head. —Horrible. Were you a wrestler, da?

—Don't mind them, says Maggit, surprisinly unwillin to go along with the charade. —Are yeh not eatin any o that? What's wrong with it?

—It's very good for you, says Sinead.

—Nutritious, says Pajo.

—Horrible, says Anthony. He sticks out his tongue.

—Here, says Maggit. —D'yeh want some Monster Munch?

Anthony beams. —Yeah.

Maggit twists in his chair and leans backwards, rummagin through his rucksack. He pulls out a six pack o Monster Munch.

—Tell yer ma yeh et yer vegetables now, yeah? Maggit says, and hands Anthony a packet. —Hear me? Don't tell her yeh were eatin these, OK?

—Yeah.

—Giz a packet, says Pajo.

—Fuck off, says Maggit.

Pajo looks hurt. He sinks back into his chair.

—This dinner smells like the funeral for Pajo's chickens, says Anthony.

Everyone laughs.

—Well done, says Maggit to Pajo. —Yer after puttin him off chicken, now. There's fuck all he'll eat as it is.

—I didn't mean to.

A woman comes over and leaves the bill on the table. Sinead picks it up and scans it.

—Where to now, Captain Oates? Ned says to me.

—Montpellier Hill, I say, swallowin the last o me Guinness. —Hellfire Club, like. Yiz up for it?

★

Fuckin hell man, I'm wrecked. Uphill all the way, like; windin gravelly roads and dirt tracks, fir trees bobbin. I haven't been up to the Hellfire Club in absolute donkeys. Not since I was a kid, when I came up with me ma and Paula. I'm dead excited about seein it again. I can't believe some o the rest o them haven't been up here at all.

Teresa and Paula are holdin hands. They'd never do that in Clondalkin, like. Too fuckin dodgy. Pajo starts complainin about his destroyed quadriceps and Ned tells him about a machine he got cheap off a chiropractor. The view from Montpellier Hill is cool. Yeh can see right out over Dublin and into the Irish Sea, a giant swathe o grey that stretches out to Liverpool, eventually minglin with the Mersey somewhere in all that mist. It's always terrified me, the sea; the thought o somethin that immense, like, that deep . . . all manner of unknown and unknowable creatures powerin through the depths, eyeless and nameless and pale-skinned. Scary fuckin shit, man. Compounded o course by the fact that I never learned to swim. Or maybe I should say related to the fact; my never learnin to swim the inevitable outcome o this immense dread o the sea.

Pajo and the girls are laggin behind. Sinead and Pajo are swingin Anthony along between them, his runners skimmin over the dirt. He's laughin and squealin.

—Wha does Sinead study? says Maggit to Ned. —Business or somethin?

—Art.

—Art, says Maggit, eyes on the trail ahead. —Does she wanna be an artist?

—Yeah. A painter.

—Yeh can't study to be a painter though, can yeh? Yiv got it or yeh don't.

—And you'd know all about paintin, obviously.

—I'm just sayin. If yer good yer good. What's there to learn?

—Loads, says Ned. —All the history and that. That's important. Yeh need to know yer place, what's been done already.

Maggit smirks and shakes his head.

—Yeh do, says Ned. —Like . . . the impressionists and cubists and all these. They all did things a certain way, they had things to say . . . well, to paint, in a new way. It's –

—D'yeh hear this, Denny? says Maggit, turnin to me.
—Fuckin cubism. Bullshitism, more like. Yeh haven't a
clue, Ned.

—And you do?

—Ned, if bullshit was music, you'd be a brass fuckin
band.

Ned looks like he's gettin pissed off now, so I decide to
wade in. Not on the fuckin art debate, though. The first
thing that pops into me head is Ned's ex Sarah, so I just
blurt out:

—Wha happened to you and Sarah in the end?

I think Ned's copped that I'm just changin the subject,
but he seems happy enough to leave cubism behind. —Ah,
complications, Denny, says Ned. —Complications.

—She was a weapon, says Maggit

—Wha?

—Don't get yer knickers in a twist, says Maggit. —She
was. She'd a head like a melted wheelie bin.

Ned looks at me, then back at Maggit. For a second I
think he's gonna say somethin about Maggit and Bernadette,
the obvious comeback. Maggit'd go mad if he did that. He
takes a breath instead, though. Calms himself.

—She had her good points, Maggit, he says. —Youse
weren't around when –

—Ned, the fuckin tide wouldn't take Sarah Jones out.

—Yer a fuckin prick you, d'yeh know that? says Ned,
quietly but with weight behind it, and he picks up the
pace, leavin us behind.

—Very fuckin sensitive, isn't he? says Maggit.

I don't answer. I just phase out o the conversation; I'm
not in the fuckin mood, like. Maggit can act the arsehole
even at the best o times. I don't know why he does it.

I mean, we're all mates, yeh know? Why's he so fuckin angry all the time? We're here to enjoy ourselves. Have some fuckin fun, like, which is hard enough to do with the thought of impendin homelessness hangin over me. I feel like everything's gettin in on me.

★

We march on for another fifteen minutes or so, corkscrewin up and round Montpellier Hill, leavin behind the view o Dublin for another one o the woods and mountains spread out below us. Maggit's ticklin Ned, tryin to make him laugh. He probably knows he was out of order back there, but it's not his style to just come out and admit it. After a minute or two they start a mess fight, kind o fencin with two old, mossy branches, and Ned accidentally-on-purpose wallops his stick over Maggit's head. It explodes into bits o dead bark and wood-dust. Yeh can tell Ned enjoyed it, and Maggit takes it in good humour. Anthony whoops. Pajo's gimpin along with his hand on his back.

—Yeh OK, Paj?

—Me back's in ruins, Denny, he says. —Think I'm overcompensatin or somethin, cos o me quad.

—We're nearly there now.

We walk a bit further, the sun well up above us now, beamin down just enough warmth that some of it gets through the swirlin wind. I'm just about to pull me runner off and smash the fuck out of a little stone in me shoe that's been slowly drivin me mental when we finally crest the hill. We pass the trees and then the Hellfire Club itself emerges to our left, a huge black shape with its shadow tumblin down the mountain. There are two big windows on the upper floor, black rectangles starin balefully out over Dublin, and a gapin maw for a front entrance. It's surrounded by a little wood on three sides, but there's nothin blockin yer view from the front, where the mountain falls away in a steep incline of loose rock. Yeh can see for miles.

The place is in bits now, like; a wreck, really. Hard to imagine wha it looked like in its heyday.

—Fuckin state o the place, says Maggit. —I could o just walked around St Marks if I'd wanted to see a burnt-out house.

—Jaysis, will yeh give over, says Ned. —Bleedin wreck-the-head today, you are.

Probably somethin to do with Anthony, Maggit's pissy mood. Or Bernadette, rather. Like I said, though, best to leave it. Fuckim, like, as he'd no doubt say himself.

We plonk down our bags. We've a load o drink and enough hash to do us for the night. Ned's always goin on about me smoking hash but sometimes I'm just in the mood for it. Won't be goin near any o that till Anthony's gone, o course. Paula and Teresa are headin back early, and they're takin Anthony with them. We brung some Slimfast with us as well. Slimfast is ideal campin food cos it's cheap and easy to make and fillin.

There are other people up here as well, which isn't unusual. There's a gang o dodgy-lookin teenagers in tracksuits and Nike caps hangin round, and a little troupe o Goths as well, a bit further down, huddled round a rock.

I stand and feel the wind whip around me, close me eyes. For a second or two I think I can hear music, an acoustic guitar bein strummed, maybe, but when I open me eyes there's nothin, sight or sound.

Paula and Teresa and Anthony are gone. Ned flaps out an oul blanket and lays it on the ground while Maggit licks some skins and carefully fixes up a joint. He lights up and takes a long drag.

—Man, that's some stuff, he says, his face contorted. He hands it over to me and I inhale a lungful.

Fuck sake.

It starts to hit me straight away; me head feels light and me vision goes a bit funny.

—Where the fuck did yeh get this mad shite? says Maggit.

—Off Tommy, says Pajo.

I hand it back over, me hand shakin.

—Mad fuckin stuff, that, I say. —I'm fuckin spaced already.

—Amateur, says Maggit. His already gaunt cheeks hollow and the tip o the joint glows a deeper orange as he pulls on it. He shakes his head and grins. Sinead takes a drag next. Smoke billows from her nose and she closes her eyes.

—Jesus, she says.

Ned looks at her, concerned.

—Yeh alright love, yeah?

Sinead nods.

—Excellent, she says, and smiles a wide, warm smile.

Sinead hands the joint to Ned. Ned looks at it and hands it to Pajo. I crack open a can and take a drink, leanin back into the cavity-ridden rock behind us.

—D'yiz know wha happened to it? I say.

All faces turn to me. I hadn't planned on sayin anythin; it just popped out.

—Wha d'yeh mean? says Ned.

I scratch me chin. It's bristly. Haven't shaved in a few days.

—Em, the Club like. The place was burnt out years ago. D'yiz know wha happened to it?

—G'wan so, says Sinead.

—It went up in flames, like. Years ago. It was –

—Where'd yeh hear this? says Maggit.

—Just know, I say.

—G'wan, Denny, says Sinead.

I take a sip from me can. —OK. So just imagine, right, that the place is still in action, yeah? Yeh get fellas and girls comin up from the city every weekend for dances and gamblin and all this. Exclusive though, it's not just commoners boppin up here, this is top o the range hedonism, upper classes only like. Anyway . . . actually, did yiz know this place was named the Hellfire Club cos o some fella called Jack St Ledger?

Headshakes and shrugs all round.

—Yeah, well, he was this Satanist fella. He founded this cabal called –

Maggit laughs.

—Cabal?

—Yeah, a cabal. A secret society like. They were called the Hellfire Club and they met up here. They were Satanists supposedly. Although mostly they just came up here and got drunk and high and –

—So we're carryin on a grand tradition? says Ned, obviously delighted.

—Suppose so, yeah. Although these saps were readin the Satanic Bible and all the rest, yeh know? Evokin the Great Horned One and all this shite. So anyway the satanic ties became more and more, like, tenuous or wharrever, as

231

time went on, till all they were doin was comin up here to play cards and dance and ride and wha have yeh. They went like the clappers apparently, with all these mad drugs and that. They were on laudanum and opium, smokin stuff. Injectin cocaine. Everythin.

—Injectin cocaine?

Maggit, again.

—Yeah. They used to do that years ago. Sherlock Holmes did that. And before yeh say, I know Sherlock Holmes isn't real, but that's wha he did in one o the books. So it's all goin grand anyway until one night this scruffy little fella turns up lookin for a game o cards.

I look round. Everyone's eyes are on me.

—Well anyway yer man has money so they let him play. They think he'll be a piece o piss, just some workin class eejit or somethin after stumblin into some cash. Course in the end he cleans the place out like, he's fuckin untouchable.

—So who's this fella? says Maggit. —Some kind o demon or somethin?

—Hang on will yeh? Fuck sake. So yer man's a total pro, yeah? And everyone's broke in a couple o hours. Course these snobby pricks aren't impressed with a smelly gobshite beatin them on their home turf so they hold out on him like, tell him to fuck off back to his coal shed. Now, yer man —

—Coal shed? says Maggit.

—Yeah. Well wharrever like. His hovel then. Anyway yer man just sits there and takes the insults. Not a bother on him. He just says, I'll be paid one way or the other, and he gets up and leaves and whumph! The table they were playin on shoots up in flames and in minutes the whole place is burnin. Totally blazin like. The doors and windows are all jammed shut and they can't get out. The whole lot o them are burnt to death and the place was left like . . .

I point at the Club.

— . . . that. Just a burnt-out shell.

—And wha about yer man? The smelly fella? says Maggit.

—Well, a youngfella and youngwan were comin up the hill, on the very same path we took like, and they saw yer man comin back down. Thing was, he was over in them fields there . . . the ones with all the rocks and that in them. Treacherous. And he was skippin along, hoppin and jumpin, cool as yeh like. Totally nimble and that. He was . . .

I stop. Bollix. I watch me audience, watch them watchin me, wonderin where I'm goin.

—He was wha? said Maggit.

—He was . . . kind o . . . it was kind o goatish like, the way he was movin. Skippin like. Actually, look . . . I was supposed to say earlier that someone saw his feet under the table and they were hooves.

Me moment in the limelight and I'm after ballsin it up. Class, Denny; well done.

—I knew he was some kind o demon fella, says Maggit. —It was obvious like.

—Well you can tell the stories next time then Dickens. Yeah?

Sinead laughs. Ned's smilin and Maggit's kind o scowlin, the way he does. I hop up.

—I'm goin for a slash, I say, as much to flee the scene o me botched tale as to relieve me bladder. There's a corner in one o the rooms in the Club where everyone pisses. I pass the Goths and duck under the blackened lintel and into the Club. It's fuckin manky. Beer cans everywhere.

Bits o blanket and crisp packets. Totally filthy. The walls are covered in graffiti. So and so loves so and so. Blah-blah was here, such and such a year. Must o seen thousands come and go, this place. DEAD DUBLIN BY NIGHT is scrawled over one o the walls in yellow paint. I head up the scummy stairs and into the big room on the left-hand side. There's a corner at the front that's smelly and visibly stained. I walk over and unzip. Splashy-splashy. There's a window next to it and I can see Ned and Sinead and Maggit and Pajo sprawled out on the blanket in the deepenin dark. Sinead's drinkin a mug o Slimfast. Smoke's curlin up from the new joint in Pajo's hand. And there's Dublin again, spread out in front o me. Looks tiny, really, when yeh can see all that water out there as well.

I'm a bit unsteady on me feet from the drink and the smoke. Bit frazzled, like. Makes the shadows seem somehow full. And then out o nowhere I feel a kind o chill on me. Like somethin's in the room with me. Visions of a runty, hairy face. Clip-clop on the stone floor and music somewhere behind it. Me spine comes alive and I turn and piss onto me runners.

Nothin there.

Fuck.

Stories though, man. The way they work on yeh. They're a kind o spell, aren't they? Or a prayer, maybe, some o them. An article o faith. How the fuck else can yeh make sense o things, like? Yer fucked without them. There has to be meanin. It's not just all fuckin . . . like . . . evolution or wharrever. Cells and impulses. There's got to be stories as well. This happened and then this happened and then this happened. And it all meant this.

It all meant this.

★

We get utterly wrecked in the lengthenin shadow o the Hellfire Club. By the early hours o the mornin Dublin's a puzzle o tiny lights in a sea o nothin below us. Everyone's in ruins, dead to the world. The teenagers are long gone. The Goths got pissed off with our singin and scarpered an hour or so ago. It gets cold – freezin, like – so we head into the Club. I wrap Ned and Sinead in the blanket and they fall asleep like one big bulky two-headed creature. Pajo follows me and snuggles up beside them like a pup.

—I'm wasted, says Maggit, back out beside the rock. —I'm a fuckin loser. I'm a loser, Denny. Amn't I? A complete fuckin cunt, a sad fuckin sack o shite.

—Shurrup, I say, and lead him upstairs, the two of us slurrin and stumblin. I plonk him down in a corner under the window.

—Night, night, I say.

He's frownin in his sleep.

I make me way into the other room. The one with the spine o the ancient chimney. So dark, here. Me head's spinnin. There's a draught whooshin down the flume, clean and cold. Patchouli. And then I get that feelin again, me spine hoppin. I knew I would, somehow; knew this feelin would come back. I stand there, for ages it seems. Dunno wha the fuck I'm doin. I press me face to the wall and close me eyes. I run me palms along the bumpy, grimy stones, then turn round in circles and laugh and come back to the chimney, sink to me knees on the shitty cruddy ground, compelled, and peer up the flume . . . up, up and into the inky tunnelled blackness above me. Stars in a small blue-black square. Smell of old soot and coal. Jesus, can yeh imagine wha it would have been like, burnin to death

235

here all them years ago? Fuckin horrific, man. Faces slidin from skulls. Skin bubblin and cookin. Hoofs clip-cloppin outside.

I turn on me phone and it says that I have two more missed calls. Both from Shane. I can't believe the fuckin prick is actually tryin to throw us out. Shane and Gino, it's like . . . It's like there's somethin wild in them. Some mad and ancient impulse. Even now that they're older and they've wives and jobs, it's still there. They were mental when they were younger. Proper lunatics. Shane was always a bit more savvy and Gino that much more savage, but the two o them were off their heads.

Probably the worst of it was over Gino's foal. I was about twelve at the time. I was arsin round in the fields on me own. There used to be loads o fields like that years ago. I knew Gino's mare was after havin her foal and I wanted to see it. I remember marchin through high grass and duckin under barbed wire and cuttin the heads off thistles with the swish of a branch I broke off a dead tree. In me mind I was miles from home and years ago, in some older Ireland. Those fields went on for miles and miles – they might as well have gone on forever. I passed a burnt-out car with the door hangin open like the broken wing o some huge and squat mechanical bird. After years o wanderin I found the field I was after. The horses were at the far end, a huge oak tree above them. I marched up and they whinnied and shifted their weight and then I saw it. The foal. It was dead. Its mother was standin over it, nudging it, and it was dead and shorn of its mane and tail and covered in all colours o paint and there was a steel rod skewered through its eye. The sun was castin a shadow across it like a sundial and it said three o'clock. Three o'clock, past the time me ma told me to be back for me dinner although that didn't matter anymore. It took me a while to realise I was cryin.

I was still cryin when I told Shane. I don't know how they found out who did it. I don't even know if they were sure themselves. Shane and Gino got their mates together. They said I had to come with them. Me da knew what they were up to. I remember it in snatches after that. Gino slappin the hurley against his palm, the same one he left in the house a few years ago, tellin me that, even though I was fuck all use in a scrap, someone had to have a weapon in the house. I was still wearin me Undertaker T-shirt and me shorts from earlier that day and I was shiverin with cold or fear or both. The first fella wasn't at home but they found him at the corner by Finches and I could smell the vinegar off his chips. A few of his mates tried to jump in but this was Shane and Gino and mad Philip Butler who could lift concrete slabs over his head, and they left them layin. The fella said he didn't do it but it didn't matter, he probably did, his chips scattered on the path and mashed into the ground. They pulled him after them through the estate and Philip Butler banged on a door. A fella answered and Gino punched him and dragged him out by the hair. His face was red with blood, his nose smashed.

They dragged them to the fields. They were me brothers and me brothers' mates but they were fuckin terrifyin; heads shaved close to their skulls and their hurleys lyin against their shoulders and all o them dead quiet. The two fellas were cryin, blubberin tears and snot and blood. I was thinkin fuck this fuck this run the fuck away and Shane put his hand on me shoulder and looked at me and I walked on. We passed the burnt car in the dark.

They brought them to the top o the field and the horses stood and parted and cantered away. The fella from outside Finches fell to his knees and started screamin and shoutin and Philip Butler brought his fist down on him. Gino walked up to the other one.

—Yeh sick fuckin cunt yeh, he said. —Yeh fuckin –

And then the kicks and punches rained down and I thought I was gonna faint but I didn't. I thought about the shadow on the dead foal and of all things the smell o vinegar and I watched it happen, watched the event that'd become Cullen myth, a story told but not fully believed but I was there, a child and a proof and I watched and felt me underpants dampen with piss, watched them pull the lads' shirts over their heads, their chests heavin and skinny-pale as they tore the boots and jeans off them and shaved them bald, their nakedness complete except the paint that Shane slopped onto them, oozed into their eyes and ears and mouths, mixin green and red and then up stepped Gino and out came the time-tellin bar – a pain for a pain, a hurt for a hurt and their screams in the dark like shocks o sheer white, sheerest, purest white – and I turned and ran and ran and ran forever.

★

There's someone here. Jesus, I fell asleep on me fuckin back, the night sky in the flume above me. There's someone . . . I can fuckin feel it. For real; in the dark. I think o me da in his armchair and the boundin devil that burned this place years ago and for a second they're one and the same. It's a mental, horrible thought – me da sittin in the dark, grinnin, his face twisted and malevolent. This is it, man, I've totally fuckin lost it. I've –

—I am meeting skinny Santa Claus, no? You bring me presents?

I scramble onto me arse as a laughin face bends down towards me.

—Are you OK, man?

The voice is odd, otherworldly. Whoever owns it squats down beside me. There's an exhalation o sharp, minty breath.

—I didn't mean to scare you, man.

The shadow puts a hand on me shin. I jerk me leg away.

—You like parties, man?

—Wha?

—You like to party? Listen man, don't freak out.

The shadow stands and walks back to the window. Or dances rather, its head noddin. It holds up its hand and gestures at the night outside the window.

—Listen man. You like it?

I can hear voices outside the Club, talkin and singin and whoopin. The shadow laughs and stamps its foot, throws out an arm, arched, a spectral matador. I can see fireflies – nah, they're sparks – sparks and rags o flame tumblin upwards, past the window, twistin into the night. Wha the fuck kind o music is that? Singin and wild fiddlin and a guitar bashed rhythmically; a crazy, intoxicatin blend o punk and Cossack folk.

The shadow twirls against the window, hummin. Then it walks back to me, holds out its hand. I take it and it hauls me up and pats me on the shoulder.

—I didn't mean to scare you man.

—Yeah, I say, wantin to say more. The arse o me jeans and the back of me shirt are cold, slightly damp.

—You wanna join?

—I'm here with mates, I say, as a kind o veiled warnin; like*, don't fuck with me, I'm not alone.*

—Take a look, man, says the shadow. It gestures for me to come to the window.

—Look.

I follow him and peer out the window, me palms on the ancient frame, the stones cool, slightly lumpy. Our fire is huge and bustlin, and there's a small crowd o people round it, dancin and drinkin and playin. I can see the fiddle player, an oldish fella wearin a flat, multicoloured cap, his face lit up by the firelight. A woman with pinned-up black hair is sittin on a rock, a djembe between her thighs, slappin out a wicked, drivin rhythm, her grinnin face to the purple sky. Men and women are stampin their feet, clappin. Two men with red hair are playin guitar. They look identical.

—Look, says the shadow again, pointin.

Pajo's down there, a small, thin shape with his lank green fringe plastered behind his left ear, cheeks hollowin as he sucks on a cigarette. He's tappin his feet and noddin his head, gaunt and smilin, lookin completely at home.

—Your friend is a funny guy, says the shadow.

—Yeah, I say again. —He's wired to the moon. His name's Pajo.

—You want to party?

—Yeah.

Why did I say yeah? This is fuckin surreal, man. Fuckin hell.

—I'm Andriy.

He holds out his hand. We shake. His grip is light and he tickles me palm with his fingertips as he draws his hand away.

—I'm Denny.

—I know man. Your friend said to me. You OK?

—Cool, yeah. Bit spaced like. I'm not dreamin am I?

—No. You a somnambulist?

I shake me head.

—Well then, you're not dreaming. This is a great spot, says the shadow. —You been here before now?

—Nah. Well, actually . . . yeah, sorry. Few times. Gets a bit . . . like . . . crowded in the city, yeh know? Yeh feel like yer trapped in or somethin? Ever get that? I feel fuckin stuck.

Jesus, wha the fuck am I on about? Givin him me fuckin life story here.

Andriy nods. —Look, there's always a way out man. There's traps on the streets, you go underground. Yeah? Traps in your room you go through the roof. You know? You get out man. Simple. Just get out.

—Yeah. Spose.

We walk downstairs, me pattin the walls, Andriy seemingly unhindered by the dark. I pass Maggit on the way – he's still asleep, wrapped up in me green sleepin bag, a huge caterpillar with a man's dreamin head – and Ned and Sinead, who're sleepin as well, in the corner. I step out o the Club, duckin under the low, lopsided lintel, and Pajo and a woman in a loose, blue wool jumper turn round and hold up their hands, yellin. A clean breeze hits me.

Andriy takes a few steps forward, twirls and bows.

—This is Denny, he says, his arm held out in my direction. People cheer. One o the redheaded men hands

Andriy an acoustic guitar covered in stickers and graffiti. Andriy takes it and starts to play, slappin the guitar rather than strummin, skippin on the spot and a hum buildin deep in his throat, findin words I don't recognise. The old fiddler picks up the rhythm, then the djembe player. People link arms and kick out their legs, dancin. Andriy stalks through the crowd and someone hands me a bottle o Tiger. I look at it, the amber liquid, the tiny bubbles, then lift it to me lips and drink and dance, dance and drink, the night long and manic, full o mad voices and mad rhythm and Andriy at the centre always, clappin and playin and howlin and laughin, his eyes bright and a stream o songs and stories on his lips; people, places, crazy getaways and doomed and drunken loves. The huge dark around us a nothingness complete and we go through it, through the roof of the night sky, bottle after bottle, dance after dance, this night unending.

★

They're still here the next mornin, the fire burned to glowin embers and the new sun swellin up from the Irish Sea below us, immense and pale.

Most o them are immigrants. Oren, the fiddle player, is from Israel. He's in his fifties and he's wearin loose-fittin, shapeless clothes, in reds and purples and deep oranges. His beard and ponytail are streaked with grey. Wojtek, Magda and Lukasz are Poles workin in Ireland to pay for apartments and college fees back home. Shavo's a zookeeper from Armenia. His eyes are nearer black than brown and his dark, curly hair bounces minutely when he speaks. He'd been in charge of an ancient brown bear in Yerevan zoo, a bear whose health we must o toasted a dozen times last night. There's even a few Irish; two brothers from Donnybrook (Nik and James; both young and redheaded, both baldin) and the djembe player, Linda (she looks foreign but she's only from Lucan, not far up the road from me). They're in a band.

The fire's smoulderin away, charred branches pokin from the embers, gnarled and blackened and bonelike. We sit in a circle and watch the fire. I'm fuckin exhausted but happy, like I used to feel after I came home from a day's graft on the sites; wrecked but content, me body gorgeously, languidly floppy, the bones loose and nearly oozy. I don't even have a hangover, which is unusual for me; not a jellyfish in sight.

The Hellfire Club looms up behind us, thick with history, covered in lichen and graffiti. Lovely view, like, in the mornin. Pajo's sittin next to me on a tasselled blanket, his eyes red-rimmed. Maggit's still asleep; he never stirred. Sinead and Ned made their way home about an hour ago, the two o them lookin dishevelled but happy enough. Ned's a gentle enough fella anyway but when he's around Sinead he's even more so, like he's scared she'll crack. Pajo kicks a branch towards the fire. Nik and James are sittin on a log, Nik holdin Oren's violin to his ear and pluckin at the strings. Magda and Lukasz are asleep, Magda's head on Wojtek's lap, Wojtek twinin her blonde hair round his index finger. Oren sits and smokes a thin cigar. Linda's sittin next to Andriy, the gypsy gesticulatin wildly as he speaks, his voice low and musical. Somethin about Australia, I think, somethin about the aborigines, some custom o theirs he'd fallen comically foul of. Linda laughs with her hand on her mouth.

He's a fuckin looper, this Andriy fella; proper fuckin head-the-ball. Even in the light o mornin he seems a bit unreal, a serial illegal immigrant out to make the world drink and dance, then puke like dogs. I vaguely remember him lecturin earlier this mornin on the empowerin nature o disbelief, sayin that, among other things, he doesn't believe in God, borders or drinkin wine from glasses. Apparently, by disbelievin in God, he becomes one himself, as the pinnacle of evolution; by disbelievin in borders, he's a citizen of the world and everywhere is home; and, regards the wine glass thing, it's the bottle or fuck-all, and by that reasonin hobos and down-and-outs are more worthy than kings. Sound by me, like; less washin up. He's wearin a close-fittin military jacket with the sleeves rolled up, a bracelet o coloured beads on his left wrist. His black jeans are frayed at the ends and his canvas runners are scuffed. His eyes have that strange Slavic quality, by turns madly alive and comic and then suddenly distant, the irises like pearls or somethin, swelled over generations from the harsh, raw grit of Balkan history. Magda, Wojtek and Lukasz are the same. Andriy's fuckin moustache is a bit much, though; handlebars on a fella that can't be more than a year or two older than meself is a definite no-no.

I like them though, this gang of oddballs. I think it's the sheer force o their determination to enjoy wharrever the fuck they're doin. I hadn't really realised that I've stopped doin that meself, that I've let meself drift so fuckin far, let meself get so fuckin stuck. Yeah, I'm out drinkin with me mates and that, but there's, like . . . a desperation or somethin to it. I'm runnin and gettin nowhere at the same time. I mean, wha am I doin with me life? I went to Wales cos I was feelin how I'm feelin right now . . . fuckin . . . like, aimless or wharrever. I remember feelin, when I first left for Wales, that I was in control. And I feel anythin but in control now.

—Yeh hungry Denny? says Pajo. Pajo's taken off his jacket and he's sittin with his arms out slightly from his body, his palms flat on the ground. The broad tips of his big, crusty boots are pointin at the sky, twitchin slightly to some unheard beat.

—Yeah, a bit. Are you?

—Kinda. Here, I think there's a few bars in me bag. Snickers or somethin. Hang on.

He stands up and brushes down his jeans. He walks over to the Club, disappearin into the dark.

The sunrise is gorgeous, the sun and the water and the city below us. The sea stretchin beyond sight, grey and smudgy at the horizon.

Pajo comes back with his bag, followed by a wary-lookin Maggit. Maggit eyes the unfamiliar faces round the fire and sits beside me and Pajo. Pajo hands me a Mars Bar.

—No Snickers, he says.

—Thanks Paj.

I was never a big Mars fan but I wolf it. Starvin to fuckin death here, like. The sun's warmin me shoulders. Nik, the sun glintin off the oddly-placed bald spot near the top of his head, saws a horrible, squealin note from Oren's violin. Oren winces and laughs softly.

—Jesus, says Nik. —Sorry about that lads.

We sit there for a while longer, chattin away. The sun nearly sends me to sleep; Pajo nudges me and I jump. There's a line o crows on the roof o the Club, squawkin away, utterly black against the clean mornin sky. Maggit throws a stone up and they fly, feathers tumblin.

—Yeh could o hit one o them, says Pajo.

Maggit shrugs.

We pack up, Oren kickin dirt over the fadin embers o the fire. Shavo collects the rubbish and stuffs it into a plastic Aldi bag. Linda slings the djembe over her back. She has a real nice way about her. She was in another world last night while she was playin, proper gettin into it. I couldn't really say anythin to her when she was like that, though. Seems kind o intrusive or somethin.

We make our way down Montpellier Hill, James (or Nik; it's hard to tell at a distance) slippin and slidin on his arse, rippin a hole in his jeans. There isn't room in the van for me and Maggit and Pajo. We could o squashed two of us in but we decide to make our own way home. I exchange phone numbers with them, then Andriy slaps me on the back and winks, before pullin me to him and givin me a firm, brisk hug.

—Remember, my friend; through the fucking roof.

Then he winks again, bows, and hops into the van. Wojtek heaves the door shut and the van pulls off, crunchin through the gravel.

—Wha did yeh think o them loopers? says Maggit.

—I thought they were alright. Did you not? I thought they were sound.

Maggit shrugs and spits into the dust, then starts the long walk home.

When we reach Tallaght we drop into a greasy spoon and I eat two breakfasts. Maggit eats two and a half. Pajo's supposed to be a vegetarian but he scarfed down a few sausages with his cereal and toast.

—Sure, Srila Rupa Gosvami wouldn't begrudge me a decent breakfast.

I'm impressed he got all that out without chokin on his bran flakes.

—Who the fuck is that? says Maggit. —Some holy fuckin gobshite I suppose.

—He, like, wrote the stuff that A.C. Bhaktivedanta Swami Praphupada translated. In ancient times or wharrever. Years ago, anyway.

—Do you practise them names?

—Yeah.

I stuff an egg, sausage, rasher and white puddin sandwich into me mouth. Maggit shakes his head and gulps at his tea.

★

I say see yiz to Maggit and Pajo and hop off the 76 on the Neilstown Road. Dyin for a piss, like: too much tea. I trudge across the green, skirtin the huge blackened patch where the kids had their Halloween bonfire, and whack the garden gate until it opens.

I stick me head into the sittin room. Paula and Teresa are asleep on the sofa, Paula's legs stickin out under a pink duvet. It's still only early by their standards, about twelve. There's a girl with studs in her nose and ears asleep on the armchair, her huge boots propped up on the coffee table, and a small, thin fella – he only looks about eighteen – conked out on the floor, an overfilled ashtray inches from his snoozin, droolin head.

I hop up the stairs three at a time and push at the bathroom door. It doesn't open, though; there's somethin blockin it. I push against it with me shoulder, slowly – there might be someone asleep in there, which wouldn't be that unusual, especially since Paula had people over last night. I get it open enough so I can squeeze in sideways, which is to say it's not open that much at all cos I'm a skinny prick. In future I'm gonna –

Fuck.

Fuckin fuck fuck fuck.

Jesus it's Kasey. Oh fuck. He's on the ground and his legs are up against the door. His face is blue. He's topless and fuckin hell fuck this fuck this his eyes are open. His nipples small and dark. The ridges of his ribs. There's an empty pill bottle in the sink, and pills semi-dissolved, small bubbly masses, by the slow drippin o the warm water tap. I hear a car startin outside, a crow cawin. Someone's mobile ringin downstairs. Paula's, a polyphonic version o The Simpsons theme tune.

Fuck this. Fuck this.

I back out and walk to me bedroom and sit on the swivel chair, next to the window. I pick up the wastepaper basket and set it on me lap. Then up come me breakfasts in a thick hot stew.

TO WHOM IT MAY CONCERN

First off please believe that I am very sorry for all the trouble I have caused. I know that I have been a worry to my mother and to my sisters. Whats Kasey up to? Is he OK? Etc. It must have been hard having a mad eejit like me on your minds all the time. I dont want to be a worry anymore. I want to go out while Im on top (joke). I miss Jackie and maybe I will see her again on the other side. Its supposed to be great in heaven but maybe they wont let me in. Im a good liar although I suppose St Peter is used to the likes of me waffling on. "Yes yes, I saved a bus of nuns and orphans from falling off a cliff, that was me." Etc. In heaven they probably have lie detectors like the Jeremy Kyle show though, which are 96% accurate. We'll see.

Anyway. Live long and prosper.

I love you ma, da, Sorcha, Gillian, Elise and Sarah. I hope you knew all along.

PS. Please take my van, Denzerino. I dont know if this is legally binding but the keys are on the window ledge. It should make up for the car. Make sure you give it a good clean.

PPS. I'll give you a shout Pajo and tell you what its like.

KC

THE SAME OUL TORTURE

I park the van up by the flats and walk through the rain. Dunno where I'm headin. Just wanted to get out. Been awake for two nights on the trot. We started in one o Paula's friend's houses in town, then made our way back to someone's gaff out towards Portmarnock and then back to ours. I'm knackered but I know I won't sleep, I popped a few o Pajo's pills last night and I feel . . . I dunno, I just keep walkin, wanderin. On and on. I fuckin hate this feelin. This has to stop, man. This really has to fuckin stop. Jesus.

Past net cafes and pubs and Dr Quirky's, the statue o Jim Larkin to me left, rain splashin on his broad shoulders, his arms lifted to the sky, implorin a proletariat that no longer gives a fuck to rise up, make a stand, be counted. I turn down Middle Abbey Street and look in the window o Chapters for a couple o minutes and then head for Liffey Street. Past the Hags with the Bags and the Woollen Mills and a fella with no shoes huddled in a doorway, sleepin, head back, his hands on his knees, the soles of his feet black. I stop at the promenade for a while, watchin the rain on the Liffey. Town is completely different when it's rainin. Dead empty, dead still. I light up a cigarette and lean against the low wall and watch. Watch the river, the rain, the grey sky. The far off sound of a busker. Me body slowly pulsin, thumpin, breathin, heavin.

Slowin down.

★

I step out o the rain and into the church hallway, then into the church proper and the place expands above me, the roof like the ribcage o some huge beast and the few people here silent on the pews, the altar a huge and ornate configuration at the front, draped with cloth and decked with candles. Smell of incense and damp clothes. I cut through the pews and head for the side door, the one that leads upstairs to the tea room, a little place above the church for the Holy Joes to have a bit o cake and a natter. Great for penniless pricks like me. I feel like a pilgrim with me hood still up so I throw it back and shake the rain off o me jacket as I wind me way up the stairs. Whitewashed walls and concrete, echo-y steps. Little leaflets and posters tacked up, kids' drawins and stuff for the scouts and jumble sales. Then through the door at the top and into the tea room.

Me phone rings as I step inside and I have a quick look. It says UNKNOWN NUMBER. Bollix to that, like; I hate answerin the phone when I don't know who it is. It might be Shane callin from work or somethin. I stick it back in me pocket and dig out a couple euro and get in line behind a couple of old women. Somethin about this place. All this faith. The oulwan in front o me lifts up one o the glass covers and takes a caramel slice and her hand is all spotty. Might have one o them meself. The caramel slices, like; not the hand. And only one sixty as well. Or one o them little scones.

I lift up the cover and plop two scones onto a saucer. The oulwan in front o me dips into her handbag and pays for her stuff and then turns and smiles at me and heads for her table. Somethin behind her smile, though. Not sure wha.

—I'll just have these, I say to yer man who's servin. He's a strange-lookin fella, big-faced, kinda like a cross between Sam Allardyce and a harmless, Jim Henson troll. Young, as well. Eyes big and unblinkin. Bit slow, like, I think.

—Would you like a drink, sir? he says.

—Actually, yeah. Sorry. A tea, please. Milk and no sugar.

He smiles, then looks up at some hidden price list above him and mouths a sum. So strange, this fella; so odd and serene.

—Two euro and ten, sir, he says.

—Cool. Thanks.

I hand him the money and he counts it and I smile and nod and take me tray and head for the table in the far corner, the one beside the little stained-glass window. Great spot, this. I plonk down the tray and stir me tea and the sound o the rain on the glass is gorgeous, tiny tributaries weavin and warpin behind the reds and blues of angels and saints. I take a gulp o me tea, cut and butter me scones. The hubbub o hushed conversation, rain on the window. I poke at a stray currant on me saucer. The walls are old, here; old ornate walls made of a dark and dull wood. Probably oak but I don't know anythin about wood. Failed fuckin woodwork at school, like.

I sit and watch the old people eat and talk. I can't believe Kasey's dead. I can see him, curled up on the tiles in the bathroom. Dead. After I gave me statement the bangharda asked me if I needed to see someone, to talk things over. A shrink, like. Nah, I said. I'm grand. It was nice of her to ask, I suppose.

I finish me tea and buy another one, yer man still smilin and when I'm back in me seat I take a peek over at him and he's more troll-like than ever. Not slaggin or anythin. Just the way he looks, a dark shape in his hole in the wall, an outcast troll from somewhere gone or never there. Some mad and storied place.

I'm takin a gulp o me tea when Tommy Power comes up the stairs. Never would've expected to see someone like Tommy in a place like this, which is part o the reason I'm here. The collar of his bomber jacket is right under his chin and his thinnin brown hair's plastered to his forehead. Not in the humour of him, to be honest. He clocks me straightaway though, and nods and winks and grabs some cake and a mug o tea and pays and comes back over, soaked and grinnin.

—How's things, Den?

—Grand, Tommy. Yerself?

—Not too bad. Cept for the bleedin rain.

An oulwan a few tables over shoots us a look. Tommy doesn't notice.

—Oul cheapo cake, wha? he says.

—It's nice.

—And the bleedin head on yer man over there. Fuckin Bo' Selecta, like.

—Wha yeh up to? I say.

—Just off work. I've to meet me missus in here in a few minutes.

I take another sip o me tea.

—Isn't it fuckin terrible about Kasey all the same? says Tommy.

—It's sad, yeah.

—I'd be headin down with yiz for the funeral meself only I'd be hung by the bollix if I was off the scene for a few days. Where's this the funeral is, up the North isn't it?

—Donegal.

—Donegal. That's right. Nah, too much on down here, Denny. I know that sounds bad, but sure wha can yeh do? I'm up to me bollix.

—Don't worry about it.

—When is it?

—Not for a while. Next week.

—His poor ma, like. Doesn't he have sisters and that as well?

—Four, I think. Pajo was sayin.

Like yeh give a fuck, Tommy. I suddenly feel offended. Kasey's time on earth has come and gone and hardly anyone's noticed or cared. I know that's obvious and there's millions like him but I'd never really thought about it, not properly. I needed promptin from a shithead like Tommy to realise it.

—Lot o fuckin tears there, says Tommy —Lot o fuckin tears. He shakes his head. —Can yeh smoke in here?

—Wha d'you think?

—Yeah, suppose. Here, yeh workin yet?

—Nah.

—Yeh lookin for a job?

—Ehhh . . . dunno.

—They're lookin for people down my way. Easy few bob, Den.

—Yeah?

I try to sound both noncommittal and curious. To be honest I don't care how easy the job is, but I'm bleedin stuck now.

—Yeah, says Tommy. —Simple. Just doin the security in Landsdowne Road. Yeh know them fellas with the big yellow jackets at the football matches? It's just that. Just watchin the game.

—Cool, I say to me mug, and a pigeon lands on the ledge on the other side o the glass. I can hear it cooin and its shape is all blurry and distorted.

Tommy jerks a thumb at the window. —Still got the loft?

—Yeah. Nothin in it though. Gino has them all out his own back.

—Course, yeah.

Tommy slurps at his tea then leans in towards me.

—Thing is, Den, the pay's not great. But –

He shoots a glance left and right. Looks dodgy as fuck, like.

—Yeh can supplement it dead easy. Sellin stuff. Know wha I mean?

—In a stadium?

—Yeah. Teenagers and that. Just a bit o blow, like. Nothin hard.

I look into me mug, at the dregs o tea and milk, the chip in the handle. Then back at me would-be conspirator.

—Nah, Tommy. Seriously, man. I don't deal.

Tommy sits back.

—Up to you. Yeh can just go straight, anyway. Just do the security. And we're playin some shitty eastern European side next week so we've a decent chance o gettin a result.

I kind o shrug, like I'm mullin it over. I should just tell him no, straight out like.

—Here, do us a favour though, will yeh? says Tommy. —Mention it to Maggit and Pajo and that. Loads o places goin. Serious. Mostly fuckin Polish and that workin there, talkin fuckin gobbledegook, could do with a few locals yeh know?

I nod.

—So will yeh say it to the rest?

—Yeah, I'll say it when I see them.

—And here, Denny. Tommy goes all quiet again. He scratches the side of his nose. —Yeh didn't hear anythin about a load o charlie that went walkin, did yeh?

—Charlie?

—Yeah. Cocaine, like. Sneachta. No?

I shake me head.

—No. Yeh sure?

—Why? What's up?

—Ah, nothin that won't keep. Sure keep yer ears peeled anyway, yeah?

—Yeah.

Tommy looks up and he makes a face like he's dyin or somethin. He nods his head.

—There's the missus, he says.

Tommy's wife is standin at the top o the stairs. She's small and she looks dead unhappy.

Tommy stands up and wipes his hands on his jeans.

—Here, I'll see yeh soon so, Denny, he says. —Good luck. Give us a buzz if there's anythin goin on in the gaff, yeah?

—Yeah. I will, yeah.

Tommy slaps me on the back then turns to his wife. They head down the stairs.

I mop up a few crumbs and listen to the rain again. There's definitely more to Tommy askin me to deal than him bein concerned about me finances. Tommy's not that bad, really, but Dommo and his mad mates are. I hop up and say see yeh to the fella behind the till and smile and nod and leave the clickin cups and the cooin pigeons and take the stairs one at a time.

★

I head down Grafton Street. No particular reason. Me body's still tryin to get rid o those pills I took – I hate the feelin, the horrible shiveriness and a sense that yer body's not yer own. I said to meself I'd stay away from stuff like that after the party but the whole Kasey business is after knockin me off track altogether.

The rain's eased off now and there are a few buskers and performance artists and that linin the street – a young fella doin Beatles covers with his acoustic guitar and a woman standin dead still on a little box, eyes unblinking, her clothes and face all painted silver. I pass them by and cross the road to Stephen's Green. I'm just at the gates when me phone rings again. UNKNOWN NUMBER. Fuck sake. I let it ring out and then it rings again, straight away. Ah, fuck it.

—Hello?

—Hello, Denny?

—Yeah. Who's this?

—It's yer da, Denny.

Fuckin hell. Knew I shouldn't've answered. I haven't spoken to me da since . . .

—Haven't heard from you since the funeral, I say. It sounds like an accusation. Which it is, I suppose.

—Yeh OK, son?

—I'm grand, yeah.

—Yeh drinkin or somethin? Yeh sound a bit –

—I'm fine. What's up?

—I've a bit o news for yeh.

God, me da's stupid fuckin accent. Where does he get it from? He sounds like Ronnie Drew out o The Dubliners. I'm sure he didn't always talk like this.

—Good or bad? I say.

—Good.

—G'wan. Is it about you and Irene?

—Were yeh talkin to someone?

—No. Is it?

—It is, yeah. We're, em . . . we're gonna get married.

—Congratulations.

—Jesus, don't sound too happy.

—Congratulations, wharrever. Well done.

I step into the park. It's fairly empty. I head for the little stream and stand there, a couple o ducks glidin by.

—We'd like yeh to be there, he says.

. . .

. . .

—I . . . I dunno, da.

—This has nothin to do with yer mother, Denny. We're split up years. Yer mother could've gone with someone else if she'd –

—You fuckin left her, da.

. . .

. . .

—Where are yeh now? I say.

258

—The park.

Jesus. Not this one I hope.

—Which park?

—Stephen's Green. Where're you?

—Yeh on yer own?

—Yeah, he says. —Yeh at home?

—Yeah. Well . . . not in the house. Just out.

I start back towards the entrance o the park.

—So will yeh be there, Denny?

—Look da, I dunno. It's too fuckin . . . I dunno. Here, someone I know's callin me, I have to run.

—Have a think about it and give me a shout.

—Bye, I say.

I look at the phone for a few seconds, then slip it back into me pocket. Gettin fuckin married? For fuck sake. The fuckin oulfella, wha? Movin on. I stand by the gate for a minute or so, temptin fate, thinking he's gonna walk by any second. Why the fuck I'm doin this I don't know. I don't wanna see him. No chance. If I did I don't know wha I'd do. Cry or shout or kick or laugh. No fuckin clue. And I don't wanna know, either. He's gone. He made the decision, not me. He's fuckin history.

I take me phone out again, thumb in a text.

SORRY DA, THINK I'LL GIVE IT A MISS. ALL THE BEST WITH IT.

I look at it for a while, me thumb hoverin over SEND. Then I press it and watch until the MESSAGE SENT notification comes up. I don't bother savin the number. I pocket me phone again and start the journey home.

★

259

In the van I start thinkin about me ma. The mad dances and voices she'd do to make me and Paula laugh. She always seemed dead different to other peoples' mas. Other peoples' mas seemed old, but my ma never did. I think of her sittin by the kitchen table, watchin jeans and t-shirts flappin on the line, whole worlds in her eyes. I wondered wha she was thinkin. I often did. She's like me in that way, I suppose. Or I'm like her, always thinkin and wonderin. I remember I was about sixteen and me da had left the year before and I was flickin through the channels on the telly, past MTV and all these crappy music stations, when me ma said:

—Did yeh ever hear o Rory Gallagher?

—Did I ever hear of him?

—Yeah.

—The guitarist, like?

—Yeah.

—Wha about him?

—Ah, I was just wonderin would anyone your age know him.

—He's on the Wall o Fame in Temple Bar with U2 and Sinead O'Connor and The Undertones and that, I said.

—Mmm.

—Why? D'yeh like him?

—A fella I knew years ago was mad into him.

—Yeah?

—Yeah. Thomas. He died a few years ago. Well, I say a few . . . it was probably ten years ago now. More even. He liked me.

—Liked yeh?

—Well, yeh know wha I mean. This was years ago. Before I met yer da. His ma used to be always tryin to get

us together. He was mad into music and he used to write
poems and all this. He wasn't like most o the other fellas
from the estate. He wrote a poem for me. He gave it to yer
auntie Denise and he asked her to give it to me. Denise
read it and she was slaggin him, sayin, God, the state o yer
man, writin poems. She couldn't get her head round it. I
thought it was nice, though.

—Did yiz go out?

—Ah no. He never asked me out or anythin. But I can
see now that he liked me. Well, I knew back then as well,
really. But nothin ever came of it. We were only kids. The
same age as yerself.

—Wha happened to him?

—Ah, he got into drugs and all that. That oul heroin.
He was one o the first. We never knew about AIDS at the
time; he must o used a dirty needle. He got off the drugs
eventually, he got himself together, but he was sick, although
I don't think he knew for a long time. No one knew about
AIDS, any o the facts or anythin. People thought you could
get it by standin too close to someone. I used to think that
meself. I saw him sometimes in Ballyfermot over the years
and he'd always ask about you.

—About me?

—Yeah. I bumped into him one time and you were
only a baby. I had yeh in the pram. He was on a push bike.
He still had his hair long, but it was after goin very grey.
He was with a girl from Ballyfermot and he had a baby of
his own, a girl, the same age as you. He asked me how was
I and all this. Grand, I said. He didn't know he was sick. He
was happy.

—When was the last time yeh saw him?

—Well, I saw him around, like I said. He'd always stop and say hello and how's Denny. Eventually I heard he was sick. It was startin to come out then – loads o the fellas and girls who were on heroin in the eighties were after gettin AIDS. As if the heroin wasn't bad enough on its own. But I had all youse, I had me own life and he had his; I didn't see much of him for a few years and then Denise told me he was dyin. His ma was after bumpin into Denise in Ballyfermot and she said would she ask me to go and see him in St James's hospital, that he only had a few days to live.

—God.

—I didn't know wha to do. I didn't tell yer da; he'd have gone mad. I couldn't believe his ma even remembered me. But I went. I got the bus. His girlfriend and his ma was there, they were in a special room. They have these rooms for families if someone's dyin, with nice chairs and all this. His ma was in an awful state but she was delighted I came. His girlfriend was probably thinkin, who's this? I felt horrible, like I shouldn't be there. Like I was an intruder. His ma gave me a hug and said to his girlfriend that I was an old friend o Thomas and I went in to see him.

—Wha was he like?

—It was terrible. He was old-lookin. He was like an old man. He couldn't see. Me heart was broke lookin at him. I just said, howayeh Thomas, and he smiled. He knew me voice. Howayeh Kate, he said. We didn't say much else. He asked after you, though. I told him you were in school and great at English and Art and he said that was good, he was delighted; he said they were the best to be good at. I just held his hand and kissed his head. I was all over the place when I left.

—D'yeh still think about him now?

—Ah no. Well . . . sometimes, I suppose. Things remind yeh.

—Imagine yeh had o got with him instead o da.

—Ah no.

—I'm just sayin. It's mad.

—Yeah. He was a lovely fella. Very gentle.

—Yid probably have been better off with him. If he was never on drugs and that.

Me da had left a year or so before. He was livin in Inchicore with a woman called Irene. They were carryin on for a while beforehand. I never really liked me da and I hated wha he did on me ma.

—Ah who knows? said me ma. —Sure I'm happy anyway.

—Yeh might o been happier.

Me ma shook her head and smiled. She took a sup of her tea. —I wouldn't have you, Denny, she said.

—Don't be a gobshite, ma, I said. She was embarrassin me. I had a funny relationship with her; it was OK to swear at each other.

—Well, if I'm a gobshite, you're a son of a gobshite, she said, and laughed. —That's worse.

We looked at each other. I remember realisin that I loved her very much, that I loved her to a frightenin degree, puttin the words together in me head with a feelin that'd always been there. That always would be there.

FIRE AND WATER

I feel compelled to go upstairs. I can't help it. I take the steps slowly, and I can feel every muscle in me legs, every sinew and tendon. I have this mad sensation of meself as a mass o tiny bits and parts all pullin together. I get to the top and look at the open bathroom door for a few seconds, look at the floor where Kasey's body was, the tap still runnin, and then I turn and walk down the hall, towards me ma's room. I open the door and go in. It's neat enough, pretty much the same as before she died; the pictures o me and the rest o the kids on the walls, the little jewellery box in front o the mirror. Slaughter's never been in here, nothin bad's ever happened here. I pass by her bed and cross the room to the window.

I look out across the green and the factories and shops are gone. It's like it was years ago, cept there's a two hundred foot tall horse cantering there, tossin its head, its shadow huge, fallin across fully grown trees. It rears up on its hind legs, titanic and wild, and it whinnies and –

★

Glass smashes. Me head's spinnin and I'm still drunk when I sit up on the bed, fully dressed, me T-shirt damp. Me clock says it's quarter past three in the mornin. Don't remember fallin asleep or goin to bed or anythin, everythin's all blurry in me head; visions o Paula and Teresa in me head, a few drinks for Kasey, somethin like that. There's voices comin from downstairs, a mad fuckin commotion. I can hear Paula shoutin. I stumble through the dark to the door, me heart thumpin and me head still spinnin. Me mouth is parchment fuckin dry.

I pull the hurley from under me bed then open the door and step out onto the landin, men's voices below mixin with Paula's and Teresa's and . . . Charly, is it? Yeah, I remember now – Charly called round and we had a few drinks in honour o Kasey cos the girls won't be able to make the funeral. I hurry downstairs, trippin on the last step and fallin into the coat rack, then into the sittin room and fuckin hell there's a huge hole in the front window, the night air blowin in and glass everywhere, glitterin. Paula and Teresa and Charly are standin at the opposite end o the room.

—The fuck's goin on?

—Someone put the window through, says Teresa, her face drained o colour.

There's people in the garden. Teresa starts pokin at her mobile, her hands shakin. There's shoutin and laughter from outside.

—Get that fuckin jungle bunny out here!

Charly looks terrified and Paula looks furious.

—The fuckin bastards, she says. —If they think they can fuckin scare me in me own home –

She heads for the hallway.

—Paula, wha are yeh –

But she opens the front door and steps outside. I follow her, the night cold pricklin me bare chest and arms, me

265

heart goin a hundred and ninety. There's a gang o fellas, six or seven o them, laughin and shoutin in the garden. Slaughter's with them, the mental fuck, with a mad, unhinged smile on his face and a can o Bulmers in his hand.

—Here's the fuckin dyke, he says, his mates cheerin him on. —And here's her brother. Although I'd say he'd fuckin love to get into her knickers. Wouldn't yeh Denny?

I wanna say somethin but nothin comes out. I'm fuckin shittin here. I grip the hurley till it hurts. I shouldn't be holdin this, though. Gino or Shane should. Wha the fuck use am I?

—Sure the last time I saw this cunt, says Slaughter, to his mates I suppose but lookin straight at me, —I was on the job with this fuckin cracker of a bird, had her bent over the bed and everythin, she was gaggin for it. And who should walk in only Captain fuckin Farrell here. Probably watchin through the fuckin keyhole the little –

—Get the fuck out o this garden, says Paula.

Slaughter takes a sup from his Bulmers. —Get that fuckin nigger hooer out o this fuckin estate more like, says Slaughter, almost gleefully. —Or here, tell me, d'yeh like them black?

Paula looks at me, then turns back to the lads. —Were youse lot born fuckin male or did yiz get yer dicks off the medical card? she says.

The lads whoop and laugh. I recognise another couple o faces; the two fellas from the bus that time, still in their blue and red bomber jackets, like they've never changed since that day. They eye me as I step towards Paula.

—I said get the fuck off o me property, says Paula.

—Show us yer tits, someone says, the provincial fuckin wit.

266

—Get yer girlfriend out!

—Yeah, give us a show love!

—Nah, hang on lads, says Slaughter. —I have a present for her, he says, and he unzips his fly and gets out his dick, then takes hold of it and flops it around. This is fuckin mental.

—Look, I say. —We're gonna –

—D'you want some as well, says Slaughter, grinnin, and it's only now I realise he's stoned, wrecked, completely fuckin gone, his eyes glazed and the pupils huge, nearly swallowin his irises. This is serious, man. This is dodgy as fuck. A car passes on the other side o the green, glidin off into the night, oblivious. Me heart's goin apeshit and inside me head is buzzin, cracklin, totally fuckin overloaded with drink, adrenaline, fear, the lot.

—Where's the jungle bunny, says Slaughter. —Does she like white cock?

Slaughter's crew laugh and whoop, one o them, a skinny fella in a Nike tracksuit, brayin like a fuckin donkey.

—She's from fuckin Dublin, says Paula. —She's as entitled to be here as you.

—Me fuckin hole she is. She's fuckin black.

—I won't say it again, says Paula. —Get. The fuck. Out.

Jesus, Paula, shut the fuck up.

—Get the nigger out first, says Slaughter.

Paula walks up to Slaughter, who's about ten feet away. I want to follow her but I feel like I'm stuck to the concrete, like me feet are cased in cement.

—Get out, she says again and, fuckin hell, she spits in his face.

It only takes a split second for Slaughter's fist to pull back and shoot forward, catchin Paula in the side o the head. She drops to the ground and Slaughter lays into her with a savage boot and I feel like pissin meself, I feel like a fuckin ghost, like I'm barely here as I run at Slaughter and raise the hurley, holdin it in both hands, and drive it down, aimin for his head but crackin it full force against his shoulder. He falls to one knee and there's a second where the rest o the lads just look on, stunned, and I take another swing, catchin him on the top o the head, a glancin blow. He covers his head with his arms as the others jump forward. I don't even get a chance to lift the hurley again before I'm grabbed and the punches and kicks rain in. I can hear Teresa shoutin. Someone hits me in the stomach and somethin hard and bony catches me in the back o the head. Lights come on in some o the neighbours' houses and dogs start barkin. I can smell somethin, petrol or gasoline. I twist and turn like mad. Bodies and arms everywhere. Me knee smacks against the wall. I try to lash out but me arms are pinned so I bite at somethin soft and warm and the owner screams as me mouth fills with blood, then I feel meself lifted off the ground and I see the sky for a second before crashin down into the concrete on me shoulder. I turn, wrigglin like Gino said he used to, yiv to be slippery as a greased trout, he used to say, yiv to keep movin and I can see again, a blurry low level view o the garden, the overgrown grass, the uneven concrete driveway and boots and runners and frayed jean ends round me. I see fire. The fuckin smell o petrol, Jesus. Somethin hits me in the head. I try to turn and I see a boot get so big in a split-second it blocks out the world. I barely get me head down and it catches me in the top o the head rather than the face. Fuck, me head . . .

—Yeh don't fuckin mess with the fuckin Slaughter –

. . . me fuckin head. I get me arms up over me. KA-BOOM. A forest o legs around me and eyes above, each agleam with fire and hate. I curl away from them, another kick catchin me in the back, up near me shoulder. But I keep movin, keep squirmin and lashin out with me feet and me balled fists, completely fuckin manic, and then fuckin hell I see her, above me – me mother with steel in her hand. Me ma as a younger woman and she screeches and lunges, fire caught in the blade. The kickin stops.

—I will, she says —I swear to yeh I fuckin will, I'll put this through yer fuckin neck –

Paula's standin over me, one o the big kitchen knives in her hand, breathin heavily. I can see fire dancin in the blade. Slaughter backs a few feet away, by the gate, his mates behind him. His mangy cock is still out and it's semi-erect, the mad fuck. He fumbles it back into his jeans and leers at Paula.

—That's not very nice, says Slaughter.

—I swear to fuckin God, I'll fuckin gut yeh, yeh prick. I'll fuckin kill yeh.

Slaughter laughs. —Yill try.

—Yer fuckin dead I'm tellin yeh. Yeh come anywhere near him.

Slaughter winks and wrings his hands together. He looks at me on the driveway and then back up at Paula. —I'm dead, am I? *Someone's* fuckin dead alright. And I don't mean yer ma yeh dirty fuckin hooer.

—Get fuckin out o here, says Paula.

—Don't worry, I'm goin. Niggers and queers and all sorts, place fuckin smells. I'll see yiz around, yeah? Good luck. See yeh after, Denny.

He grabs the gate and shakes the fuck out o them like The Ultimate Warrior used to do in the wrestlin, years ago, and he makes a weird sound, a kind o mad animal howl with his head thrown back. Then everythin's quiet. Slaughter spits towards the house and turns and walks away, his mates followin. Each one o them spits in the same direction. Towards Charly, I suppose. And me. Paula hunkers down beside me.

—Jesus Denny, yeh OK?

—Yeah. Grand.

—Yeh sure?

—Yeah, well. Not great, like.

—I phoned the police, says Teresa. —And the fire brigade.

I turn round, painfully. Teresa's at the front door. There's smoke billowin out o the hallway behind her. Paula kneels down beside me, her hand on me knee. We sit here for a good long while.

I'LL MEET YOU AT THE FOGGY DEW

I pull Kasey's van in outside Mr Kinsella's shop just as he's openin the gates, a once big Mayo man hunched by years and the mornin rain, his wispy white hair dancin in the wind as he struggles against the weather. The shop is in the middle o the estate and it's surrounded by ten foot walls caked in graffiti and with squiggles o barbed wire tacked on top. Mr Kinsella latches the gates in place and squints at me through the rain-streaked window o the van. He raises his hand in a hasty sort o greetin then hurries back to the shop. I kill the ignition and hop out, me runners crunchin through the gravel as I jog after him, me shoulder still achin from me kickin and the rain comin at me in all directions, fierce and fiercely fuckin cold.

★

Mrs Kinsella is stackin the fridge with cream and butter and milk, her broad back to me and her apron tied in a loose bow. A radio talkshow is babblin away somewhere. Mr Kinsella places his drippin jacket on a peg behind him and rubs his hands together and nods at me. His nose is like somethin yid see growin inside a smoker's lung; blotchy and red and lumpy. I've been comin here since I was a kid but I haven't been for ages and I don't think he recognises me with the beard and me hair so long. The shop doesn't do that much business now, with the new Centra down the road. I heard it's supposed to be closin up soon.

Mr Kinsella rolls the sleeves of his shirt up past his elbows and places his spotted, farmer's hands on the counter. —Grand morning, what? he says.

—Lovely, yeah.

—I'll get me bikini out if it keeps up, says Mrs Kinsella, still busy at the fridge. She shoves a two litre o milk onto the top shelf, then turns round, wipin her hands on her apron. She has a wide face and a slow, motherly smile. —Is this what they call them, bikinis?

—Think so, yeah, I say.

—I'll get up on the roof and catch a few rays. Isn't that what they say? Catch a few rays?

—Yeah, I say, smilin. —Somethin like that.

Mrs Kinsella winks and turns back to the fridge. Mr Kinsella looks at her back for a second and then turns to me. He shakes his head slightly.

—In a bit of a scrap there son, were yeh?

—Ah, nothin really. Just a few drunk lads.

I unconsciously touch me right cheekbone, where it's sore and discoloured. They wanted me to stay overnight in the hospital after the Slaughter thing but I wouldn't. It was the first time I'd been in a hospital since I seen me ma and it freaked me out. I told the police I didn't know who did it – too much fuckin hassle, man. Gino and Shane said they'd sort it themselves. I don't even wanna think about that, to be honest.

Mr Kinsella nods and looks like he's mullin wha I said over. Wharrever conclusion he comes to, though, he keeps to himself.

—What can I get yeh so? he says.

—Em, I've a bit of a list, like. I'm headin off wirra few mates.

—Well for yiz. On yer holliers are yiz? Yiz picked the right day.

—Well, headin out for a funeral. Donegal, like. Might have a look round on the way back, though. Check out the lay o the land. Haven't really been round Ireland much.

—Ah be jaysis, says Mrs Kinsella, turnin round again. —Yer own country!

—I know.

—I'll tell yeh where's a lovely place, she says. —Glencolumbkille. Now that's a gorgeous place, isn't it Aidan?

—Grand, says Mr Kinsella.

—Ah it's more than grand, says Mrs Kinsella. —Grand he says. It's like something out of a story book. Knock the shite out of these places yeh see on the telly, anyway. Spain and all this. Did yeh ever see that show where they go to live foreign for a few days, to try the place out? Where was it they were, Salamanca? Yeh try this place yill never be back. Feckin Salamanca!

—Sure we'll have a look, I say. —Think we'll be headin through it, anyway. That's in Donegal, isn't it?

—It is. And sure headin through it's no use, says Mrs Kinsella. —Get out and have a look. Stretch yer legs. And drop by the Tapper's Yard as well, they do a fierce whiskey. Home-brewed.

—Sure isn't the fella drivin? says Mr Kinsella. —Yill have him killed on the road. Did yeh not see in the paper about them fellas killed in a car in Kildare? There's more deaths on the road than I don't know what.

—Ah sure stop for the night, yeh might as well, says Mrs Kinsella. —And here, tell oul Seán that Carmel sent yeh. He'll look after yeh.

Mr Kinsella glares at his wife. —Have you that milk sorted yet?

Mrs Kinsella rolls her eyes, then winks at me again. —God, I'd better hurry up and sort the milk before the ravening hordes bate the doors down, she says, the wind drivin the rain across the gravel in the empty yard.

★

I slam the doors shut and hurry round to the front o the van. Hop in. The rain drummin on the roof. I watch the wipers shuckin the rainwater from side to side for a few seconds, then turn the key in the ignition and swing the van back onto the street. There's no off-licences open yet so the drink'll have to wait. Have most o the rest o the stuff, though.

Feels a bit weird, like, drivin Kasey's van. It's wha he wanted, though, I suppose. It occurred to me that turnin up at his funeral in his own van might seem a bit weird but, like I said, he wanted us to have it.

Every time I close me eyes I can still see Kasey's face. Dead in the bathroom, lookin up, the big un-seein eyes. Dead in a fuckin bathroom. And not even a top o the range bathroom, like these well-off pricks that die after mad coke binges are found in; no, a poxy, grimy bathroom in me own fuckin house. Where's the fuckin dignity like, yeh know? That's two people dead in the house now, Kasey and me ma. Well, not me ma, really; she died on the way to hospital, in the ambulance. Paula was in it with her, drunk. And yeh know wha, I fuckin envy her. I do. I envy her the fact she was the last one with me ma.

I cut through Rowlagh and out onto the Neilstown Road. I can see a couple o little girls in school uniforms hurryin along in the rear view mirror, huddled under an umbrella, so I wait for them to pass and as they do they look up at me and giggle, then hurry on, skippin through the rain. One blonde-haired, the other dark. The streetlights are still on and the way the flickerin sodium light hits the road it looks like a canal, slick and shimmery. A little bit further up the two girls stop and skip across to the other side o the road, meetin a third girl who huddles in with the first two. Then it's back again, weavin between traffic, all three o them beneath the one outsized umbrella, bone-dry and walkin on water.

I press play on the old tape deck in the dashboard. There's a tape still in it and Metallica's Master of Puppets blares out. Haven't heard this in years. I crank it up and drive on.

★

Ned's already standin in the porch when I pull up outside his garden. Sinead's with him. He kisses her and they hug, then he hurries over. He throws his swanky-lookin rucksack into the back o the van and then hops into the passenger seat. Sinead waves and I beep the horn as we pull off.

—Nice to see yer eager, I say.
—Ah yeh know me.

I nod.

—And here, we've to drop into Tommy's on the way.

Me heart sinks. —He's not comin is he? Fuckin Tommy?

—Ah no, no. Tommy? Nah, he's holdin a bit o stuff for me. Wait and yeh see.

—Stuff?

—Yeah, says Ned, tappin the side of his nose. —Stuff.

★

Pajo's gear is squashed into a plastic bag. His chin's restin just over Ned's shoulder. Pajo's fuckin devastated, like; he was closer to Kasey than any of us. Ignatius is yappin away somewhere in the back.

—So we've to collect Maggit in town? What's that all about?

—He'd to see someone, says Pajo. —He gorra call last night. He said to ring him. I know Denny, that's not cool. I said that to him but he said he had to go. I think it might o been Bernadette.

—Bernadette?

—Yeah, I don't know for sure, like. Could o been.

—What'd she want Maggit for? says Ned.

Pajo shrugs. —Maybe she wants him back.

Ned raises an eyebrow theatrically. —Ah here now Pajo. She wants him back? She wants a knife in his back more like.

Pajo scratches at his slightly yellowed incisor. It looks like he's gonna say somethin but he just shrugs again and pats Ignatius on the head.

—Did he say wha time to ring? I say.

—Just in the mornin was all he said.

—Betcha he doesn't go, says Ned. —Assumin he's still alive.

—Ah no, he will, says Pajo. —He will. He said he would.

—Yeah, cos he's well known for his reliability, isn't he? says Ned. —Paragon of honesty wouldn't yeh say, Denny?

I nod.

—Ah no Denny, he will, says Pajo. —He kept sayin. Seriously now, he'll be there.

—Is he not over Bernadette, Pajo? I say.

—Don't think so Denny, no. He says he is, like, but . . . nah, I think he still likes her.

—Ah well, says Ned. —It's his own fuckin fault, lads. Not bein bad like, but it is. It's one thing bein mates with him but imagine havin a kid with the cunt.

There's silence for a while. The low whine o the wipers. Patta-patta o the rain.

★

Pajo and Ned chatter away as I drive. Ned rang Maggit and we've to meet him at the Foggy Dew in about a half an hour. Apparently it was Bernadette he was with. Ned asked him were they back together but unsurprisingly they're not. Wonder wha it was all about, though? Course, there's no chance Maggit'll actually give anythin away; loves his fuckin mysteries, Maggit does.

We've to stop off at Inchicore to pick up this stuff, wharrever it is. Tommy's new place is near the Black Lion, just round the corner in a little estate. I swing in and pull up outside a new-lookin house with a concrete garden and the blinds still pulled down. There's a big black satellite dish stickin out o the side o the house. Ned unclips his seatbelt and hops out. Not sure wha I feel about gettin supplies off Tommy. I mean, we're sittin in Kasey's van, and it was Kasey robbed all that cocaine off Dommo, Tommy's brother. There's no real way o tyin it to us, though. Not even Ned or Maggit know that it was Kasey, that's strictly between me and Pajo.

—D'yeh reckon Kasey'd mind us gettin stuff off Tommy, Paj?

Pajo shakes his head. —Nah. Don't think so, Denny. He wouldn't want us, like . . . goin hungry or wharrever.

Pajo strokes Ignatius and nods and we natter away for a few minutes before Ned appears at the window again, this time with Tommy. Tommy's wearin a housecoat and a pair o shorts but he has a raincoat thrown over him and he's peerin out from under it. He could do with a shave. There's a pile o somethin, about three feet tall, on the ground. It's boxes or trays o some sort but I can't see wha of.

—How yeh keepin Denny? says Tommy.

—Cool. What's all this so?

Ned picks up one o wha I can now see is a covered aluminium tray and passes it through the window. I open it up. There's cocktail sausages, chicken wings, sandwiches, sausage rolls and god knows wha else, piled on paper plates and wrapped in cellophane.

—Where'd yeh get this? Is it alright?

—Course it is, says Tommy.

—It was supposed to be for a weddin reception, says Ned. —One o Tommy's cousins.

—And why have we got it?

278

—Munchies, says Ned.

—Yer man called her last night and said it was off, the prick, says Tommy.

—Jilted her?

—Yeah. He was in the airport when he rang her, headin for Spain, the cowardly cunt. Can yeh believe that?

—Fuckin hell.

—He'll be in for some hidin if he ever comes back here, tellin yeh.

—And so we're the beneficiaries?

—Suppose so, yeah.

—They'll do for the drive, says Ned.

—So this stuff is definitely OK, yeah? I ask. —Not gone off or anythin?

—Yeah, it's sound, says Ned. —It was meant for today.

—Ye of little faith, says Tommy.

—There's not much vegetarian stuff, says Pajo.

—God love yeh, says Tommy. —Yer gettin it for next to fuck all.

—Don't worry about it, I say. —He'll live. Thanks. Right, we'd better get movin.

—Good luck lads, says Tommy. —Write me a postcard.

—I'll bring yeh back a turnip.

—Fuck off. Grab us a bottle o poitín if yeh can.

—We'll see.

—Ah, go on, so. Be off with yiz. Watch out for randy farmers' daughters. They'd fuckin crush skinny cunts like youse to death.

—We'll be grand.

—Ah yiz will. Good luck, so.

Tommy slaps the side o the van and steps back. We pull away and head for town.

★

It's only early so the Foggy Dew's still pretty empty. I trail me fingertips along the polished near-yellow wood o the bar and scan the taps. The girl behind the bar is Chinese, with a small mouth and brown eyes. Looks a bit like yer woman out o Wayne's World, can't remember her name, like, but she's younger, this girl, probably a student or somethin. She smiles at me by way of enquiry and absentmindedly touches the lobe of her ear. It looks dead cute, actually, the way she does it. I fancy somethin lighter than a Guinness but since the bargirl's after catchin me early in the decision-makin process and for some reason I don't wanna look like an indecisive sap I knock on the Guinness tap with me knuckle and smile. The girl ducks down and grabs a glass and holds it at an angle under the tap and draws the pump back, fillin the glass about three quarters full and then leavin it to settle. Proper way to pull a pint o Guinness, that. Loads o the foreign bar staff just fill it straight up and hand it over.

The cash register bleeps. I hand over the money and she places it in the till and hands me the twenty-cent change and nods and wipes the bar. I should have told her to just keep the twenty cent but it's too late, if I gave it to her now it'd look like awkward charity rather than a tip. Someone with a bit o savvy, someone like Ned, would o been on the ball and the second she turned he would o held up his hand and said nah, it's grand, and smiled. Although it's only twenty cent so fuck it, like, I could be James fuckin Bond, a suave, debonair prick and it'd still be a poxy, unworthy tip. Yeh couldn't get a packet o Chickatees for twenty cent these days. All go in the Celtic Tiger, like.

I turn and lean back against the bar and scan the pub while the Guinness is settlin. Ned's already after gettin a round in and I said I didn't want one, I'm drivin. But after lookin at the lads tuckin in I can't help it. One for the road, as they say. There are a couple of oul lads in one o the booths, chattin away loudly. One o them starts laughin this big harsh brass laugh and his shoulders shuck up and down. There's a giant cluster o warts on his cheek and he has small eyes, deep and pooled with memory. There's a couple o pints o Guinness in front o them, with rings o froth at intervals above the inch or so o dark left at the bottom o the glasses. Sign of experienced Guinness men, them rings. Each one measurin a gulp, well formed and evenly spaced; another ritual I'm aware of but personally indifferent to. Badge of honour among these old-school boozehounds, though.

I turn back to the bar and I can see the Chinese bargirl from three different angles because o the mirrors. She's leanin against the till and without lookin directly at her I can see that's she's worryin over a tatty pad and she's rubbin her earlobe like it's part o some spell she's castin to make wharrever bad sum she's glarin at add up. I can see this in both profiles, left and right, and over her shoulder the back of her head and the red scrunchy that's holdin up her hair, the tip of her ponytail dyed white. She catches me gaze and smiles and puts down the pad and biro, then tops up the Guinness and places the pint on the bar. I thank her and she smiles again and I take me drink away towards the back and wonder wha her voice sounds like.

Maggit's sprawled out in the back room, a huge weary grin on his face. His long skinny legs are crossed, one giant laceless workboot on top o the other. His blue jumper sits snug on the beginnins of his beerbelly and the sleeves are rolled back to his elbows. The fucker looks exhausted and he raises his half-gone pint o cider to me and winks. Ned's sat on the opposite side o the table with Pajo, and he smiles and gives me a mini-salute.

—Fucker stole a march on us, says Ned. —Sneaked a few while he was waitin.

Ned's fingerless gloves are on the table, on top of a pile o newspapers. Pajo's sittin beside him with Ignatius's head pokin out o his jacket. I have to push the papers aside to make room for me pint. There's a copy o the *Daily Star* flopped across Maggit's lap.

—Paper round?

—Celebratin, says Maggit. —Fuckin deadly.

Maggit hasn't shaved in a while and his oversized ears are especially noticeable today cos he's after gettin his head shaved. It was gettin fuzzy the last time I saw him but it's dead short and bristly now. He keeps subconsciously pattin his skull with his non cider-holdin hand.

—Looks nice, I say, lookin at his head.

Maggit shrugs and looks kind o uncomfortable for a split second. Maggit can be weirdly sensitive when it comes to his looks. Especially his ears. They used to call him earoplane when we were kids. Jesus, the amount o scraps he got into over them ears. He's always sayin, when he's drunk, like, that he's gonna get them pinned back, but I think admittin any ear-related abnormality while sober, even to himself, is too acute a pain for him to bear. And so the ears abide.

Maggit sits forward, kind o hunched over his drink. After the momentary wobble over his haircut the smile's back in place, a big wide grin showin teeth that are surprisinly well kept.

—Fuckin Man U went out yesterday, didn't they? he says. —Deadly. Readin all the post-match discussion while I'm havin me breakfast. There's an article by Dunphy. And stupid Ferguson's excuses as well. Fuckin delighted I am.

—They're out?

I'm usually well up to speed on football but the past few days have been mental so I've completely lost track.

—On their poxy arses. Deadly. I was out watchin it with a few heads last night. Some fuckin laugh, I'm tellin yiz. Went on a mad one after that. I'm fuckin wrecked, like. But yeh have to read the papers as well, that's the icin on the cake. All the excuses and that.

—Thought yeh were seein Bernadette?

—Wha?

—Were yeh not supposed to be seein Bernadette last night?

Maggit looks into his pint. —Yeah, he says. —I did.

—Everythin alright?

—Yeah, grand.

—How come yeh ended up out with the lads?

—Ah, leave it Denny.

—Yeh didn't propose to her, did yeh? says Ned.

Maggit eyes Ned.

—Yeh didn't, did yeh?

—Yeah, says Maggit.

—I'd say she jumped at the chance, did she? says Ned, winkin.

Maggit places his pint on the table and looks at Ned. —Will you ever shut yer gob yeh mouthy cunt? Now yer ridin that posh slapper yer God's gift, wha?

—Leave it out Maggit, for fuck sake, I say. —He's only messin.

Maggit takes a big gulp of his cider, finishin it off. We sip at our drinks in silence for a minute or so.

—Were yeh serious, Maggit, askin her? I say. I have to be careful, here, I don't wanna annoy him. I mean, he's a pain in the fuckin arse but still, I don't wanna see him down.

—Yeah, says Maggit, and to be honest I'm surprised I'm even gettin this much out of him. —I got a ring. I got it off a fella in Cork. That's where I was when them poxy knacker fucks were hasslin yeh.

—Yeh still that hung up on her?

—I have a fuckin kid with her, Denny.

—I know, yeah. But . . . doesn't mean it's gonna work, does it?

Maggit shrugs. —No fuckin chance now, anyway. I dropped up to the house a few weeks ago, like, to talk to her. We went for a drink and that. I told her I was still into her. But then a few days ago she saw me with that knacker youngwan, Niamh, and that was it, fucked.

—So yeh still proposed? Wha did yeh expect?

—Don't know. She's a fuckin cunt, anyway. Does she expect me to believe she's never been with a fella since we split up? She's a fuckin hypocrite.

—Yeah, but after yeh said yeh were still into her, like, she probably thought –

284

—Ah, fuckin . . . just shurrup about it Denny. I'm not in the mood.

I take a sup o me pint. Maggit's fuckin deludin himself. There's no way in hell Bernadette would ever o had him back, one way or the other. But he has an excuse now, a reason to be angry. The world makes sense again.

—Nice pint, I say, noddin me head, even though it's just that same smoky gloop. Just feel like sayin somethin positive, yeh know? Liftin the gloom.

—Pulled it right, did she? says Ned, obviously completely uninterested one way or the other. He looks like he's fumin after wha Maggit said about Sinead, and I don't blame him. This is turnin into a total fuckin mess. But it's Kasey's funeral so fuck it, we have to go through with it.

—Yeah, she did, I say, and I smack me lips to emphasise the point, like yeh see the oul lads do. —Grand.

Maggit glances over at the bar. —Pulled right? I'd fuckin pull *her* right.

Ned rolls his eyes.

—Seriously, says Maggit. —Them fuckin Asians. See them on the internet? Tommy was showin me on his mobile a while ago. Fuck sake.

—Wonders o modern technology, wha? says Ned. —The spread o information, the exchange of ideas. Meetin o cultures. Porn.

—Hilarious, yeah. I didn't put it there, did I? I only watched it. Mental stuff though all the same. Them fuckin Asian youngwans, tellin yeh. Saw this video where about fifty chinky businessmen wank over this bird. Head to toe in spunk, like. I was . . . actually, there's Triads holed up off Parnell Square, know that? Serious. Fuckin gang warfare;

it was in the *Herald*. Put yer fuckin eyes out, them Chinese. Stick them in formaldehyde.

Ned looks at me.

—Fuckin chinks, like, says Maggit. —Tellin yeh. Near as many chinks over here now as there are fuckin Polish, swear to God. Breedin us fuckin out. Maggit fishes a packet o cigarettes from his pocket and sticks one in his mouth.

—Smokin ban, yeh sap, I say, and Maggit, shakin his head, sticks the cigarette back into the packet. —You fuckin losin it or wha? I say. —Gerra grip.

—Fuckin country's goin to shite, he says. He folds up the *Daily Star* and puts it on top o the pile o papers. He looks at me. —One more before we head, so? Your round, Pajo.

★

There are a few more tapes in the glove compartment o Kasey's van – Kill 'Em All by Metallica, Seasons in the Abyss by Slayer and Peace Sells . . . But Who's Buying? by Megadeth. None of us are that mad into old-school thrash metal but I stick Kill 'Em All on all the same, like a tribute to Kasey or somethin. The Four Horsemen blares from the tinny speakers, which is pretty appropriate I suppose.

Fuckin weird oul thing, death, isn't it? Hard to get yer head around, like. I remember readin somewhere that Mark Twain said there was no point in him fearin non-existence cos he hadn't existed for millions o years before he was born; death is just more o the same. I'm not sure if that makes me feel better or not. Or if I wanna see life, existence, that way. Maybe things are more connected than that. I mean, stories, like – they don't ever actually end, do they? They go on. All I know is that I still miss me ma. Does that ever get better? Does the sadness ever go? I don't think it does, really; I think yeh just get used to it, maybe, over time. I hope so.

—Pull over, says Ned.

—Wha?

—I'm gonna fuckin die if I don't have a shite. Jesus. There's a McDonald's over there, look. Pull over. Quick.

—Havin an oul McShit, wha? says Maggit.

—Yep. Anyone stops me I'll tell them I'm buyin five Big Macs after I've . . . relieved meself. Fuckin hell.

Ned's wincin. He looks round desperately.

—That's it. Oof. Jesus Christ I'm gonna fuckin gick me knickers. Wouldn't touch that fuckin food if I was youse, lads. Jesus. Wait and I get me hands on that bastard Tommy. Tellin yiz, I'll do fuckin time for the cunt. I'll –

Ned lets rip with a wet, spluttery fart.

—Ah Jesus!

—Yeh smelly prick!

—Fuck youse, I can't fuckin help it! Shoddy fuckin merchandise, like . . . fuckin Tommy . . . fuckin scammy bastard!

THE HOUR OF
OUR DEATH

The priest is a fat Dubliner with a stammer and a thick black beard. Looks a bit like the da out o The Royle Family, that Scouser fella. He doesn't walk, this priest, he waddles instead and he cups his belly in front of himself like yeh see pregnant women doin sometimes. I can smell the sweat off him from three rows back. Maggit's been gettin more and more stressed listenin to him; I can feel the tension buildin, buildin.

—It is a s-s-s-s-sad day when a mother and father outlive their s-s-s-s-suh-suh-son.

Yid never get a priest with a speech impediment like this in Dublin. This is like a Father Ted sketch. I mean, I don't wanna sound like I condone discrimination but when yer job entails public oration maybe it's time to look elsewhere. It's not so bad when he's speakin on his own but when he's leadin the mourners it's a joke:

—N-n-nuh-now and at the hour of our d-d-d-d-d-death . . .

Ned looks at me and makes a face. Pajo's away with the fairies and he doesn't even notice. The whole church is stutterin the Our Father with the hapless priest, the mourners developin their own sympathetic, syncopated speech impediment. Sounds like a room o spazzos. Ned's only just holdin the laughter in.

— . . . Ay-ay-eh-eh-ay-ayyy-m-muh-muh-m-m-m-muh . . .

Maggit shakes his head, a look o disgust on his face.

—. . . muh-muh-muh . . .

—Ay-fuckin-men, says Maggit, loud enough that people in the rows around us can hear him. A fella in a too-big suit turns round and glares at us. Maggit steps out o the pew and walks along the aisle, his footsteps huge and clamorous. Ned whispers 'sorry' to the fella in front of us. Pajo stares at his boots. I look over at Kasey's ma, her eyes ringed red and her face sunken and pale. She looks ancient although she's only in her fifties, near enough the same age me own ma would be now. Kasey's sisters are beside her, and his da, a tall fella with a slight belly and shaggy grey hair. None o Kasey's sisters look like him.

The rest o the funeral drags on. It seems perverse in a way, dawdlin over Kasey's death, the fat, stuttery priest behind his altar eulogisin about him, even though he never knew him from Adam. So impersonal. I mean, I'm pretty sure Kasey didn't believe in God, or not the God o the Bible at least, so what's all this about? This is all for us really, isn't it? The priest stutterin away, Jesus this and Mary that, the resurrection, the assumption. What's it all about? I doubt anyone is even listenin. I can barely remember me ma's funeral. I was standin there in the same suit I'm wearin now, standin and kneelin a split second after everyone else, takin me cue from others, Gino and Shane and me da quiet and dignified and me mad auntie Denise wailin and Paula beside me, tremblin, and I wanted to take her hand but I didn't. I wish that I had.

★

—Ah ye're very good lads, says Mrs Cassidy. She takes a sip from her vodka and orange and looks at each of us in turn, smilin and blinkin, then heads over to her daughters. Mr Cassidy's up at the bar, gettin a ludicrously expensive round in. Not bein bad but I hope this isn't a round we're supposed to reciprocate; he's after takin orders from at least twelve people, us included.

Kasey's ma and sisters are sittin to our left. They're against the wall, behind a long, narrow table and all sat on the same side, oldest to youngest, like a graph showin the female Cassidy agein process.

It's the usual mix of post-funeral moods in the pub, some people in good form and others sombre, silent. Pajo looks like he's a million miles away; hard to tell wha goes on in his head sometimes. Ned looks like he doesn't know wha to look like, caught halfway between solemnity and the drunkenness which always puts him in a good mood. And I'm ... well, hard to say, isn't it? Don't really know. I'm in conspiracy theory mode, here. I mean, did Kasey killin himself have anythin to do with the drugs he robbed?

I hope I'm projectin a look that's at least partway respectful and suitably morose. Hard to judge occasions like these, especially when, and I know this sounds bad as fuck, I don't really feel anythin. Cept, at the moment, annoyed at Maggit. Which makes me feel like a bit of a fraud.

That wasn't on, Maggit stormin out like that. I mean, if he'd any time for Kasey in the first place I could allow for him feelin frustrated over that stuttery priest, but he didn't, it was just pure selfishness, pure childishness. He hasn't even turned up for the afters yet and he has his phone switched off. Fuck it, anyway; I'm not bothered.

I take a gulp o me Guinness.

—D'yiz wanna go out the back for a bit? I ask.

—Wouldn't mind a smoke.

—Sound, says Ned.

—Yeh alright Denny? says Pajo.

—Yeah, grand. Yiz comin out?

The two o them nod and we head for the back door.

★

It's early evenin and the sun's settin over the trees at the back o the pub. It's nice enough, warmish and windless. Unusual for Donegal, I'd imagine. We're sittin round a little rough-hewn wooden table, our drinks in front of us, suited and booted and uncomfortable as fuck.

—No word from Maggit? I say to Pajo.

He shakes his head.

—Fuckin arsehole, I say. And I mean it. Me head's done in with that prick.

—We could leavim here, says Ned, smilin. —Leavim stranded.

We sup at our pints and Pajo and me light up. I'm tired. The Guinness is goin down nicely though. I need a piss but I don't wanna go back inside yet. I can hear the odd car passin on the other side o the pub, and the hubbub o the mourners from the open windows. I down the last third o me Guinness.

—Dyin for a piss, says Pajo, makin a face.

—And me, I say. —Don't wanna go back in yet though.

—I'm gonna go in them trees there, says Pajo. —Keep an eye out, will yiz? Don't want any, like, ladies or anythin to see me. Seems kinda –

291

—G'wan, says Ned. —We'll give yeh a shout.

Pajo stubs out his cigarette and stands up. He smoothes his slightly too-small trousers and nods and heads over to the trees. He turns back as he's standin under the shadow o the little wood and waves, the sky pink above him, then ducks under the lowhangin branches and disappears. The little stupid wave makes me think o Pajo as a kid, and I can see it so clearly it actually makes me feel . . . I dunno. Us watchin the wrestlin as kids. Me cheerin for The Undertaker and Pajo mad for Bret Hart. Pajo as a ten year-old for a second . . . seems like . . . ah, it's mad, isn't it? Tick tock, tick tock. He's barely changed since I first knew him. I mean yeah there's the drugs and that, the gear, but he's still the same. Too fuckin delicate for this world.

—D'yeh think he'll be OK? I say.

Ned looks at me. He scratches his cheek. —He'll be grand.

—No, like, I meant, in general. With the –

—I know wha yeh meant. He'll be grand, Denny. Doesn't need you worryin about him, anyway. No one does. Yiv yer own troubles.

I take a deep drag and blow the smoke out slowly.

—Will you be OK, more to the point? says Ned.

—Will I . . . ?

—Just . . . how's things with yeh, like?

I tap me cigarette. —Not bad, I say.

—Yeah?

—Yeah. Well. Could be better, like.

—D'yeh think about her much?

—Loads.

—Yeah?

—Yep.

—It'll get better, man. Takes time.

—That's wha they say, anyway.

—Yep. That's wha they say.

★

We're back in the pub and another few pints are behind us, the pub full and warm when Pajo says:

—I saw Kasey.

Ned raises his eyebrows and sips his Guinness. Pajo's smilin. It's not one o these weak, watery smiles like Kasey's ma has on; it's the real deal. He's beamin, his wonky teeth bared and his eyes crinklin.

—Wha? I say.

Pajo shrugs. —Out in the trees. There was someone with him.

I look towards the window. The evenin's dyin light.

—Yeah? I say.

—Yeah, Denny. Serious.

Ned nods. He's sound, Ned. Never judges. Unlike me.

—Hundred per cent, says Pajo.

—Did he do anythin? asks Ned.

—Nah. Just smiled. The two o them did.

Two o them. —Who's the other one? I say.

—Dunno. A girl.

—Yeh serious?

—Yeah. Him and a girl. They were smilin and they waved. She'd black hair with blue bits in.

Ned smiles. —Here, he says. —A toast for Kasey, wha? Ghost Kasey.

Me and Pajo raise our glasses and clink them together.

—To Kasey, says Ned.

—To old friends, says Pajo.

—Old friends, I say, and I can't help smilin. I take a massive gulp from me Guinness and set it down carefully as the women o the Cassidy family start up a verse o The Fureys' Sweet Sixteen, surprisinly well sung, sad and happy and just fuckin perfect.

★

The pub door swings open and the priest waddles in, followed by two pious-lookin oulwans with shawls on their blue-rinsed heads. Ned calls oulwans like them God groupies; old women obsessed with the clergy and countin down the days to the next weddin, baptism, funeral. Ned nods at them as they come in, a glint in his eye.

—Check it out, says Ned. —Couple o –

—God groupies, I say.

Ned and Pajo laugh. I feel a bit better now. Mr Cassidy comes over to us with four pints o Guinness in his big hands and places them on our table. Mr Cassidy's a big man, a Dubliner, tall and well built. The top few buttons of his shirt are open and his tie is off. Yeh can see the grey hairs on his chest.

—Yiz alright there lads? he says.

—Grand, yeah.

—Sound. Thanks for these, Mr Cassidy.

—Ah, no problem lads, he says. He runs a hand through his thick hair, then takes a huge swallow of his Guinness. He brushes the froth from his upper lip.

—Very sorry for yer loss, Mr Cassidy, says Ned.

—Ah, says Mr Cassidy, shakin his head. —Ah sure, was it a surprise, lads?

Ned looks lost momentarily and then recovers enough to make a multi-purpose sigh. The priest orders a brandy at the bar.

—Sure the way he was carryin on, lads, was it any wonder? Mr Cassidy nods surreptitiously at his wife. —Poor oul Brid is knocked sideways. But this is it lads, if yeh carry on like Kasey did. God love him. Ah sure he was always very soft.

I'm not sure whether to bring this up or not but, fuck it, here goes:

—Emm . . . it said in the note he left about a girl called Jackie. Who was that?

—Ah, a girl he was very fond of years ago. She died of an overdose. That oul heroin, lads. Fuckin scourge.

—I never heard him talk about her.

—Well. Sure aren't we all mysteries, lads? There's more we don't understand than we do. Mad oul world, wha? And here, speakin o mysteries, I'd better say hello to the Father.

Mr Cassidy gulps another huge measure of his Guinness and stands up. He nods at us and walks back over to the bar, where the priest with his brandy and the two God groupies are standin. The priest pats Mr Cassidy on the shoulder and the two oulwans look up at him and shake their heads, two pious vultures, their eyes filled with gleeful sorrow.

THE PINK AND BLACK
ATTACK

The wind from the Atlantic's dead cold. I'm sittin on top o the van, me palms flat against the dew-damp roof and the toe-ends o me boots pointin at a wide black sky. There's a trad band playin in the pub behind me, mad, wild fiddlin and tin whistle spillin into the night. The rest o them are inside, drunk and dancin, their shadows flashin at the old border pub's windows. Don't fancy it meself. Not yet, anyway. It's been a week nearly since Kasey's funeral and home seems dead far off. Rossnowlagh, Carrick, Derrybeg, Ardara. We've driven through each and stopped and drunk and danced and puked. Dungloe, Annagary, Glencolumbkille. Never even heard o these places before, never mind been to them, and yet, I dunno why, it all seems dead familiar. Mad that, isn't it? This feelin I get that nothin is new, not really.

Me watch beeps. Ten o'clock. The ocean's shiftin in the dark. I can hear it, the low roar and crash and hiss o waves. The smell, as well. Dead fish and smashed, buckled crabs and beyond that the salty tang o the sea.

This place o wind and wetness. The outer edge of an island already on the edge o things. How much has this place changed? Cabbages yer head to think like that, doesn't it? I mean, this place has been here thousands upon thousands o years. Me ma brung me to the natural history museum in town, years ago, and the thing that I remember clearest is the Irish elk. So big. So fuckin massive. What sights would that elk have seen? An older Ireland. A world o dense forest and clean skies and green and purple hills. An immense elk in silhouette on the mountainside, its antlers huge and ornate, a strange four-legged chieftain o the high places.

Me mobile buzzes. It's Paula.

—Hello?

—Heya Denny. Yeh alright?

—Yeah, I'm grand. What's up?

—Nothin much. Where are yeh?

—Donegal. Sittin on the roof o the van.

—Very nice. Where's the rest o them?

—They're in the pub. I just came out for a bit of air.

—Shane's just after callin round.

Fuckin hell. —Wha did he want?

—He dropped round to Slaughter's.

I hesitate for a few seconds. —Dropped round? Wha d'yeh mean?

—Him and Gino. They dropped round to him. They said everythin's sorted.

—In wha way, sorted?

—Yeh know wha way, Denny. They went round, them and a few o their mates. Yeh know yer man Butler and that. Philip Butler, I think his name is. It's sorted, anyway. He won't be comin anywhere near here again.

—Wha, like they –

—Look, Denny, I'm gonna have to go. It's all sorted, there's nothin to worry about. I've hardly any credit and

I've to ring Teresa. She got that new job. We're after doin the house up a bit. And here, one last thing. I think we should have a bit of a think about sellin this place.

—Wha?

—Just have a think about it. Shane mentioned it and he said we can split some o the money, help us get on our feet. I'll talk to yeh soon. And remember, everything's grand with Slaughter and that. Shane and Gino sorted it. Yeah?

—Yeah.

—Right, I'll see yeh, so.

—Bye.

★

I grab the three pints and carefully pick me way back to the table, me fingers spidered round the glasses, strainin to keep them all together. Another mad, improbable but inevitable comeback from Liverpool. Peach of a goal from Alonso, as well. Top quality signin, he was. Benitez's best so far. Maggit was already after givin up, he was in the jax and he missed it. He legged it back out with his belt floppin when he heard the roar from the pub and as soon as he saw the score he jumped up on the table and started dancin like a madman. Nearly got us thrown out. Dermot, a local GAA head with shoulders as wide as the van, winks at me as I pass him at the pool table, still strugglin with me stout overload and the people millin round me.

—Some fuckin game, what? he says. —Should watch soccer more often.

He's after sayin this about ten times already. He said he's callin it soccer rather than football to assert his Gaelic roots; a continuation o the great struggle against Britain on a linguistic level. I give him a wink back and then finally set down the drinks in front o Maggit and Ned.

—Sound, says Ned.

—Cheers, says Maggit. I gave him a bit o stick about his lack o faith earlier on but he insisted he never gave up; accordin to him he turned to God while he was in the jax; he got down on his knees in the cubicle and prayed for an equaliser and lo and behold, Alonso's volley rocketed into the net.

I take a sip from me Guinness and then it's back to the bar for the double vodka and Coke for yer woman Maggit's after pickin up with. As usual I can't remember her name. She's from Belfast anyway, a student. Seems nice, like; there's somethin really cool about her. She's the same age as me but she's after goin back to uni, to finish an English degree she started a few years ago. She writes stories. Fair play to her, like; gettin on with things, gettin ahead. Or tryin to, anyway, which is more than most people do.

Feelin pretty drunk now. Nice though. Cool little pub this, the Tapper's Yard. Dead small like, only the one room, and apparently oul Seán does a lock-in every night if there's people up for it, and there usually is. Fuck-all pubs like this around Dublin. The jukebox is free. Not great stuff on it mind, but there's some Dylan tunes and Thin Lizzy and a bit o Neil Young as well, so it'll do. Heart of Gold's playin now, for probably the fifth time since we've been here – Ned loves that song.

—Thanks very much, Denny, says the girl as I place her vodka and Coke on the table.

—Yer grand, I say.

Lovely eyes, she's got. Not sure if they're brown or a deep, shiftin green. The place is buzzin, packed. We're sittin on the little bockedy red corner couch, dead snug and warm. Dermot is up at the pool table with Pajo, rackin up a new game, his hair pulled back in a tight, short ponytail. There's a wind blowin in from the sea and yeh can hear it shakin the window in the frames. Deadly atmosphere. There's loads o locals (oulfellas with papers at the bar, a dolled-up oulwan teeterin on her stool) and a few students from the local university. A few o Dermot's mates as well, musicians and that. One o them, Lorcan I think he's called, pulls out a stool and plonks down his pint o Bulmers beside me Guinness.

—Up for a lock-in then boys?

—Deffo, says Maggit.

—Bit of singsong and that, ey? Yeh up for it?

—Yeah, I say. —Sound.

—Got me guitar in the car, and Dermot's. Back in a jiffy.

He gulps the last of his pint and hops up, pickin his way through the crowd towards the door. When he opens it the wind whooshes in with a howl. He runs out into the dark with a whoop. A broad-shouldered fella in a denim shirt slams the door shut behind him.

The girl tucks one of her dreads behind her ear and smiles at me. They're green, her eyes. She has a small stud in her nose. She's got high cheekbones and she's wearin a slightly shabby, buttoned-up denim jacket. Maggit looks put out already, now that the attention's not on him, and makes a bit of a face. Which is stupid cos I'm not interested. Well, I would be, like, if I'd o bumped into her first but there yeh go. I wonder if he told her he has a kid? I doubt it. And anyway, I don't wanna annoy her, like. I mean, she's out here to have a laugh, to enjoy herself, not to have gobshites like me doin her head in.

Maggit laughs at somethin but I didn't catch wha was said. I didn't see him at all the day o the funeral. Well, after he walked out, like. Then, the next mornin, he rang me. Asked me to meet him at some greasy spoon in the village. He was sittin by the window, the remains of a fry on a plate in front of him; the skin o the white puddin and the pale fat of a rasher.

—What's the story? I said. I knew somethin had happened. Somethin had changed. I sat down across from him. It was a nice mornin, the village comin to life outside. Maggit looked at the back of his hand, then up at me.

—Well? I said.

—She's movin away, he said.

I knew who he meant. —Where?

—Fuckin Bulgaria for fuck sake. Or Albania or one o these mad fuckin places. Her da's after buyin her a house. Supposed to be dirt cheap over there.

—She takin Anto?

—Wha d'yeh think Denny? For fuck sake.

I nodded and that was that. I tried to talk to him about it but he wasn't havin it.

He didn't wanna know.

Maggit's still laughin when the door flies open and Lorcan falls in backwards, the two guitar cases clatterin off the floor. Seán howls drunkenly from behind the bar, his fat round head lollin on his shoulders.

—Few tunes, ey? That's the stuff, man! Few tunes! And remember now boys to tell Carmel that I was askin for her!

A beautiful woman so! Ah boys I tell ye, it's an awful pity ye never saw her when she was young! An awful pity!

★

Mrs Kinsella was right about the whiskey. Fuckin hell, I take one shot and the head's nearly blown off me. Seán slaps me on the back and laughs.

—True enough, ey? Is that or is that not the finest whiskey yiv ever tasted?

Finest? Fuckin strongest, anyway. I cough and nod.

—Aye, it is so, says Seán. —Me own grandfather came up with the recipe. Good stuff, ey?

—Yep, I manage to blurt out.

Ned's standin up on a stool, beltin out a rebel tune about Wolfe Tone with Lorcan below him, bashin away on his guitar. Pajo's doin a mad little jig beside him, his arm linked with a short-haired woman with rings in her nose and a swishy, multi-coloured gypsy skirt. Maggit, the dreadlocked girl, Seán and Dermot are sittin at the table with me. Maggit seems a bit off, still. We've all been tryin Seán's patented, top-secret recipe whiskey and to be honest, we're all well gone at this stage, fucked, totally AWOL. Great fuckin craic, though. Mad, like. We've a load o whiskey glasses in front of us and out o nowhere Maggit says, eyes on his whiskey:

—Know wha I'd love to do?

Here we go. —No, I say. —Wha?

He looks up. —D'yeh know what'd be me ultimate fantasy? Like, even if I could win the lotto, I'd rather have this. Top, top fantasy.

—G'wan, I say, takin a sip at me whiskey. Everyone's lookin at Maggit. He's drunk but he's not quite wrecked.

—Serious now, he says. —Wha I'd love, right, is to be locked up in a . . . like, a kind o big tanker thing. A big steel room with no way out. And it's full o midgets.

Dermot and the dreadlocked girl laugh, puzzled. Seán looks perplexed.

—Wha yeh on about? I say.

—With midgets, like, he says, dead earnest. —Locked up. Say about thirty o them. A big gang. And like, for me ultimate fantasy, I'd batter them all to death. Fuckin cream them. I'd have one in a headlock, *bam bam bam*, diggim in the head. Boot another one. *Schmack*, up against the wall. Dead. Batter them, the lot o them.

He starts laughin. —Best fun ever.

—You for real? I say. —That's yer ultimate fantasy? You on somethin or wha?

—For real, he says, lookin round. —Fuckin hate midgets, like. Little bastards.

—How many o them did yeh say?

—Dunno. About thirty.

I set me whiskey down. —For one, Maggit, that's a mad thing to say. And two, I reckon thirty midgets'd kill yeh. They'd wear yeh down.

—Me bollix they would.

—They would. Thirty's too many. Yid probably kill a few o them but they'd get yeh, they'd overrun yeh. Yid be dead. Killed by a tanker full o midgets.

Maggit fills himself another measure o Seán's whiskey. He's thinkin somethin over. He takes a sip then says, lookin at no one in particular:

—Wha a fuckin way to go though.

★

Seán shakes his head again. He's been regalin us with tales about the Troubles and it looks like another one's on the way. Apparently this place was used as a safehouse for IRA heads on the run. And he says that Mrs Kinsella was – and is – a staunch Republican. She lived up here for a while when she was younger.

—All madness aside, he says. —I'll tell ye this for nothin. Worst mistake I ever made in me life was lettin that woman slip between me fingers. Too busy with the cause so I was, with stupid dreams. At the end of the day it's all about now, what ye can have right now and hold onto, not what's in the past or fuckin worse, what's in the future. Sure who knows what the future holds, ey? Ye take stock o what's in front o ye, what's fuckin important. And before ye say it, yes, of course the cause is important, of course it was worth fightin for. But sure what's the use when in the end it's not about yer country, it's about yer life, it's about yer happiness.

Seán sighs and runs a hand through his thinnin hair.

—Don't say that to Carmel now, OK? It's too late for all that so it is. She's happy enough where she is and that's an end to it I suppose. Still, here's me bringin the mood down! Would ya listen to me! Sure get some more o that down ye! C'mon now, show an old gunrunner what ye're made of in the capital!

And another round o whiskies is poured. We hold them out over the table and clink glasses. I catch the dreadlocked girl's eyes and she smiles at me again. I wink at her.

—Ready now? says Seán. —Sláinte!

—Sláinte! we shout, and down the whiskies in a fit of coughs and gasps and barely suppressed, pukey heaves.

Everythin's swimmin round me, spinnin and soft-edged. I try to focus on a picture o the Hunger Strikers on the wall by the window but it keeps goin blurry. Everyone's sittin now, the ten or so people that are still here at wharrever time it is, swayin and nursin their pints. I look at me watch. Half five, I think. Jesus. The dreadlocked girl is sittin between me and Maggit and we've been chattin away for ages. I'm not sure wha about, but it's cool. The feel of her thigh against mine is gorgeous, fuckin electric. She takes me hand to look at me ring.

—That's nice. Where'd ye get that?

—It's me ma's. Well, like, used to be.

—It's lovely.

—Yeah.

I wanna say more, like, but I can't think of anythin else to say and me voice is kind o slurred so I just nod and smile and take a sip o me pint.

★

There's an air o sadness about Seán as he locks the place up, and after he's stumbled upstairs we sit outside for a while, by the van. It's gettin bright now, the sky turnin purple and the sea emergin from the dark, the first mornin light caught in the waves. Pajo and the short-haired girl are sittin beside each other. She's got faint tattoos on her arms, thin bluish lines interweavin. Ned's snorin away, his mouth open, lyin on his back in the gravel, absolutely stinkin o the booze he's spilled over his shirt and jacket. The others are all sittin or hunkered down, weary but content. The dreadlocked girl (and wha a fuckin joke this is, why don't I just ask her her name?) is sittin between me and Maggit again. It's gettin a bit weird now, this seatin arrangement thing, but fuck it. I can feel Maggit willin me to get up and fuck off but there's no chance, I'm stayin here. Fuckim, like.

We swap stories and sip bottles o beer and cider. I tell them about the campin trip in Wicklow, the gardaí and the sheep and the money in Pajo's boot. Everyone laughs and the dreadlocked girl squeezes me arm. I can tell by lookin at Maggit that he's not happy but I press on anyway, tellin them about the upside-down car, and Andriy, and Wales. That and a half-dozen other stories. I catch meself thinkin – is that really how it happened? Did I say that? Did Pajo, or Maggit? Who knows. This follows that follows this, and the world abides, makes sense. The dreadlocked girl squeezes me hand and God, it's such a nice feelin. Her touch and warmth. Her smell. And then Dermot nods and says that he's got one.

—Tell me this now, boys and girls, he says. —Do ye believe in the wee folk?

—I do, says Pajo, kind o sheepishly.

—After ten bloody whiskies we do, anyway! says the short-haired girl beside him, slappin him on the thigh. Pajo grins and blinks.

—That's as well so, because I don't want to give any of ye Dubliners nightmares. If ye believe in the wee folk already then well and good. But I never believed. Never. I'd always be gettin off me nan and granda, Dermot, don't go out near the fairy rings at such and such a time, and stay off such and such a field and what have ye, there's pookas and spirits abroad. Me arse, I says. I'm a man o the world, nan; I've been to Thailand, I've seen ladyboys, I've seen fuckin New York, I've no time for fuckin leprechauns

306

and bloody banshees. So anyway, one mornin I'm on me way home from this very establishment, after a good long session not unlike tonight's, slaughtered on whiskey and pills and I'm well gone so I am, when, back in the village, what do I see outside Mulligan's newsagents, only a fuckin wee sprite! Tellin ye! So much for me fuckin worldly ways, what? There she was, a wee sprite, peepin out between the gaps in the railings! Funny little eyes and a sad, doleful face. Well fuck me, I says, and I start goin over in me head what me nan and granda used to tell me. Thing was, I couldn't remember what ye're supposed to do, what rituals and such to protect yerself, so I took off me jacket and I was gonna throw it over the wee thing's head, bring it back home and show me nan, ask her about it, when out of the shop comes a woman and says come on now, Áine, we're goin, yill be late for school. So the little sprite ambles over to the woman and she scoops her up and sticks her into a car parked by the side of the road.

Dermot stops for effect and looks out at his audience. I already know what's comin next. I glance at Maggit and he's pretendin to be inspectin his nails. Why I gave the fucker the benefit o the doubt in Wicklow that time I'll never know.

—Turns out the so-called fuckin sprite's a wean with Down syndrome! I hurried the fuck off thankin me lucky stars I never stuck the jacket on her! Can ye imagine? Done for fuckin molestation or child abuse or somethin! So let that be a lesson to ye – don't believe in fuckin wee people!

Some o the crowd laugh and some look a bit uncomfortable. Maggit gets up and wanders off up the beach.

—Jesus, lighten up! says Dermot, and he takes a swig from his already empty bottle o beer.

★

I'm just slippin into sleep in a patch o beach grass when Pajo shakes me shoulder. I open me eyes. The others are all sprawled out, sleepin. The girl with the dreads is asleep beside me. I don't remember lyin down. She looks gorgeous. Her jacket's open now and I can see in the growin mornin light that she's wearin a Bret Hart T-shirt, with 'The Pink and Black Attack' written across it. Fuckin hell. A girl who likes wrestlin. I have to slowly pull me arm out from under her. I stand up, me legs like jelly.

—What's up? I say.

—C'mere, says Pajo.

—Wha?

—Just c'mere.

Pajo starts off back towards the van. I follow him, me body floppy and deadened by tiredness. Have a massive headache comin on, as well. This one's gonna be a killer. I stumble through the sand and up the wooden steps and back to the yard. The pub's dark against the mornin sky. Pajo's standin by the open door o the van, on the driver's side.

—Wha? I say.

—Look. I was tryin to get the seats down, like. Tryin to see if I could make somewhere to sleep or wharrever, cos o me back. Me back's at me now cos o me knee. Ned said I'm probly overcompensatin so me back's –

—Jesus, Pajo. OK. Get on with it.

Pajo reaches under the seat. He fumbles round then pulls out a see-through bag filled with white powder. He hands it to me. I weigh it up in the palms o me hands, bouncin it. It's heavy. Dead fuckin heavy.

—There's loads o them, says Pajo. —On the other side as well. What'll we do?

—Fuckin hell . . .

—What's up then, lads?

I turn round and it's the dreadlocked girl. She yawns, stretchin her arms over her head. Her Bret Hart T-shirt rides up a bit, showin her white stomach and a bellybutton ring. She looks at the packet in me hands and her eyes widen.

—Jesus, is that fuckin cocaine?

I nod. —Yep. Sneachta.

—Ye dealers or somethin?

—Long fuckin story, I say.

★

I'm standin on the edge of a cliff, a ten minute walk from the others still sleepin on the beach, Pajo and the girl beside me and the Atlantic crashin below, waves breakin on the rocks and white spray risin and fallin. There's a small fortune o coke in a pile o bags at me feet.

This leads to that leads to this.

We could try to sell it, I suppose. God knows I could do with the money. I could pay back Teresa the few quid I owe her, get some stuff for the house. Do it up a bit, specially since Slaughter and his mad fuckin mates burnt the place. The solution to a whole lot o fuckin problems is lyin here. Mad Kasey's haul. I'm not an expert on charlie but there's got to be a fuckin shitload o money to be had sellin this stuff. A fuckin fortune . . .

But there's no chance.

Not really.

There's the instinct for self-preservation for one thing. Yeh have to factor in that I'd be kneecapped if Dommo and his mates ever found out wha happened. Course, we could try sell it on to a proper dealer, broker some deal, or sell it bit by bit on the sly ourselves, dole it out. But would it be worth it? I mean, yeah, I could have a holiday or somethin, go away. It's a chance for a new start and all that, a means to an end. New beginnins, all yer clichés. I mean, this fuckin life, man. Tick fuckin tock.

I'm probably gonna regret this at some stage but fuck it. I tear open a bag like it's a crisp packet and look at Pajo and the girl.

—Sorry, I say.

They nod, the girl tuckin a dread behind her ear again.

—Yer mad, she says, smilin.

I toss the bag out towards the sea and immediately we're engulfed in a cloud o swirlin cocaine, the wind hurlin the powder back at us like that bit in The Big Lebowski, a chemical whirlwind ghostin around us. It gets into me eyes, up me nose, down me throat, stingin the fuck out o me. Pajo and the girl are coughin beside me, howlin and laughin. I start buzzin, the powder workin already, and we laugh and start hurlin punctured bags into the air, the small white packets sailin through the mornin sky with plumes o powder sprayin out behind them, engulfin us, then plummetin towards the wide and hungry sea.

The girl hugs me and twirls me and we hug again, her cheek against mine.

—I can't remember yer name, I say.

—Aoife, she says, into me ear.

—Sound, I say, and step back from her, holdin her hands, lookin at her, her fierce eyes, her smile, the powder in her hair.

STANDING STONES

I first read about Cúchulainn in that old book Victor bought me. I was only a kid and it fascinated me; the cattle-raid o Cooley and evil Queen Maeve and then how Cúchulainn was killed by an enchanted spear brung to Maeve by the hideous children o Celatin. It was the first book I ever read.

It's sad, and full o great deeds and loves. And loss as well, I suppose, in the end. Or a kind o loss. I'm sittin at the wheel o Kasey's van, flippin through the pages o the book. Victor found it in Belfast, in a secondhand shop. Brung it down to me from the North for a Christmas present cos he thought Emer looked like me ma. Dunno why I brought it back up here with me. Aoife's sittin in the passenger seat. The others are outside, Maggit loungin on the sand and Ned and Pajo, mad eejits that they are, splashin in the sea fully clothed. I place the book on the dashboard, lyin open on the page with the picture o Cúchulainn, dyin.

—There, I say. —Look.

Aoife tilts her head. The early evenin's fadin sun glints orange and yellow on her dreadlocked hair and the rings in her ear. I watch her as she studies the picture, the slope of her nose, the slight partin of her lips. She softly closes the book and looks up and out through the window, towards the beach. About fifty yards distant, black against the sinkin sun, is a stone pillar.

—Yeah, it's not bad, is it? says Aoife. —I mean, it could be. Ye never know. I suppose you've just got to trust in somethin, at the end of the day.

I nod. In the minutes before his death Cúchulainn lashed himself to a pillar so he could die on his feet, and even in death his enemies were afraid to approach him. Always stuck with me, that. The defiance, the triumph over dyin.

Aoife smiles.

—Will we have a look, so? she says.

★

The pillar's eight feet tall and pocked with tiny holes. Tufts o beach grass are sproutin from the sand around the bottom. I run me hand across the uneven surface. Grains o sand stick to me palm.

—Did Cúchulainn actually exist, though? says Ned, shiverin slightly, his wet clothes clingin to him.

I shrug. —Dunno.

—He might have, says Aoife. —In the way, say, King Arthur might have. You know, there might have been an Arthur, or whatever, someone like him anyway, and then all these stories got added on. Myths springin up around an actual historical figure, ye know?

—Spose, says Ned.

—So ye never really know, says Aoife.

The ocean is a glitterin reddish gold. Pajo and Ned hunker down on the reedy sand, chattin between themselves. Maggit is standin behind them, his hands in his jeans pockets, starin at nothin. He hasn't said much since we left Tapper's Yard, a few days ago. I feel sorry for him. I dunno why, really. Aoife slips her arm around me waist.

—It could be yeh know, Denny. For all we know, a man called Cúchulainn, a chieftain or whatever, might of stood here, years ago. Imagine. I mean, I know it's probably not the actual stone. That's supposed to be in Louth or somethin I think, is it? That's what the mythographers and that say, but sure look around ye, Denny. How could he not have been here? A place like this? So old and wild.

I place me hand on the pillar again. This isn't Cúchulainn's stone. No chance, like. But it'll do. This link to the past. Everythin leadin here, now. And on and on. I close me eyes for a few seconds and take in the cool damp air, the salt and dried seaweed. I see me ma as a young woman, standin on Bray beach, a bucket o seashells at her feet and a hand raised to keep the sun from her eyes. The breeze flaps her long skirt and her unbraided hair. I'm watchin her watchin the sea. She takes a step forward and a wave breaks around her pale ankle.

OFF ON YOUR TRAVELS

I park the van across from the house and hop down from the driver's seat. Aoife's already out by the time I've made me way to the passengers' side, me chivalrous gesture wasted.

I struggle with the gate and the hinges creak as it swings open. I lost me key somewhere on me travels so I ring the door bell. It makes a kooky ding-a-ling sound. Aoife winks at me. A minute later Paula opens the door.

It seems like I haven't seen Paula for years. She's tired-lookin and wearin paint-spattered jeans and a dead old Italia '90 Ireland jersey. She smiles. The bruise under her left eye's gone a faded purple colour.

—The wanderer returns, she says.

I smile.

She looks at Aoife. —Who's this?

—Aoife, I say. —This is Paula. Paula, Aoife. Yeh not invitin us in?

—Sorry, yeah, says Paula. She stands aside and we step in. I feel weird about tellin Paula. But I say it anyway:

—I won't be stayin long.

Paula tilts her head. —Wha?

—I'm gonna check out Europe. Wanna see Poland. And Ukraine and that. I've the numbers of a few people from over there. There's a live wrestlin show on in Germany as well, so we can go there afterwards. We'll see if we can get tickets.

—When?

—Tomorrow. Well, not the wrestlin show, but we'll be leavin tomorrow.

—Serious?

—Yeah. Me and Aoife.

—Fuckin hell, Denny. Where yeh gettin the money?

—We'll be grand, I say. —We'll take the van and slum it. I can still draw the dole with me bank card from abroad. Pajo's signin on for me.

—Jesus. Wha brought all this on?

The three of us are standin in the hall. I can hear the radio from the kitchen, Eamon Dunphy dismantlin Ireland's latest European Championship qualifyin shambles.

—Just need a change, Paula, I say. —It's doin me head in. I need to get movin.

Paula looks at me. Properly looks at me. —God, she says. —We better have a drink tonight, so.

Same oul Paula. I smile again.

—Is everthin OK? she says.

—Yeah, cool. Everythin's deadly.

She nods. Her eyes still on me. Searchin. —Here, she says. —I've a bottle o cheapo wine in the fridge. Will I open it?

—G'wan.

The three of us walk through the hallway and into the kitchen. The place is completely different. The walls are a pale, smooth cream colour. It smells o fresh paint and turpentine and the windows are open. There's a clean breeze movin through the house and an empty paint can beside the sink. Paula takes the wine from the fridge and pops the cork and it ricochets off the fridge door and pings against the window. She grins, her eyes on Aoife for a second, who's standin in the doorway, takin in her new surroundins.

—Fuck. Could o broke the window, says Paula.
—Again.

—Where's Teresa? I say.

—In work. Her new job.

—Deadly.

—Ah yeah, she's delighted. Will yeh have a glass, Aoife?

Aoife looks at me and then back to Paula. Fuckin hell, man; she's beautiful. They both are.

—Yes please, says Aoife.

—No need to ask you, Denny, says Paula.

I grab the glasses from the shelf by the window. The back garden's unrecognisable; the grass cut, the weeds and bushes chopped back. Me mountain bike's leanin against the shed. The front wheel's still buckled. T-shirts and underwear flap on the line.

—The place is lookin well, I say.

—Ah I couldn't put up with it the way it was. Ma'd have a fit if she saw it. We're not gonna sell it. Me and Teresa and Shane had a chat about it yesterday. We're gonna keep it. We'll always have somewhere to come home to, yeh know? I think ma would o wanted that.

—Cool, I say. I think about sayin somethin else as well but fuck it, that'll do. Keep it simple, like. Keep it cool.

Paula raises her drink and all three of us clink glasses.

—Cheers, she says.

—Sláinte.

—Sláinte.

I down the wine in one and lean back against the sink, me palms flat against the counter. Paula's smilin behind her glass, her eyes bright and young. Me mother's eyes. She grins at me and winks.

ACKNOWLEDGEMENTS

I'd like to thank the following people, all of whom helped in some way to get me here, now. First and foremost, a huge thank you to Louise and Brian, me ma and da (for everything) and Fallon and Gary, me sister and brother (for what's gone and what's to come). I'd also like to thank Pauline Duffy (for ages I was writing for you), Selina Whiteley (for your belief, forever), Keith Lynch (mo cara), Desmond Barry (for being me first CW tutor, for help getting this book out there and for pointing me towards Cormac McCarthy, who I now know isn't Irish, despite the name), the Irish Arts Council (for money when I badly needed it), Francis Bickmore (for the shape), Karolina Sutton (for making me realise saying 'yes' straight away isn't always the best thing to do) and everyone I've ever laughed, danced, jammed, protested, drunk or watched wrestling with. Go raibh maith agat.

And finally, extra special thanks to Rob Middlehurst (for all the awesome advice and selflessness, for the endless chats – hope they're endless, anyway – and for being a genuine scouser and a wonderful teacher).